Michael Shew was inspired first novel, after working as a head teacher in two London comprehensive schools for many years. "All of life was there," he says, and the idea for this story began to form as he faced the daily pressures and exhilarations of being a Head. A 'Writing Fiction' course at Kellogg College, Oxford, motivated him to turn his plot into a novel. He loves hill-walking and travelling and is fascinated by politics. Michael now lives with his partner Francesca in Derbyshire, where he wrote this book; they have an adult daughter Tania.

To Barry,
As if you haven't got
enough on your plate –
you're now got this bloody
book to read.
All my love,
Mick

To Ruby, our Irish Red Setter, who lay at my feet while I was writing this book, keeping me focused, patiently waiting for her walk.

Michael Shew

LESSONS IN LYING

AUSTIN MACAULEY PUBLISHERS™

LONDON • CAMBRIDGE • NEW YORK • SHARJAH

A CIP catalogue record for this title is available from the British Library.

ISBN 9781528916776 (Paperback)
ISBN 9781528916783 (E-Book)

www.austinmacauley.com

First Published (2019)
Austin Macauley Publishers Ltd
25 Canada Square
Canary Wharf
London
E14 5LQ

My thanks to Elizabeth Garner, my tutor at Kellogg College; to Philip, Farquhar and Bill for their thoughtful comments and suggestions on my early drafts; Neil for his ideas on marketing; and most of all to my wife, Francesca, for her invaluable advice, love and encouragement.

Act 1

1

Summer 1994

Robert continued to glare at Janice, Winston and Toby as they chatted in the centre of the field, ignoring him completely. "Which part of 'please go to the cooking tent and start preparing this evening's meal' do you three not understand? Everyone else has cooked for the last five evenings, now it's your turn. Just go there, now."

With a herculean effort, they all stood up and moved glacially over to start preparing the meal.

"Keep calm, Mr Mason, it's only five o'clock. It doesn't have to be served up for an hour and a half," said Toby.

With some effort, Robert kept his cool. Toby, the precocious 15-year-old son of a Labour MP, had been winding staff up since they'd arrived six days ago.

"Thank you for pointing that out, Toby; where would we be without your guidance? That's a rhetorical question by the way."

"I didn't think teachers were supposed to use sarcasm with pupils, sir."

"They're not, but I make an exception in your case. Now stop prevaricating and start preparing."

"What's prevaricating, sir?" Janice joined in.

"It's the special pasta dish for this evening's meal, isn't it, sir?" replied Winston, to laughter from those in the field who appreciated his whip-crack humour.

Robert walked back to his tent, smiling. Of course some of these kids are going to push the boundaries with staff on a school camp. But he had to admit he was enjoying the relaxed banter and goodwill that had quickly developed. There'd been a happy atmosphere in the camp since day one, and several staff had congratulated him. *We're half-way through, with no incidents or upsets,* he thought. Even the weather, notoriously unreliable in the Brecon Beacons, had been benign, with little rain and two sunny days.

He saw the note on his sleeping bag as soon as he unzipped the tent flysheet and sat on the grass to read it.

Hardly spoken to you since we got here. Come over to my tent for a chat when the kids are in their tents? Sue x.

Sue had begun to irritate him with her unsubtle demands for his attention. It was as if she thought their casual fling four weeks ago meant he owed her something.

After the evening meal and various games organised by the staff, pupils had free time until they went to their tents for the night. While teachers not on duty could relax over a beer or glass of wine in the staff tent, this was one of the times that Robert most felt the burden of responsibility as he'd insisted that staff taking the evening duty couldn't drink. He remembered the uproar when he'd read out the relevant section of his 'guidelines for staffing the school summer camp' at their final meeting two weeks ago.

On those days when a member of staff is on evening or night duty, he/she must not take any alcoholic drink until their shift is over.

He'd stuck to his guns in spite of threats from some of his colleagues to drop out in advance. None did, and he'd only had to speak to one of them about it since the camp began.

When all the pupils were in their sleeping bags that evening, he went over to Sue's tent.

"I thought you weren't coming. Where have you been?"

"Come on, Sue, I'm in charge of the camp. I've got to be around, especially when we're getting the kids into their tents."

"Yes, Rob, I know how important you are, and where I am on your list of priorities. Do you really think anyone's going to be at risk if you took an hour off now and again?"

"Let's leave it, shall we? I don't think either of us are in the mood," and he turned and went back to the staff tent.

The positive atmosphere in the camp continued the next day, apart from an incident between Tom, a boy with Asperger's syndrome, and Sam, an older pupil. It started, as these things often did, with name-calling directed at Tom, then escalated when Tom responded by hitting the older boy. It wasn't a vicious blow, but Sam wasn't the type to lose face. When he delivered a much harder punch to Tom's stomach, leaving him doubled up, Tom ran to a corner of the field and stayed there, refusing to join in any activities, tying up a member of staff for the rest of the day.

By the evening, he seemed less distressed. Sue had helped to bring about a reconciliation of sorts between the two boys, which Robert felt he should acknowledge as they sat down for the evening meal.

"Thanks for getting that sorted and calming Tom down, Sue. I was getting worried that I might have to call his parents if he didn't respond."

"Don't mention it, you're welcome. Sorry about last night, I didn't mean to be a pain. Any chance of a chat tonight? I could bring some wine round after my duty ends."

"As long as it's after your duty. I'll see you 'round eleven, then."

It was clear to Robert that Sue wanted more than a chat as soon as she pulled the flysheet back and crawled in. She complained at some length about another member of staff, then launched into a long moan about her boyfriend never showing any interest in her. He could smell drink on her breath.

"We had a good time in Wales, didn't we?"

"It was nice, Sue, but for me it was in the moment. I'm seeing someone now, and it wouldn't feel right."

"But it was OK to screw me when I was with Martin, was it? You're such a hypocrite, Robert. Come on, she doesn't have to know."

Robert tasted the whisky on her tongue as she planted her mouth against his. For a second, he thought of responding, before pushing her away.

"I mean it, Sue, it isn't going to happen. I'd like you to leave, please."

"Christ you're boring. I'll get back on duty, then."

"What do you mean back on duty? I thought we agreed you wouldn't come here until your duty ended?"

"Calm down. After Henry handed over to me, I went 'round the tents a couple of times then came here."

"Bloody hell, Sue; you shouldn't have done that. Please, get back out there and check everything's OK." Robert started to put his boots on; he'd better walk around and check on the tents himself. *Why do some people turn a consensual shag between colleagues into a love affair?*

Sue re-appeared after three minutes, wrenching the flysheet door open, clearly distressed,

"Tom's tent is empty. I've done a very quick search of the site and can't see him anywhere. What should we do?"

Robert's immediate fear for the worst brought a horrible tightening in his stomach; he forced himself to think rationally. *The odds are that Tom's somewhere near the camp, but it's vital that we do everything to find him in the next hour.* He took a couple of deep breaths and answered her as calmly as possible.

"OK, wake up John and Frank, then go 'round to every tent and check he's not with anyone else."

He had to consider the possibility that Tom had wandered off into the Beacons with no map, warm clothing, compass or even a torch. In the dark, he would quickly get disorientated. In which case, anything could happen.

By the time he'd put on his weatherproof gear, the other three had finished looking in the tents.

"He's not there," said Sue.

Her face was drawn, and she looked scared. Robert knew she was thinking about only one thing; if anything has happened to Tom, it was because she wasn't patrolling when she should have been. But, of course, he was culpable too. Not only culpable, but as the trip organiser and camp leader, he was ultimately responsible. If Tom had come to any harm, he would need to agree a story with Sue—fast—and stick to it; otherwise their careers could be over.

"John, can you round Brian, Justine and Frank up, please? The six of us can then search the immediate area around the camp. Everyone will need a torch, whistle, map, compass and walkie-talkie. If we don't find him soon, I'll need someone to go to the phone box and alert the mountain rescue team and the police; tell them we've got a missing child and give them our grid reference. Four of us will then divide up the wider area into quadrants on our maps and search each one. The fifth person should stay on the camp and inform other staff what's going on when people wake up. Have I missed anything?"

John spoke up. "Isn't this a bit over the top, Robert? I mean, he's probably hiding near the camp and will walk back in, big grin on his face, as soon as he starts to get cold. Shouldn't we wait until dawn, that's only four hours away?"

"I don't want to assume the worst, but we need to act as if anything's possible. If he walks back in the next ten minutes, fine. But if he's lying out there with a broken a leg, then the sooner we find him the better. Whoever finds him, use the walkie-talkie to inform the rest of us about his condition and location. Sue, once we've finished searching near the camp, would you be OK to stay here and check in regularly with the rest of us, while Frank goes to the call box to alert the police and mountain rescue?"

"Of course. Let's get our equipment, meet back in three minutes and get started."

Robert saw that she was hiding her fear with a composure she clearly didn't feel.

"Thanks, Sue. And please remember, all of you, tread cautiously out there. We don't want another casualty."

When the initial search around the camp perimeter found no sign of Tom, Robert, John, Frank and Justine set off on the wider search, and Frank left for the phone box. Sue would call in regularly so that the others could check if they were still in range.

Robert felt a growing despair as he trod carefully over the bracken, sweeping his torch slowly over the ground ahead, calling Tom's name. He knew the odds on finding him in the dark over such a wide area weren't good. He had to hope that Tom had the luck to find his way back to the camp, or the sense to find a hollow to lie in and cover himself with heather and bracken until dawn.

There was the other massive problem; how to explain how Tom had managed to slip away unnoticed during Sue's shift. They needed to agree a story before the others began to ask the question, which they surely would.

Sue's voice came over the walkie-talkie.

"Please reply to this in turn everyone, so that I know you're still in range. You first, Robert."

Robert stopped, switched over to 'Talk' and acknowledged, then listened as the other three responded. He carried on cautiously, careful of the misleading shadows cast by the torch, his boot laces occasionally snagging on the bracken, aware of the cold slowly seeping through his clothes and boots. *If I'm feeling like this with all my gear on, what's it like for Tom?*

Suddenly, the beam picked out a faded white sign on a fence ahead. As he got closer, he could see part of the fence had collapsed. He read the sign:

"DANGER: KEEP OUT, OLD MINE WORKINGS"

Heartbeat pounding in his ears, he walked gingerly up to the fence. Now that he was next to it, he could see some wooden bars had been dislodged. The dank, peaty smell was overwhelming, as he crawled on his hands and knees to the edge of the collapsed mine shaft and shone his torch down into the blackness. At first, he saw nothing, but the wave of relief that swept over him was instantly snatched away as the torch beam picked out a small body on a ledge, fifteen feet below. From the angle of Tom's limbs, he was probably seriously injured. Or even worse.

In desperation, he began shouting repeatedly at the body below.

"Tom, can you hear me, are you hurt?" But there was no movement or response.

Gripping the torch between his teeth, he braced his arms and legs against either side of the shaft and started to edge downwards. It was crazy; the moss on the rock made the sides of the shaft slippery, and God knows how he'd climb out. But he had to try.

2

The explosive disintegration of the toilet window was followed instantly by a shower of glass splinters scything into the urinal, missing Robert by the scariest margin.

It was mid-morning break on the first day of his first teaching post. He'd already managed to offend over half of his previous class by miss-pronouncing their names—leading to a mini riot, duly witnessed by the deputy head—and abandoned his third-year lesson on the refraction of light in chaos, having been given the wrong apparatus.

"Another waste of space, just out of teacher training," he overheard the head technician muttering not so quietly.

He looked at the large jagged hole in the centre of the window and then saw a huge stone on the floor. Through the hole he saw a group of Year 11 pupils rapidly gathering in the playground outside, which was overlooked by the staff toilets. One or two were trying to peer in—should he tell them to back away? As he was giving this careful thought, he heard Jack Smith, a PE teacher known to pupils as 'the enforcer', bellowing,

"Right, who's responsible for this?"

Robert had learned enough basic child psychology on his post-graduate teacher training course to know that it was asking for trouble—at the very least—to demand that a group of excited fifteen-year-olds name the culprit.

"The IRA," yelled Marcus, fortunately for him unseen by Smith. Pupils erupted with laughter, even though IRA bombs had been going off for years now, with another one recently near Dover. Robert decided it was time to leave the men's toilet and quickly made his way to the staff room.

What the fuck have I got myself into? he reflected as he walked along the corridor, dodging oncoming pupils. His thoughts were interrupted by Molly Atkins, an art teacher who'd introduced herself on the training day before term started. He'd been wondering ever since whether she was just being friendly or chatting him up when she'd suggested that he join the rest of her department in the pub at the end of the day. As it turned out, the science department meeting overran, and he couldn't make it.

"God, what on earth happened, the kids are going mad outside?"

"A huge stone came through the window of the toilet as I was taking a leak. Glass everywhere, and some of it a little too close for comfort to a part of me I'm very attached to."

Molly looked at him, unsmilingly.

"I'm sure you'll recover quickly enough," she said, walking away towards the art room.

He queued for his tea and biscuit, smiling at two or three people he recognised, then found one of the few vacant chairs in the staff room and slumped down into the sagging upholstery, his buttocks almost forcing their way through the remaining springs. As a probationary teacher in his first year, he had a reduced teaching load, but had learned that he would be given a couple of difficult groups to test him out. Thankfully, his first class after the break was a top set in 'Year 9' with an easy reputation.

Looking at his new colleagues, animatedly exchanging anecdotes from their summer holidays, he tried to bolster his confidence by reminding himself that he'd achieved what he'd set out to do three years ago, during his first year at Sussex University: to become a science teacher and build a career in the profession. His father was disparaging, of course, repeating ad nauseam that he was setting his sights too low, but there was nothing new in that.

The five-minute warning bell brought him back to reality.

The Year 9 lesson went well—he'd felt the majority of the class were interested and wanted to learn—but he was anxious about the class in the afternoon. Derek, his Head of

19

Department, hadn't helped when he'd told him that most of them hadn't wanted to take the Science and Society GCSE.

"It's a dog's breakfast of general science stitched together with bits of cod sociology. None of us wanted to take it so we gave it to our lucky probationer. Congratulations! Show me what you plan to do."

Two hours later, sitting in the deputy head teacher's office at the end of the day, Robert proceeded to recount, in stomach churning detail, the catastrophe that was already the talk of the staff room.

The pupils had taken control of his lesson—'To find the best aerodynamic shape for a car'—from the start. His demonstration, dropping various shapes through water to see which was fastest, held their attention for about 30 seconds.

"This is crap, sir, it's not realistic."

He had to admire the hutzpah of the way they added 'sir' to the end of every insult.

"Cars don't drive through water, we need to see what happens when you drop shapes through air."

"That's a good point, Carl, but you'd need a long drop to detect any difference and this room isn't high enough."

"But if you go up to the Ecology garden on the roof, you could drop them off there and we could stand below and time them."

Inexplicably, he'd agreed to this. Why? He wanted them to like him. Standing near the precipice on the third floor, shouting "3, 2, 1 go!" at the top of his voice to the oddly reduced numbers below and releasing a selection of objects watched by scores of distracted pupils from classrooms that overlooked this spectacle, was bad enough. Learning that half the class had walked out of school thirty minutes early and indulged in a shoplifting spree at Londis, completed his humiliation.

After Robert had finished his account, Sally said nothing for several seconds; she just sat there, staring at a point on the wall above his right shoulder.

"Robert, I know how deflated you're feeling at the moment. But you must understand that any teacher that tells you that they've never had a lesson like this at the start of their career is a liar. However, there's no point in pretending that this afternoon was anything but a bloody disaster."

Robert breathed in deeply. Sally Franks had a reputation for being fair and supportive, but this seemed harsh. Too harsh. It was only his first day, for God's sake. He struggled to think of the right response—if there was a right response.

"I'm devastated about the disruption and damage I've caused, Sally. I feel I've let you down personally, as you appointed me.

"Here's what we're going to do. You will lose this class for the next term. Derek will take over."

Robert thought how pleased Derek would be about that.

"You will shadow a number of the best practitioners in the school, teaching a range of classes. I will drop-in to your lessons as often as my normal duties allow and meet with you once a week to discuss what I've observed.

"Do you have a problem with any of those proposals?"

He felt this level of support was demeaning but knew he shouldn't say so.

"None at all, Sally. I can't deny that this afternoon hasn't been a humbling experience, but I'm determined to learn from it. I know I can."

"Please don't dwell on today's events, Robert. Go home, phone a friend and relax. I'll see you tomorrow."

Sally walked him to the door. She felt disappointed with their meeting. When she'd offered him the job, back in May, he'd impressed her. Confident, but not full of himself, he knew his stuff and talked passionately about teaching science. She was surprised he'd made such a litany of basic errors. He'd seemed edgy just now; was that something to do with her? Hopefully, he's humble enough to take advice.

Robert was feeling angry, not humble. He had a couple of books to pick up from his locker in the staff room before going home. An abnormal silence descended almost as soon as he walked in, followed by the resumption of murmured conversations.

There was no option but to tough it out. As he got to his locker, Ron, the staff comedian, called out and broke the atmosphere.

"Ah, young Robert, I hear your experiment dropping objects from the roof caused some disruption earlier today. I just hope you understand the gravity of the situation."

Ron roared with laughter at his own joke.

At that moment, Robert despised him; he loathed all the smug bastards sitting there, enjoying his humiliation. *So much for the supportive staffroom culture that I was told about. One day, colleagues, you'll regret this.*

But he knew he had to show he could laugh at himself.

"I'm sorry to all of you whose lessons were ruined by my stupidity today. Not the start to my career that I would have wished for. I'd like to say it won't ever happen again, but it probably will—how could I deny Ron the opportunity for another one liner?"

Ron walked over, put his arm round Robert's shoulders and loudly re-assured him that everyone in the room had probably done something just as embarrassing at the start of their career.

That seemed a good point at which to collect his stuff, make an exit and drive home.

As he walked up to his ageing Mini Cooper in the car park, he saw a note on the windscreen, scribbled on a page torn out of an exercise book. As he pulled the note from under the wiper, his heart sank further at the thought of an abusive message. But he smiled, as he read,

"Thanks for letting us out early today, Mr Mason, see you Thursday. Signed, 11SS."

The Mini was almost ten years old and rarely completed a journey of more than ten miles without breaking down. He'd bought it for a couple of hundred pounds from a fellow student; it stopped in heavy rain, was excruciatingly uncomfortable, unreliable, noisy and self-destructed over speed bumps.

There was a touch of humidity still in the air in the bright September evening. At this time of day, the traffic in north London was snarled enough to make the speed humps irrelevant. Even with the short cuts, it took him half an hour to drive back to Stroud Green, near Finsbury Park, the sunroof open and Paul Simon on the cassette player. *Still crazy after all these years sums up the day perfectly.*

Susan, his landlady—a BBC producer—had left a note saying that she'd be out all evening, which was a relief. He'd decided not to take Sally's advice to meet up with friends over a few pints. He'd stay in, cook something simple and reflect on the implications of the day's events. If he could put his feelings at being publicly put-down behind him.

His experience today, coupled with Sally's brutal appraisal and his colleagues ridicule, had re-awakened the chronic self-doubt that he'd suffered as a teenager, fuelled by his father's unending disparagement. "Oh, Robert, surely you could have done better than that?" was the typical response to any hard-won achievement.

He cleared away the crockery, poured a glass of red wine and sat at his desk. *How bad was I; can I retrieve my career before it's started?*

Two hours later, he had a strategy for the next three months. He'd take all the support Sally could offer, more if necessary, and build a good relationship with her. He might need someone at the top to fight his corner. He'd mix more with his science department colleagues, picking their brains and harvesting all the tips he could. Most of all, he would focus single-mindedly on his own self-interest.

By Christmas, he'd know if he was cut out to be a teacher.

It didn't take him that long. Soon after half-term, he felt confident that his teaching and class control had improved significantly; coming up to Christmas, he was actually looking forward to his end of term review with Sally.

Sitting beside her in an armchair in her office, her body language was very different to their meeting at the end of his first day.

"Looking at the feedback from Derek, the colleagues you've shadowed and my own observations, you've made significant improvements with behaviour management, the pace of your lessons and pupils' engagement. As is to be expected after just one term, there are still areas that need to improve; but overall, Robert, good progress. Well done."

Robert allowed himself a smile and relaxed.

Marking a pile of Year 10 books at the end of the day in his lab, feeling on a high after his meeting, he congratulated himself on the systematic way he'd turned his performance around. He'd engaged with the support he received—that was a big factor—but the turning point came when he'd read a copy of 'The Craft of the Classroom' by Michael Marland.

The central message was simple and made a lot of sense to him. The author, a well-known head teacher, argued that teaching is a craft that can be learned and honed like any other, and every teacher needed to find the approach to their craft that works for them. There was no infallible model for success, but there are specific generic skills involved, like any craft.

After that, he'd approached his lesson observations forensically, noting the techniques used by the best teachers to make their lessons engaging and free of disruption. He applied those he felt would work for him to his own practice, with increasing success. Obvious stuff like involving every pupil, not only those putting their hands up, using eye contact and body language, and changing his plans mid-lesson if things weren't working.

The end-of-term was a revelation as staff-pupil relations relaxed and extra-curricular activities encroached more and more on the formal timetable. By the penultimate day, Robert realised he was probably the only one still planning lessons. The school took on a happier, almost anarchic, feeling.

He'd seen Sally a couple of times on the corridor when she was on duty, and she'd reminded him about the end of term meal for new teachers that week. He now understood the value of encouragement from someone you respect; her approval and support had made a big difference.

There were nine of them crowded around the table in the bustling Greek restaurant that Friday. It was far enough from the school to make sure there wouldn't be any pupils and parents around, with reliably good food and close to a tube station. Sally booked the same place every year, and the restaurant staff knew her well. Supporting and guiding these nervous, fledgling teachers through their first year gave her more satisfaction than any other part of her job; she'd refused point blank to relinquish it when the Head had wanted to change her responsibilities.

She looked at the energised, carefree faces around the table and congratulated herself on the difference she'd made for every one of them; she was sure they'd all pass comfortably at the end of the year. As her gaze caught Robert's, he raised his glass, mouthing "Thank you," as she lifted hers in return.

Standing amongst the group on the pavement outside the restaurant at the end of the meal, she went over to Robert.

"I'll see you in January. Make sure you enjoy yourself and wind down over the holiday."

"You too, Sally.

Robert felt upbeat and optimistic as he drove into the school at the start of the spring term, a sharp contrast with his first day, four months earlier. Even finding another car in his parking space failed to piss him off. Walking up to his classroom, he passed a number of pupils who were in school early for the breakfast club.

"Morning, Mr Mason, you've come back then?"

"My sister said she and her mates saw you before Christmas with a load of teachers, all a bit pissed, outside some Greek restaurant in Camden, sir."

He knew that he hadn't cracked things in one term, but he was confident that he would become a good teacher before long. He was particularly enthused about trying new approaches instead of playing safe all the time.

Some of his colleagues in the science department complained about the new national tests for fourteen-year-olds, fearing they would be used to penalise teachers with poor results. But Robert saw them as an opportunity to compete with his colleagues and show that his classes did the best. He didn't care that his attitude might be resented and lead to problems in the future.

Three weeks later, Molly appeared beside him as they were leaving a staff meeting.

"I'm very pleased to see you back, Robert. Some of the staff were betting you'd had enough last term and would be among the early quitters, but I noted that our dynamic deputy head had taken you on, and I bet them you'd be here. How was your holiday?"

"Yeah, OK, thanks, Molly, the usual mix of parties and family. I guess I should be flattered that I was noticed, even if it was just to watch me mess up."

"Oh, don't let that crowd get to you. They've all been in the job far too long, can't wait to take early retirement and their only pleasure now is watching new staff fail and berating the kids. I don't have much to do with them and they're not too fond of me, or of anyone else who's enthusiastic about teaching children."

She must be around thirty, he thought, catching the smell of her scent, its impact enhanced in the overheated corridor. As usual, she was dressed flamboyantly in a long, flowing dress, chiffon scarf and big jewellery. Not a look he was usually attracted to, but it worked on her.

She interrupted his thoughts.

"What are you doing next Friday? I'm having a couple of old friends round for a meal, and four always works better than three, so do you fancy coming 'round? As long as you promise not to talk about school."

Taken aback by her invitation, he recovered to accept enthusiastically.

"That sounds great! I'd love to. You live over in west London, don't you?"

"That's right. I'll put the address in your pigeon hole. Let's say eight o'clock; just bring yourself and a nice bottle of wine. Have a good week, if I don't see you before then."

Sitting at his desk after school that afternoon with two boys in detention for letting off a stink bomb, he pondered Molly's invitation. Presumably, she wouldn't have asked him over for a meal unless she was interested in him. 'Four works better than three' was a bit obvious. He liked her, and he'd found himself looking at her admiringly several times; she had a lovely smile and a great figure. He wasn't sure he wanted another casual relationship, particularly with a colleague, but hadn't slept with anyone since a two-week fling with a fellow student nine months ago.

Ringing the doorbell to her flat in St Charles Square on Friday evening, he felt excited and apprehensive, as he sometimes could when not entirely in control of events. The white stucco houses in the square had been magnificent, once. Early Victorian, four stories high with grand porticos and even grander columns, they'd almost all been badly converted into one- and two-bedroom flats by landlords seeking to squeeze the maximum profit from their investment. *Still impressive, though*, he thought, as he heard her coming down the stairs.

Molly was looking forward to the evening ahead, pleased with herself for inviting him. Though she'd always found him attractive, she'd been wary at first. He may be around six feet tall with a fine face, dreamy eyes and a gorgeous smile. But his gauche remark, on the first day they'd met, demonstrated an immaturity that had made her wary. With time, though, the strength he'd shown by coming through in his first term, to prove people wrong, had impressed and attracted her. And he was funny, when he wasn't trying to be.

She opened the door and there was the smile. He looked a little nervous. Well, let's see what happens—it could be an interesting evening.

"Robert! I'm so glad you could make it. Come on up, the others aren't here yet, but we'll start on the wine and I can tell you a bit about them. I should have asked if there was anything that you didn't eat, but it's a bit late now. Nothing special, it's sea bass in a wine sauce with the usual nibbles to start and cheese to finish. Mind the step before the top, it's rotten, but the bastard landlord doesn't do a thing."

Clearly there aren't going to be any awkward silences, he thought, as Molly, still talking, showed him into her flat

27

and gave him the tour. The décor was Indian chic, with Batik fabrics and throws hanging from walls and covering the second-hand sofas. *How many art deco lamps does it take to light a room?* he thought. In the bedroom, she'd used the high ceiling to create a platform bed with a ladder, giving space for a potter's wheel underneath. Looking at the ladder, Robert wondered who led the way the first time. Seeing him looking, Molly laughed.

"I know what you're thinking, and the answer is me, usually; now why don't you open your wine."

He handed the bottle over, waiting for her reaction.

"Pouilly Fume, I'm impressed, I don't often drink something that good. You've obviously got independent means. Do you mind opening it while I check on the sauce? I'll get the cork screw."

Robert poured two glasses, put them on the side table and sat down on the lumpy sofa, feeling pleased with himself for going with the expensive white, which had cost him a fortune. He was looking forward to the evening and decided to relax and see how things developed.

She walked back into the lounge, placed a tray with nuts, humus and carrot sticks on the balsa wood side table and joined him on the sofa. He noticed her lipstick and eye liner, which she never wore at work, and caught the smell of her perfume again.

"Cheers," she said, raising her glass and chinking it against his.

"Ohh, that's really good. Thank you for bringing such good wine. Now, about Sue and Dave who are coming this evening."

She took him through the history of her old friends, whom she'd known since they'd met at art college. Robert found it difficult to pay attention, distracted by her pale green eyes, shoulder length auburn hair and the outline of her breasts, which he could see clearly under her light cotton blouse. He wondered what it would be like to be beside her, naked, in bed.

The evening should have been the perfect way to wind down at the end of the week. Molly was an engaging host, attentive to her guests, eccentric but great fun. Sue and Dave had been living together for the last four years, and the evening was clearly an attempt by Molly to help them put some life back into their relationship. Dave was a member of Socialist Challenge, a group on the far left; he spent a large part of the evening voicing his opinions about the American-led war against Iraq, following Saddam Hussein's invasion of Kuwait, in a way that conveyed there could be no other possible opinions on the subject.

"Saddam had no option but to invade Kuwait as the Kuwaitis were forcing the price of oil down in order to bankrupt Iraq. The Americans then manipulated the UN vote to legalise their military assault, which was all about ensuring that the US continued to have access to cheap Arab oil. Kuwait will become yet another colonial outpost of the American military-industrial complex. It was blood for oil. You haven't said much, Robert. What do you think?"

He'd deliberately said nothing, becoming increasingly irritated by Dave's hectoring style. *I might as well go for it*, he thought.

"From what I've read, Saddam's excuses for invading Kuwait don't stand scrutiny. Hundreds of Kuwaitis have been murdered and tortured since he invaded, and the UN was unanimous in instructing him to withdraw. When he ignored that, I don't think the west had any choice but to invade. The guy's a monster and deserved to be kicked out, so I'm glad we invaded."

As Molly's eyes went towards the ceiling, Dave erupted.

"What the fuck, man. Before coming out with shit like that, you need to read some history about the way the US and Britain have been meddling in the middle east throughout this century."

Molly jumped in. "The UK and the US vetoed several diplomatic initiatives that could have resolved this without the huge loss of life, Robert. Just because Saddam is a brutal thug, that doesn't give us the moral right to kill thousands of Iraqis, many of them civilians. Horrible things happen when you go to war. I've read of Iraqi soldiers being buried alive by bulldozers. This is being done in our name, and it didn't have to happen."

Robert excused himself and went to the toilet. As he came out of the bathroom, Molly intercepted him and asked him not to leave when Dave and Sue went.

They left shortly afterwards, their goodbyes to Robert noticeably cold.

"Can I get you anything else to drink—whiskey, vodka?" she said as she came back upstairs from seeing them off.

"No thanks, I think I've had enough. That was a really lovely evening. I hope I didn't spoil it at the end."

"Not for me. Dave can get too fond of his own voice, and I think we avoided a meltdown."

If she was going to sleep with him tonight, she wanted to draw him out. He'd given little away about himself so far.

"Have you got any brothers and sisters? Tell me a little about your family."

Robert rarely spoke about his family to other people. But he felt very relaxed with her, and he thought opening up about his feelings might lead on to something more intimate.

"My dad died when I was sixteen, but we'd been distant for some time. In fact, both my parents seemed to belong to another species really, so while there was a hole in my life, I felt surprisingly unaffected emotionally, which many people couldn't understand. Mum and I got on well enough but had relatively little to do with each other; then she got married to this company director who I can't stand, so since university I've only seen them twice a year. No brothers or sisters, though I did have a twin sister who died suddenly from a previously undetected heart defect, when I was eight. She was my father's favourite; I don't think he ever forgave me for not dying instead of her."

"That must have been really tough to deal with."

"Yes, it was."

Robert remembered the day his parents had returned from the hospital, without Chloe. He'd been hurt that he hadn't been allowed to visit her; they were very close, and as her older brother (by thirty minutes), he'd always felt it was his job to make sure no harm came to her. So his grief was compounded, many times over, by guilt that he'd been unable to save her. At first, consumed with inexplicable feelings of loss, he didn't notice the increasing coolness between his parents. But from the day Chloe died, it was clear that his father wanted little to do with him anymore. The more he tried to regain his father's love and approval, the more he disparaged his son.

"Sorry, Robert, I shouldn't have asked."

"No, that's OK. I haven't told many people, that's all. I was taken back fourteen years, for a moment. You're an easy person to talk to."

After a second's hesitation, she put her hand on his thigh and moved to kiss him. Their lips touched, gently and dryly at first, then more urgently as she felt his tongue inside her mouth, pushing against her teeth. He cupped her breast with his hand, feeling the nipple starting to harden.

Molly broke away.

"I haven't slept with a warmonger before."

"There's a first time for everything."

They stood at the bottom of the ladder, kissing, their hands all over each other, pulling their clothes off. Smiling at Robert's evident arousal, she said, "Be careful not to catch that on the ladder on the way up; it would be a pity to damage it now. I'll see you on top, as they say." As she climbed the ladder, he fondled her bottom and she let out a shriek.

"Didn't your parents warn you about messing 'round on ladders, Robert?"

"They did, but I never listened."

"Now, where were we?" she said, as he climbed onto the mattress.

The next day, on the tube journey back to his flat, he sat slumped in his seat, exhausted. Given the unusual sleeping arrangements, whenever either one got up to pee, waking the other, Molly would initiate further engagement. Around eight in the morning, with little sensation left in his increasingly sore penis, he wasn't even sure whether he'd come or not.

That morning, after sharing a bath, they'd sat round the little Formica-covered table that filled the kitchen, drinking coffee and eating croissants from the corner deli.

"I think I'll need to sleep for the rest of the weekend if I'm going to function at all on Monday. I haven't slept with anyone for months; last night has been a shock to the system," he said, smiling.

"It was a lovely night, Robert. I hope you enjoyed it as much as I did."

She paused, then continued,

"I enjoy being with you, Robert, though I'm not sure I can read you yet. So—I'm doing most of the work here—do you want to carry on seeing me, see where this goes?"

Robert sat listening, impressed by her self-confidence, her honesty in expressing her feelings so openly. He liked her. More than that, he sensed being with her would be good for him in a way he couldn't articulate.

"I'd like to. I'll get really fit, going up and down that ladder."

"You know, it is possible to connect with someone without wrapping up your feelings in a joke."

They carried on seeing each other for several months, surviving a close call when lust overcame them in the art department office after school, pupils waiting impatiently outside to collect their GCSE artwork. They would talk for hours about education and teaching, which not all of his colleagues seemed interested in. The more he questioned how children learn and what he was teaching, the more enthusiastic and confident he became.

So, when two roles with extra money and responsibility were advertised within the school, he decided to apply. *I know I'm more capable than the other young teachers here*, he thought; *it's time to start building my career.*

Sally cornered him in the car park one evening.

"I hear you're thinking of applying for both new jobs? I know you're on top of most of the classroom stuff now, but don't you think it would be better to only go for one at this stage?"

"I've thought about it, but if I'm spending time preparing for one, I might as well apply for both. That way, I'll stand a good chance of getting one."

She knew the other candidates and was far less sure than Robert about his chances.

He was devastated when, after two stressful days of interviews, he failed to get either job. He went to see Sally for feedback on his performance.

"There were two issues. First, you talked too much, then you got argumentative with the panel, which antagonised them. In interviews, how you say things is more important than what you say, most of the time."

Robert began to feel the same sense of injustice that he'd felt years ago, when his father had expressed disappointment at another perceived failure on his part.

"I don't understand how they can say that, Sally. They were the ones trying to pick an argument, the way they came back at me after some of my answers."

He left her office feeling just as aggrieved as when he went in; it would be months before he understood what she was getting at.

Molly quickly picked up his change in mood. Two days later, they went to the pub after work.

"The interviews seem to have left you low. What are you feeling?"

"I'm just angry that those two idiots got the jobs that I should have got. That's pretty understandable, isn't it?"

She ignored his sarcastic tone.

"Being pissed off is understandable. But you seem different to the guy I got to know a few months ago. Almost sorry for yourself."

How dare she accuse him of being sorry for himself, he despised that in others. As he looked away, he saw his face reflected in the window, the angry image staring back. *I've got to calm down*, he thought, *this isn't her fault.*

"It might seem like I'm over-reacting, but I can't get over my failure to get either job."

"Look, you've been teaching for just under a year and you've made a real success of it. You could have a good career if you're ambitious, which I think we both know you are. But these are early days, so take time to think about what you enjoy, rather than going for everything that comes along. Other jobs will come up. I was unsuccessful three times before getting this job. It didn't feel great, but it wasn't a tragedy, and you need to put it in perspective."

"I know everything you've said makes sense, and thanks for the advice. But I can't just put the injustice behind me and move on."

Injustice? Molly hid her concern; he clearly had deeper issues to deal with than she'd realised before now.

"Robert, underneath your outward confidence, I believe you're as insecure as the rest of us. Everyone experiences self-doubt after a knock back like this; the resilient ones move on."

They'd already made plans to stay at a Bed and Breakfast in St Ives for a week in August and had such a good time in and out of bed that, for a while, it seemed their relationship would revive. But their feelings for each other never fully recovered from that conversation in the pub, and Robert sank back into a mood of despondency about his future—or lack of it—in teaching. They parted as friends, before the new term began.

3

Reckless Moves

At the end of August, Robert arranged to see three university friends he'd remained in regular touch with. While Robert had never had any trouble making friends—his humour and initial ease around people made that easy—he'd never felt the need to gather a large circle. Apart from the few colleagues he socialised with after work, Mike, John and Andy were the only people he thought of as close friends. They'd all gone into jobs in the private sector. One after another, on an overcast evening in a faux, Tudor, Chiswick riverside pub, they bragged about their successful careers and high salaries, each one trying to trump the others.

Embarrassed, Robert exaggerated his own salary and promotion prospects and went home feeling depressed and resentful.

I'm nearly twenty-five, still a classroom teacher at the bottom of the pile, apparently not considered good enough for a minor promotion. It was easy for Molly to say that I should try taking the pressure off myself, but I can't get this sense of failure out of my head.

Three weeks into the new school year, missing the stimulation and intimacy of his relationship with Molly and with an empty weekend ahead of him, he forced himself to go to a stand-up comedy night with an open mike slot at the King Arthur in Crouch End. Volunteers had a minute to get a laugh or get booed off; the first three that tried didn't get past their first joke. It was humiliating, but survivable. After three pints, he got up on stage, told his one good joke about the porcupine and the Porsche and managed one more minute before being heckled off.

He fought his way to the bar, ending up next to a young woman with a mass of dark, curly hair. She turned towards him.

"That took nerve. There's no way you'd get me up there, and I'm used to performing in front of an audience. I'm Jane by the way; can I buy you a drink?"

"Thanks, Jane. I don't know what I was thinking. I've never done anything like that before. I'll have a pint of Original, please. What do you do?"

"I play violin in an agitprop band called Act Out. That's them over there, why don't you join us?"

They lived together in a semi-official squat in Finsbury Park. The group's appearances at gigs and fund raisers hardly covered their living expenses, so they all had part time jobs in the straight economy. Jane, who'd gone to the Guildhall School of Music, played violin and guitar, and tutored middle class kids in north London.

Introductions over— "You don't teach in a fucking private school, do you?" —the conversation moved to the 'Repeal Section 28' gig that three of them were involved in the following day.

Robert had never been interested in political activism, believing it to be a waste of his time; it never seemed to fundamentally change anything. The same people always ended up running the country. Luckily, he could wing his way through their discussion about the Thatcher government's Section 28 legislation, which banned schools from 'promoting homosexuality' as a 'pretended family relationship', as he'd recently attended a union meeting about it. But when one of the group members told him he should be encouraging his pupils to strike in support of the 'Repeal Section 28' campaign, he'd just laughed.

"What planet are you on?" he said, getting a frosty glare in return.

Relaxing within the background clamour of the pub, watching the four of them, he noticed Jane's dominant role. She was different from the women he worked with.

36

Normally, he wouldn't have seen her as his type; you'd be cautioned under the Trades Description Act if you described her as classically attractive. But she had a striking oval face with violet eyes under her dark, curly hair. And a sharp wit. Judging by the number of times she'd smiled and caught his eye, she clearly fancied him.

As they got up to leave at closing time, she said, "Do you fancy coming back to our place? It's only a mile away in Hanley Road, not luxurious, but we've got some wonderful Columbian coffee and a spare bed if you want to crash."

"Sounds great; it will make a change from the instant stuff I drink."

Jane's house mates quickly left them alone in the communal space, chatting and drinking the excellent coffee. The four of them had clearly worked hard on the house to make the space comfortable. Jane and Robert relaxed, talking easily about teaching, performing and the similarities between the two. As she spoke passionately about the potential for the arts to bring political change, leaning forward and occasionally touching him, he became increasingly turned on.

After an hour or so, she said, "I have an admission. The spare bed is not very comfortable, but I've just bought a new mattress that is. Would you like to sleep with me tonight?"

He grinned mischievously. "I thought you'd never ask."

Lying awake at three in the morning, Jane sleeping deeply beside him, he thought back to the matter-of-fact way she'd undressed and got straight into bed. He'd been fascinated by the contrast between her slim, pale body and abundant, black body hair.

"Are you waiting for the orchestra to play or what?" she'd said, as he'd stared a moment too long before getting into bed. She'd taken control the second he'd got under the duvet, sitting astride him, guiding him inside, coming twice and then bringing him to a loud, groaning orgasm.

"Christ, do you always make so much noise? You must have woken the whole house, John included. I don't want to rub it in for him."

"What's it got to do with John, for fuck's sake?"

"We occasionally sleep together. Nothing serious, but he finds it difficult when I sleep with someone else."

"He's going to find the news of our engagement a shock then, isn't he?"

"You know, Robert, you're a funny guy, but you can't go through life treating everything as a joke."

"I've learnt that over the last couple of months, but that's another conversation. Maybe I enjoy the attention from making people laugh. But I would like to do this again. John permitting, of course."

She kissed him, turned over and was asleep immediately.

Jane's side of the bed was empty when he woke in the morning. Laying there, taking in the Cuban revolutionary prints and posters against the Poll Tax on the walls, he felt at ease for the first time in weeks. He got up and stumbled into her collection of guitars and violins stacked in one corner. As he was picking them up, naked, she came in, dressed, with two cups of coffee.

"Good morning, Rob. You're just as sexy in daylight. I was hoping to take you back to bed and continue where we left off, but my co-artists are keen to start rehearsing. True to form, John is being really moody, so would you mind leaving discreetly after you've had your coffee? It was great last night, and I'd like to see you again, but I've got to sort things out with him first."

He tasted the coffee on her lips as she kissed him.

"Can I at least have a pee. I'm bursting."

Sure, but please don't hang about in the bathroom. I feel rotten about this. I know it's inhospitable, but we can't afford a bad vibe during rehearsals today. Why don't you come and see our next performance this Thursday; I'll leave you the details."

"That would be great. I'd like to."

"Don't be a stranger. I'll talk to John and hope to see you on Thursday."

"Don't start the revolution without me, comrade," he replied as she left the room.

Robert had an empty weekend ahead of him with books to mark that he didn't intend looking at. On the spur of the moment, he drove to Lewes to walk part of the South Downs. He needed to think through his feelings about last night. *Was Jane anything more than a one-night stand?*

Setting off from Rodmell around 11am, heading for Beachy Head in the warm, autumn sunshine, he mulled over the previous night. *In many ways, Jane isn't my type at all. Too fervent, active in left wing politics, living collectively in an open relationship (though it wasn't very open in practice). Just a few weeks ago I was on holiday with Molly, and I've never gone from one relationship to another this quickly—is it too fast? But why live by self-imposed rules? There is no appropriate time between relationships, and Jane's difference intrigues me.*

Back in London, sitting in his room staring at two piles of exercise books, Robert determined to take pressure off himself and stop obsessing about the jobs that might have been. *I'll do the minimum necessary and no more to stay on top of the job, go to Jane's gig on Thursday and see how things work out. My career plan can take a sabbatical until the New Year.*

Jane's performance on Thursday was in West London at a benefit for people arrested during the poll tax riots. It was the kind of event that he'd normally avoid at all costs. The poll tax was a stupid move by the Tory government, utter hubris on Thatcher's part, but from pictures he'd seen on TV, many of the protesters seemed to be asking for a beating. But Jane had got under his skin, and he wanted to see her again.

The event fulfilled Robert's worst expectations, with aggressive proselytising from the Socialist Workers Party stall and speeches full of hyperbolic imagery. Act Out were great though, particularly Jane on her electric violin. He'd worked his way to the front of the stage, and she gave him a big smile as soon as she came on. John wasn't with them. At the end of their set, Jane mouthed 'Wait for me outside' as she left the stage. Ten minutes later, he met her at the stage door.

"It's great to see you. I wasn't sure if you'd be here; my guess is this isn't exactly your thing. I've told the others to go back without me. I hope that wasn't presumptuous on my part."

"I thought you were fabulous. I'm really glad I came. You really can play; your violin seemed to be a part of you during the last song. Do you fancy a curry? My treat."

"Wonderful! I'm always starving after a performance. I won't argue about the treat either. I'm broke at the moment."

Over their meal at the Bengal Lancer, they talked non-stop about her journey from the Guildhall to Act Out, the downsides to living in a collective squat, tastes in music, what he liked and hated about being a teacher, and what happened if older students came on to you.

"So, what's the score with John; was he upset about the other night?"

"Yes, but he'd been getting clingy for a while, and we needed to clear it up. House rules are that we can't sleep with each other exclusively. If that happens, one or both have to leave the house. So, John's agreed to go as he's admitted he can't accept me sleeping with other blokes."

"Poor guy, that's pretty drastic. Does that mean you can't ever go out exclusively with someone?"

"No, anyone outside of the collective is fine. Why, are you planning to make me an offer?"

She laughed as she saw the look of surprise cross his face.

"Ah, the teaser has been teased. Don't worry, Robert, if we decide to carry on seeing each other, I was going to suggest taking things a week at a time."

He looked at her, smiling, holding the image of her on stage, violet eyes staring down the neck of the violin as she attacked it.

"A week at a time sounds good."

Back at his place, he told her about his landlady's house rules.

"Not exactly collective living, is it? OK if I have a quick shower. I stink after a performance."

"Of course, you can. I'll warm the bed."

As she came out of the tiny shower room, he was struck again by the contrast between the glacial whiteness of her skin and her dark, untrimmed body hair. He pulled the duvet back, embracing her as she got into the bed and kissing her deeply. As she went to move on top, he gently pushed her leg back.

"Let's try something different, this time."

He woke early the following morning and looked at her, sleeping, her hair covering the pillow. Last night they'd talked for an hour after sex about her dreams as a musician and his as a teacher. He felt relaxed with her. Their political differences didn't seem to be an issue, and they began to finish each other's sentences. She was grounded, in spite of her outwardly freewheeling lifestyle, and he envied the confidence she had in her own abilities. Actors' and performers' work was judged and scrutinised at every performance; they needed resilience by the bucketful. *Just what I didn't demonstrate last term*, he thought.

He had a shower, made them coffee and started to get dressed.

"Don't go just yet; come here and give me a cuddle."

As their relationship developed, Jane began staying at Robert's place on week nights as well as weekends. Act Out was becoming more successful and Robert went to as many gigs as he could. Punctuality, marking and planning came lower down his list of priorities, taking up less of his time. He was relaxed, enjoying living in the moment. *Ironic*, he thought, *if this relationship has helped me to regain a measure of inner peace and self-confidence.*

The week before the end of term, Sally asked to see him. He assumed it would be a casual chat about punctuality and unmarked books—he'd almost been expecting it.

"I'm sorry for not having this conversation earlier, Robert, but I needed to see you to warn you informally about concerns I have about your work this term. You've been late to your tutor group ten times, the book check showed that you'd only marked the books of two classes once this term and your top GCSE class has complained that the other group is getting on faster. I need to know what's going on."

He looked at Sally, hardly believing what he'd heard. He was trying to control the surge of anxiety engulfing him, pushing considered responses aside. *I've been found out again, as always. Except Sally isn't my father and I'm not a little boy. Get a grip, Mason.*

He was being naïve—she was responsible for the standard of teaching in the school, so of course she's being blunt. Controlling his voice, he replied, "I accept my punctuality hasn't been great this term and agree that I've let my marking slip with two classes. I feel the complaints from the GCSE class are unfair, as we've been covering different topics. I'm not going to make excuses, especially to you, and I guarantee it will improve next term, from day one. I can honestly say that I'm enjoying my teaching more than ever now, after a low patch following those interviews. What does an informal warning mean?"

"There'll be no written warning on your record, but I'll keep a note of this conversation and the issues raised. As long as your work returns to the previous high standard, the note will lapse at the end of the year, which I'm sure it will. You're far too good a teacher for any other outcome. Are you having problems that you'd like to tell me about?"

"Thank you for asking, Sally, but there's nothing that I can't sort out."

Sally's reprimand had shocked him. He'd get the marking up to date by the start of next term and talk to Jane about the week day mornings. *I don't have to neglect the job to enjoy myself—she doesn't.*

He hadn't seen her for almost a week when they met at the Kenwood House café in Highgate for a walk on Hampstead Heath. It was a cold mid-December day, snow had been forecast and he was wearing a fleece and walking boots. He saw Jane's big, black, wavy hair as soon as he walked in and caught her eye. She got up and gave him a warm, lingering kiss.

"Wow, that was nice. I'm pleased to see you, too." He paused and looked at her. "You look lovely, if a bit underdressed for a walk on the Heath at Christmas. Don't you have a decent coat?"

"You sound like my mum. Let's order. I want to hear your news."

Back at the table with coffee and cakes, Robert told her about his meeting with Sally and its relevance to 'our morning cuddle' as Jane called it.

She sat back, appraising him.

"Looks like we'll have to set the alarm clock half an hour earlier," she said and beamed at him a beautiful smile.

I just adore her, he thought, *she's smart, funny, loves life...*

"I love you," he said.

His words came out without thinking. The look on her face—nothing dramatic, just a slight downward movement of eyebrows and mouth—said everything.

"Shit, sorry. I was thinking what a lucky guy I am to have met you. Don't get worried, I'm not about to get a ring out."

"It was just a bit of a surprise, that's all. No one's ever said that to me before. There's no need to apologise."

She paused, thinking how to pick up the conversation.

"What about this meeting with Sally? Are you worried for your job?"

"No. I know Sally and she's always straight with me. If she says the slate will be wiped clean if I raise my game, then I believe her, and raising my game will be easy."

"Good, I'm pleased. I've got some news too. It turns out that the mother of one of my tutees is the Director of Music in Education at the Battersea Arts Centre. I must have mentioned Act Out to her at some point because she came to see us at the Chiswick gig. She's asked me to apply for the job of Music in Education co-ordinator at a new centre they're opening."

"That's fantastic! You'd be brilliant in that role. Tell me all about it on the walk."

They wandered over the hard, frosty, ground for over two hours, covering every corner of the Heath and talking excitedly about her job. Near the end, she told him her concerns about what it could mean for the collective.

"I haven't told them yet because I might not get it, and I'm not sure how they'll react. Perhaps my uncertainty says more than I care to admit about the real feelings within our collective. Do you mind coming back to my place tonight? It sounds a bit feeble, but until I get the job and tell them, it's almost as if I'm deceiving them. I'd feel better if you were with me."

His low mood, hanging over him since his stupid proclamation of love, lifted a little.

They next met a week before Christmas Day. Jane's interview had been several days earlier, and when they'd spoken that morning, she still hadn't heard the outcome. They'd agreed to meet in a pub in Holloway with a reputation for good food, so he'd got there early in order to grab a table. As he waited, he realised how much he wanted her to get the job.

He knew she'd got it the moment she came through the door, though she was making an effort not to show it. She was wearing a new black dress that clung to her petite frame, and he noticed several men and women turning to look as she walked over, which made him feel good.

She couldn't keep up the poker face, breaking into a huge smile before she got to his table.

"You got it!" he yelled, leapt off his chair and kissed her.

"I did! It's amazing! I've never had a proper job before, ever. I'm going to be asking you for advice."

He hugged her, lifting her off the floor, to cheers from people on nearby tables.

As she sat down, he caught the eye of a waitress and asked for two glasses of champagne.

"A proper job and champagne—two firsts in one day!"

"I can't believe you've never had champagne before! Is that dress new? It really suits you."

"Yes, I treated myself when I heard I'd got the job. Dead cheap, though. I saw it in a charity shop in Crouch End and knew it would suit me."

"I'm really glad you did, and so are those guys over by the door."

The waitress arrived with the champagne. "Celebrating?"

Jane looked at Robert, then at the waitress and said, "Yes, I've just got a new job and my lovely boyfriend has bought us champagne."

Robert chinked his glass against hers and made the toast. Had she called him her boyfriend in public before?

"To the next big thing in music in education. I'm so proud of you; they won't know what's hit them. Cheers. So, tell me all about it—when do you start, what will you be doing?"

As Jane went over the interview, Robert had a growing sense that she was holding something back. She finally told him that her new job was based in Brighton, not London.

"I know that's a drag for us, but it doesn't take long on the train and we can see each other almost as much as now."

Robert's joy evaporated. His next words hardly made sense.

"But that's terri... I mean it's fantastic for you, it all sounds wonderful, but what about... I mean, what does it mean for you and me? Are you going to move down there? Did you consider telling them that you'd need to discuss this with me?"

Jane had been expecting Robert to be surprised, even disappointed, by the unexpected news, but the intensity of his reaction—his distress, even—alarmed her. She enjoyed being with him and the sex was exciting. Only now did she understand the gap between her feelings for him and his for her.

"Robert, please keep this in perspective. Lots of couples live in different places and have a great relationship. I will have to move down there—it will make leaving the collective easier, that's for sure—but we'll see each other every weekend at least, more when I come up to London for meetings."

"I'm sorry, it's just such a shock, Jane. Of course, we'll carry on seeing each other, but I don't see how this won't affect our relationship over time, and I'm gutted about that."

As they carried on talking, Jane's doubts about their future and her concerns about the strength of his feelings grew. She didn't show it—in fact, did everything to reassure him—as she wanted time to think. After the meal she agreed to come over to his place for the weekend, their last before Christmas, which seemed to calm him down.

By the time he got home, his mood had lightened. He'd begun to convince himself that he could easily commute to Brighton once a week as well as weekends. Plus, she was bound to come up to the London centre sometimes. They could make it work.

At the weekend, Jane behaved as if their conversation in the pub hadn't taken place. They discussed practicalities like finding somewhere for her to live in Brighton, and she told him about the unpleasant reaction from her housemates. Robert felt he helped her get over the distress their response had caused, which increased his optimism that things were still good between them.

Over the Christmas holiday Jane went to Brighton for a few days to look at flats to rent while Robert spent two days with his mother. He used the time to catch up with all the marking he should have done and plan four weeks ahead into the new term.

She was on a high when they next met at his place in the New Year. Lying together in bed on Saturday morning, Jane was excitedly updating him about her new job.

"It's a bit scary, Robert. The team at Battersea are putting such trust in me to get the education side in the Brighton Centre underway. But they're all brilliant, the Centre is in a great location and I'm moving in to my new flat in two weeks. I gave your name to the agents as one of my two referees, I hope that's OK?"

"I think I can find something positive to say, if I put my mind to it, though I expect payment in kind. What about moving your stuff down there?"

"The Centre said they'll arrange for one of their vans and a driver to take everything down and help unload at that end.

As you know, I don't have a lot apart from my instruments, clothes, a bed and a chest of drawers."

"I could help you pack this end if you'd like. Give you some moral support with your ex-house mates."

"Oh, Robert, that would be fantastic, thank you. I'm dreading it; they've been really shitty about everything."

She rolled on top and kissed him.

Two weeks later, in the cold, half-light of a January morning, he met Jane and the driver outside her house. A row broke out as soon as they walked in. When they realised her new mattress had been swapped for a horribly stained one, Robert confronted the culprit and persuaded him to give it back. Her room had been used, clothes were missing and one of her violins damaged.

As they finished loading the last of her stuff into the van and slammed the doors shut, Robert's mood sank. *Is this the beginning of the end for us? How realistic am I being about still being together in a few weeks' time?* If Jane noticed, she didn't let on. She blew him a kiss as they pulled away, promising to ring in the evening.

She rang around seven, excited and upbeat.

"I can't quite believe I'm here, in my own little flat, no bitchy housemates with weird hang-ups and light fingers to worry about. If I stand on tip toe, I can see the sea when I look out of the front room window! Geoff, the driver, was brilliant. We carried everything inside in less than an hour. He's having a cup of tea before he drives back, then I'm going to have a walk 'round the area, grab a takeaway and have an early night. Are you still coming down next weekend?"

"Absolutely! I thought I'd leave early on Saturday and get down to you by ten. Any plans for tomorrow?"

"Unpack, go shopping for some kitchen stuff and other bits and pieces, then read the proposals for the Centre's programme this year, which I should have read days ago. How about you?"

"Marking. I can't contain my excitement. I'd much rather come down to Brighton and spend the day with you."

Jane ignored the hint—they'd already agreed she needed time in the flat on her own for the first few days—and said goodbye. She put the phone down, walked into the bedroom and smiled at the figure lying on her bed.

"Now, Geoff, I think it's time to christen my new flat, don't you?"

Robert strode over to his car, parked across the road from Jane's flat. Her voice cut through the fury that had hold of him, threatening to obliterate all rational thought.

"Robert, please don't leave in this state. I feel awful you found out like that, but we never said that we couldn't sleep with other people."

"Fuck you, Jane, you deceiving bitch. We've got nothing to talk about, now or ever."

He threw his bag onto the back seat, jumped in and accelerated hard down the narrow street, a couple crossing the road shouting at him as they ran to the pavement.

By the time he was out of the town on the dual carriageway he'd regained some control, although he'd no recollection of driving out of Brighton and onto the A23. His thoughts jumped around the events of the last 36 hours as he drove the little car as hard as it would go, foot to the floor.

He'd arrived at her flat yesterday, feeling anxious; how would she greet him? He needn't have worried—Jane was warm and welcoming. They'd spent a lovely day together wandering around the Lanes then walking all the way to the new marina and back, Jane talking enthusiastically about her first week and the people she was working with. She's just the same, he'd thought, we're just the same; this can really work, and I was stupid to be worried. The air in Brighton suited her; she was glowing. They'd gone to bed when they got back to the flat, went out for a meal at Pizza Express and made love again before falling asleep.

Jane hadn't put curtains up yet, so he'd woken early the next morning. As he'd got out of bed, he'd picked up his two used condoms from the floor; he wanted to put them in the bathroom pedal bin—they tended to hang around in the toilet bowl. As the lid opened, he'd seen the unmistakable ring of a condom underneath some face wipes and tipped the contents onto the floor.

He'd sat on the toilet, staring at the pile of tissues, face wipes, empty toothpaste tube and three used condoms.

"You're up early…" Jane had stopped in the doorway, horrified, as she'd taken in the contents—all of them—on the floor in front of Robert.

He'd seen the fear in her eyes as she'd registered his fury.

"You cheating cunt, who was it? The van driver?"

Jane had given a half nod with her head.

"Twelve hours after you leave me, you're shagging someone else. Did you even wait to unpack before fucking him? Three times—he was obviously a great lay. Better than me, I presume. All your sweet words about how moving to Brighton wouldn't affect us, just lies from the word go. I adored you; I wanted us to be a proper couple. What a fucking hypocrite you are, Jane. All this crap about treating people decently, caring for their feelings."

As he'd got off the toilet and moved towards her, she'd jumped backwards, holding onto the door frame.

"Don't worry, you cow, I'm not going to hurt you. I think you'd almost welcome that, turn yourself into the victim, but I won't give you that satisfaction. Just get out of the way while I get my stuff. Don't say anything; I don't want to hear it."

He'd got dressed, thrown his stuff into his bag and raced downstairs.

Two hours later, back in his bedsit, the questions he wished he'd asked her at the time kept going around in his mind. He picked up the phone and dialled her new number.

"Hello? If that's you, Robert, I'm going to put the phone down if you start being abusive. I'm not going to be spoken to like that, whatever you think of me."

Robert counted to five and got himself under control.

"I just need to know if our relationship ever meant anything to you, other than the sex and having someone there for you."

"Of course, it did. We were good together. I really liked you, fancied you—that was obvious, surely? I'm sad we won't get the chance to see if the London/Brighton thing could have worked for us."

"But how can I believe you had those feelings for me if you then fuck some van driver, just because he's available?"

"Oh, Robert, the two things aren't connected in that way for me. I'd just moved into my first flat, feeling really happy. We opened a bottle of wine, he's a good-looking guy and one thing led to another. I didn't do it because I was tired of you. I thought we both had permission to sleep with other people. I was wrong about that, and I'm sorry I hurt you."

"When did we ever discuss fucking other people? Was I asleep for that? You know we didn't. And you knew me well enough to know how much I'd be hurt, otherwise, why didn't you tell me? Admit it, you weren't going to."

"No, I wasn't, you're right. And I admit that I was worried that you were getting more involved than I was, but I didn't know what to do. I'm sorry."

Robert's voice rose, cracking a little.

"I'm sick of hearing that you're sorry. You're a cheat and you led me on because it suited you to have someone around. You lied to me the whole time we were together. I loathe you for that, Jane"

He put the phone down.

She doesn't deserve to be doing an important job like that, after what she's done, he thought. If she was capable of deceiving him and the Arts Centre, she shouldn't be working with impressionable young people.

The following day, he wrote to the Battersea Arts Centre, explaining that they should be aware that they'd recently employed—no doubt unwittingly—someone with a conviction for dealing 'class A' drugs. Did they think a person who'd lied about such a conviction should be employed to work with young people? Jane had told him, early in their relationship, that she'd once been caught with cannabis in a stop-and-search operation. As the quantity was above the amount for personal use only, she'd been charged and convicted.

Reluctantly, the Centre had to dismiss her.

4

Nice Guys Don't Win

Slowly, Robert began to put his feelings of betrayal behind him. He went for another job without success, but the feedback was encouraging, and he remained positive, managing his disappointment. When the Head of Year 9 announced that she would be taking maternity leave from the end of May, he realised her role would need to be covered for up to a year.

Robert had little experience of a role at that level, although he'd been praised for his work as a tutor. Sally encouraged him – "I've no worries about your commitment any more" - but warned there would be another applicant, a young woman called Judith. She had two years' more experience than him—a big advantage—and he decided he had to counter that, somehow. He began to ask around, discreetly, as he knew little about her.

He found out that Judith and her friends went to a pub several miles from the school on most Friday nights for a serious drinking session. The pub had a small stage with a dancing pole, and apparently it wasn't unusual for some of them to get so drunk they performed on the pole, leaving little to the imagination. *How fucking stupid*, he thought. *She deserves to be found out.*

Robert called his friend Mike and asked him if he would go to the pub on Friday night with his girlfriend and discreetly take pictures of any incriminating behaviour, as he wanted them for an end-of-term surprise. Mike was amused by the idea and agreed. He phoned Robert the morning after he'd gone to the pub.

"Now I know why you've stayed in teaching! I couldn't believe what they were getting up to. I thought Jo and I would have to be careful so that they didn't suspect, but they were all too drunk to notice. I'll get the film developed and send you the pictures."

Robert knew he was onto something the second he saw them. Some just showed the usual Friday night excesses, but several were explicit. One revealed Judith with glazed eyes, one leg wrapped round the pole, her mini skirt around her bottom; in another, she was grasping the pole with both hands, straddling it between her legs.

If I use these, it can't be half measures, he realised. He posted one set of incriminating pictures to the head teacher. The only problem was Mary, a friend of his, who unfortunately appeared in one of the shots with Judith. But it was too incriminating to leave out. He sent a second set to the Hackney Chronicle, just in case the head teacher tried to bury them to avoid bad publicity.

Just as the Head was meeting with Judith and Mary to 'discuss an issue of some concern', the pictures appeared on the front page of the Chronicle, under the headline 'Shame of Pole Dancing Teachers: Parents Demand Answers'.

Copies were all around the staff room by break time. The press, including reporters from two national papers, were camped outside the school gates interviewing pupils, in spite of the senior team's efforts to stop them. The journalists were getting wonderful copy:

"My mum says I'm to walk out if either of them takes my class next year."

"I've seen them doing stuff like that in the gym after school."

"She's a great teacher; she lets us do whatever we want in her lessons."

Judith and Mary had to be smuggled out of the side gate and sent home pending a further investigation.

The head teacher was apoplectic. Sally disappeared into his office for over an hour and came out with prepared statements for the press, parents and staff. At the especially convened staff meeting after school, Sally rallied the staff around their colleagues and stressed the importance of not talking to the press and further damaging the school's reputation— "Which, of course, affects us all."

Some hope, thought Robert, as he stood in the staff room listening to his colleagues. There was much sympathy, understandably, for the two teachers, especially Judith, who was both more recognisable and more exposed, literally. Even Ron held back from making any remarks.

Robert thought that Judith would be lucky to keep her job, and there was no way she could be appointed as Head of Year. Providing no one else applied and he kept his nerve in the interview, the job should be his. He felt no guilt about what he'd done. Judith had been utterly stupid to behave like that, given her position, and it was bound to come out sooner or later. Imagine how much worse the publicity and consequences would be for her if this happened after she'd got the Head of Year post. And he knew he would do a much better job than her.

Incredibly, Judith initially wanted to remain a candidate, but withdrew her application once Sally made it clear that she'd brought the school into disrepute, a charge that could lead to dismissal.

Two weeks later, after he got the job, Molly took him out to celebrate.

"Congratulations to our new Head of Year 9, who I know is going to be a huge success. Not bad going, after less than two years in teaching; I hope he remembers his friends as his glittering career progresses. Well done, Robert, I'm proud of you."

"Not without a little help from my friends, Molly. Thank you for being there when I was behaving like a prat."

"You're welcome. What do you make of the pole dancing thing? Why would any teacher take such a crazy risk? Judith is sure there were no parents in the pub, but how could she know that?"

"Maybe one of the bar staff knew a parent and suggested they come to see what their kid's teachers get up to. Or maybe there were a couple of journalists out for the evening who got lucky?"

"Could be. So, when does Kate start her leave and hand over to you?"

"The beginning of June, so I've got a few weeks to prepare."

Robert knew that his biggest test in the new job would be managing his team of tutors. They'd all been in teaching longer than him—some much longer—and he guessed, correctly, that some would resent having a young and inexperienced colleague as their boss. They would probably assume that he wouldn't be introducing many changes as Kate would be returning within a year. They'll be in for a few surprises.

Sally was delighted when Robert showed her the ambitious changes he had planned for his new team. Pleased too, as she knew Kate had been coasting for the last year and pupils' results had suffered as a result.

"I'm impressed, Robert. I can see you've been busy over the holiday. You may get kickback from some of the tutors, but avoid getting into arguments, if possible. Listen to their views but keep referencing the evidence of poor progress to show why the changes need to be made.

"Have a couple of things in your proposals that you're willing to give up, so that they'll think they've achieved a compromise. Let them know that I've approved the plans and expect them to be introduced."

Robert was less than half way through explaining his proposals to the tutors at their first meeting, showing how they could make a real difference to pupils' progress, when one of them interrupted him.

"So, we're working our butts off, staying here till God knows what time, marking and preparing, and now you're telling us, without any consultation, that you expect us to take on a load of additional work, collecting data. I'm going to carry on working exactly as before and will be taking this up with the union rep tomorrow."

After the team went to see Sally with their union rep, she called a meeting with all involved. Robert knew that the rep had a short fuse, and decided his best tactic was to encourage him to go over the top.

Sally began the meeting.

"I want us to leave this meeting with a solution acceptable to everyone, so I'd like to begin by—"

The union rep interrupted her.

"That will depend on Robert agreeing to stop increasing my members' workload in contravention of the national agreement between this union and the Department for Education."

"Thank you, Frank, can I continue? Unfortunately, many of our Year 10 pupils are underachieving, and have been for some time. Our research shows that additional, targeted support can make a big impact and tutors are key to identifying those kids who need it. The system that Robert wants to introduce does that, and the tutor team will be given additional support to help them. So, what's the problem?"

"The problem is that my members are overworked as it is, and Robert is trying to bully them into doing this extra work. The union won't accept that."

Robert jumped in, seizing his opportunity.

"Accusing me of bullying a fellow member of staff, in front of my senior manager, is a serious accusation. Either give Sally the evidence for that accusation or withdraw it. If you don't, I will take out a grievance against you."

Sally cut in. She was enjoying this, but it was getting out of hand.

"Well, Frank? Robert is right. I have to take any accusations of bullying seriously and formally follow them up, as you know. If you wish to leave that on the record, then I'm going to need written statements from all of you by the end of the day."

The rep turned to the others, who looked back blankly.

"Can we adjourn for ten minutes and discuss this, please?"

"Please go ahead."

As soon as they'd left, Sally said, "True to form, Frank got carried away by the soaring heights of his own rhetoric. He'll come back and withdraw, I'm sure. However, I can see he senses we're on weak ground if we instruct them to do this, and he's right. Any ideas?"

"Why don't I offer to do the analysis for them, providing they give me their registers with all the reports they've received from subject teachers? They can't possibly object to that, and at least that way I can monitor their registers."

"If you're prepared to do that, great. It's your idea, so you should propose it. Everything going well otherwise?"

Robert laughed. "Up to this moment, yes."

The accusation was withdrawn, and Robert's proposal accepted. He could see the two tutors realised the implications of handing him their registers to check, but they'd cornered themselves.

By the end of the summer term, Robert knew he'd made the right move. He loved the variety and responsibility, finding the daily interactions with parents and pupils hugely rewarding. *Thank God I fought to get this post. From now on, I'm going to fight for every promotion as hard as I did for this one.*

Just before the school broke up for the summer, rumours began to spread that Judith had taken an overdose of sleeping pills and been rushed to hospital. She was discharged after four days but continued to suffer periodically from depression and never held a teaching job again. Robert felt little guilt or remorse; he told himself that she was always going to be found out.

He spent most of the summer holiday walking the streets of Hackney, looking for a flat to buy. The London housing market had weakened during the last two years of recession and high interest rates, and he'd begun to study the property ads in the Evening Standard. With his increased salary, he worked out he earned enough to afford a mortgage on a small flat, even with interest rates at ten percent.

With two weeks to go before the new term, his offer on a one bedroom flat in a Victorian house in Clapton, east London, was accepted. Separate bathroom, a small lounge with a kitchenette attached, walls covered in magnolia-painted wood chip paper and in need of decorative TLC. But, as the agent said, it had potential; it was vacant, and he should complete on the deal in six weeks.

He moved in at the beginning of October. He felt good every time he turned the key in the lock, walked in and looked around, getting pleasure remembering where each piece of furniture had come from. Antique shops in the East End, mostly.

"I love the feeling of being able to put my stamp on a place of my own. I was inspired by what you'd done in your flat when I saw it over two years ago."

He was talking to Molly at the end of the day.

"Then I think you owe me an invite and a meal, at least."

"Agreed. How about Friday evening?"

"Lovely. I'll bring some good wine, like you on your first visit to my place."

"Let's meet in the Eagle at 7.30, just down the road from my flat. You can get a feel for the area."

Up to now, his part of Hackney had escaped gentrification, though a few young professionals were beginning to take advantage of the slump in the market to buy and refurbish old houses. There was a noisy but relaxed atmosphere when he walked into The Eagle on Friday. He ordered a pint for himself and a glass of white wine for Molly, then sat at a table in the corner to watch the diverse crowd and wait for her. He felt at ease within himself, in a way he hadn't since the break-up with Jane.

Molly walked in five minutes later, dressed in her usual bohemian style.

"This is nice; I like it. Reminds me what North Kensington was like ten years ago. Thanks for my wine. Cheers, here's to your new home."

As they walked the two hundred metres back to his flat, neither was in any doubt what was about to happen.

"You can feed me after I've taken you to bed, Robert. I haven't slept with anyone in months."

"Your command is my wish, Molly."

From the moment they got into bed, the combination of the forbidden and the familiar made sex with his passionate ex-lover particularly intense. The following morning, Robert brought her a cup of tea in bed.

Half awake, she looked at him and smiled.

"No regrets, I hope. To be honest, I've never quite understood why it didn't work out between us. We had a memorable holiday last summer, in Cornwall."

"It had nothing to do with you, Molly. I was in a strange place after screwing up those interviews; you tried hard to bring me out of my self-obsessed depression, but in the end, I had to work things out for myself, one way and another. Why, are you thinking we could try again?"

Molly put her tea down, suddenly awake.

"A relationship? Absolutely not, don't worry. I think we've both moved on from there, don't you? But we don't have to pass up an opportunity when it comes along, do we? I don't have to go for a couple of hours; put your tea down and come here."

She contemplated him as he took off his dressing gown and got into bed next to her, pulling her on top.

"I can see you agree with my suggestion."

Robert happily took all the credit from Sally and the head teacher when the tests in November showed a big reduction in the number of his pupils under-performing. Sally tipped him off that she'd heard Kate may not come back from maternity leave and to prepare for another interview after Christmas. At the end of term, he felt confident enough to invite all the tutors round to his flat for wine and cheese.

He'd reluctantly accepted his mother's invitation to visit over Christmas as it was several months since he'd seen her. Spending Christmas and Boxing Day morning with her, her husband and their friends, listening to the conversation about the weather, terrible car journeys and young people these days, brought the sense of alienation he'd experienced as a teenager flooding back. He returned to his flat on Boxing Day afternoon with a sense of relief. Sitting at his corner table in the Eagle, he studied the mixed crowd and reflected how, as London had become younger and more multicultural, people from all classes now dressed in a similar way and adopted the same accent. It was becoming more difficult to judge background and heritage at a glance, and he loved that.

He was in there again five days later, seeing in the New Year. Walking home at one in the morning, with the taste of numerous midnight kisses lingering, he reflected on 1992. He'd put Jane behind him, made a breakthrough in his career, faced down the awkward squad on his team, bought a flat and seen his pupils' results start to improve.

He remembered the scene in the staffroom after his disastrous first day. *Who's laughing now*, he thought?

A week into the new term, news that Katy wasn't coming back after her maternity leave began to circulate in the staff room. Robert took Sally aside and asked her what she knew.

"It's not official yet, as the Head hasn't got it in writing, but from what I hear, I'm sure she won't change her mind. You'll be a strong candidate, but the post will be advertised so there could be serious competition."

The job advert came out at the start of February. He remembered Sally's advice after his first disastrous interview and asked Molly to give him a mock interview. After the first run through, she didn't mince her words.

"You're like a scared rabbit, holding yourself in. There's none of the passion I know you feel for this job; be more expressive, make eye contact and smile, for fuck's sake. Don't come across as if you're remembering lines, be yourself and don't get stroppy with the panel. Apart from that, not bad at all"

Two sessions later, Molly signed him off.

"You're as ready as you'll ever be."

Waiting in the staff room before his interview, unable to recall any of the things he'd rehearsed, his nerves almost overcame him. But as he walked towards the head teacher's office, Molly's advice kicked in. Knocking on the door, he knew he could do it.

On the Friday afternoon before half term, Sally asked him into her office and told him he'd got the job. Elated, he strode over and gave her a hug.

"Careful, Robert, I have a fiancée these days."

"You're engaged! That's brilliant. Are you going anywhere romantic over half-term?"

"We've booked a skiing break in the French alps."

"Wonderful. I've always wanted to learn to ski. Take care of yourself; you're a special person. As far as my teaching career goes, I owe you everything."

Robert walked back into school on the Monday after half term, acknowledging the congratulations of his colleagues. At the end of the day, there was an announcement over the school's creaky address system: 'Will all staff please go to the staffroom as quickly as possible.'

The hum of conversation, as everyone recounted their holiday experiences, stilled immediately when the head teacher walked in. He'd clearly been crying and looked as if he could start again at any moment. He steadied himself against a desk, then began,

"I've just had the most dreadful news from Sally's father. Sally and her fiancée were tragically killed two days ago when the mini-bus carrying their ski party left the road and plunged down the mountainside. There were no survivors. I know that you will all be desperately shocked and distressed at this news as will many of our pupils. I'm sending a letter home informing our parents, and I've asked the local authority to arrange counsellors for the children, and also for any staff that need it. I will, of course, inform you about the funeral arrangements as soon as I know. Forgive me," he said, as he choked back more tears.

Robert felt his legs giving way as he went into shock. Colleagues grabbed him just in time, then helped him into a chair where he sat weeping silently, unwilling to be comforted. Half an hour later, seeing him about to leave, Molly insisted on going home with him.

"You can't drive in that state. Give me the keys and I'll take you back."

She stayed the night, holding him, until he eventually fell asleep.

At Sally's funeral, he broke down again, angry that one of the few people he'd relied on for guidance and support had been senselessly taken away from him. It was so unfair.

For the rest of the 1992/3 academic year, he immersed himself in his work, pushing himself and his tutors hard. He missed Sally badly; she'd always been there for him.

5

Meeting his Match

During the autumn term of 1993, Robert finally silenced the remaining doubters on the staff. Three months earlier, he'd persuaded the head teacher to move two teachers out of his team, and even Robert was surprised at the impact. His tutors now competed to try and make certain their group achieved the most merits.

Eric Hatton, the head teacher, had returned from a conference in October, brimming with new ideas for the school. One involved a programme of residential activities, including a school camp, and required a co-ordinator. The job was only available to internal applicants, and Hatton made it clear it was Robert's, if he wanted it.

Some of the older teachers felt that another promotion, at this early stage in his career, was too much, too young. But their sniping had little impact. The gainsayers were the same people he'd heard in his first term in the school calling anyone aspiring to a senior post a sell-out.

Robert went for the post and got it.

But by February, well into planning the summer camp, he realised he'd underestimated the work needing to be done, particularly health and safety training. At the Council's insistence, he'd had to agree to put the camp on the lower, safer, slopes of the Brecon Beacons, but even this would be a challenging environment for some pupils and staff.

His most pressing task was to recruit enough teachers for the camp. Although August was five months away, his colleagues would have to give up two weeks of their summer holidays for no extra pay, and many would soon begin booking their own holidays. He was very relieved when a dozen people turned up to his first meeting for teachers wanting to sign up.

For the Council to approve the camp, at least half of the staff needed to successfully complete a basic mountain leadership course. He persuaded Hatton to fund a weekend course at a training centre in south Wales, on the understanding that staff would have to pay their travel expenses.

He'd scrapped his Mini three months ago and bought a beautiful, second hand Alfa Romeo Sprint, and was looking forward to driving it to the Beacons for the training weekend. Everyone was car sharing, and he'd agreed to give a lift to Sue Goodall, the head of special needs.

She'd been at the school longer than him, and he guessed she was about five years older. He'd only got to know her in the last few months, since he started as a head of year, as they often discussed pupils in his year group. She was one of those people that carried around a sense that her life had been a disappointment, and it was everyone's fault but hers. There was a brittleness to her, a fragility under the surface. Robert wasn't sure they'd have much to say to each other outside of school gossip.

He couldn't have been more wrong. Soon after they passed the Heathrow turn-off on the M4, Sue began talking frankly about her personal life. By the time they'd got to Newport, Robert knew much more than he wanted to about her unhappy relationship with her live-in boyfriend.

"Frankly, Robert, I'm glad to have a break from Martin for a weekend."

"That's sad. I mean, once it gets to that stage, you must question why you stay together, surely?"

"Just habit, really. What about you—anyone significant in your life?"

He was relieved to quickly close down her questions about his love life,

"I'm afraid not, Sue. There hasn't been anyone serious since Molly."

He saw no reason to mention his relationship with Jane. Schools thrived on gossip, so why reveal more than necessary?

As soon as they arrived, he made his way to the warden's office and introduced himself. As the group leader, he'd been given a room of his own. He'd warned everyone that the accommodation was basic, the showers communal and the food filling but dull. No one complained—they wouldn't have volunteered to spend two weeks of their summer holiday in a Welsh field with forty kids if they did.

After the evening meal, the quality of which confirmed his earlier assessment, the warden took them through their programme for the weekend: activities on the lower slopes of the Brecon Beacons, lectures about safety in the mountains and role plays on how to deal with the more obvious dangerous, scenarios. Everyone kept their questions to a minimum as they were keen to get to the village pub before closing time.

Sue approached him as they were leaving. "Aren't you joining us, Robert?"

"I won't tonight, Sue, if that's OK. The warden has asked to go through a few things. Tomorrow night, definitely."

The next day was sunny with a few clouds, perfect for hill walking. He tried to get to the South Downs as often as possible from London. *But let's face it*, he thought, looking up to the summit of Pen y Fan, *you don't get views like this*. Everyone enjoyed the day, even the classroom sessions, and they were all looking forward to the camp. The warden ended the day by complimenting everyone on their commitment and reminded them that, "If you want a shower, there's just one communal shower room, so ladies and gents separately, please?"

Sue suggested that the men go first, and be quick about it, so that the women could then take their time, which was agreed.

Robert and his two colleagues had been in the shower for less than a couple of minutes when Sue and three friends walked in with towels round them, screaming with laughter.

"Your time's up, our turn now."

Robert stood there, annoyed, and continued to rinse himself. He realised Sue clearly had this bit of nonsense in mind when she suggested the men went first.

"See all of you at dinner, then," he said as he left the shower room. Sue looked at him, laughing.

In the pub that evening, Robert noticed how much some of them could drink and apparently maintain control, including Sue, who was clearly coming on to him. *A combination of the physicality of the walking and alcohol*, he thought. *Not a good idea*. He made a note to tell everyone at the appropriate time that they couldn't drink like this on the camp; having responsibility for forty teenagers in the Brecon Beacons meant staying sober.

Robert was in bed, looking at the programme for the next day, when there was a knock at the door.

"Who is it?" he said.

"It's Sue, Robert. Can I talk to you?"

He opened the door to see Sue in her dressing gown, steadier than earlier.

"Is anything the matter?"

"Not really, I just wanted to apologise for barging in on your shower; it was my idea and very childish, so please don't blame the others. I had too much to drink earlier, but I'm OK now."

Her dressing gown hung revealingly open at the top, the cord tied loosely around her waist. As he looked at the swell of her breasts, he felt himself getting hard.

"Apologies accepted. Was there anything else?"

She smirked and raised her eyebrows quizzically. Robert stepped aside, holding the door open, and Sue walked forward. He pulled her into his room and kissed her, cupping his hand around her bottom. Undoing the cord, she took off her dressing gown and got into his bed.

They slept together once more after returning to London. She wanted to keep the affair going, but he'd felt emotionally distant after sex and told her he only wanted friendship. When a science teacher colleague invited him to a party, it didn't occur to him to take Sue.

Five minutes after arriving, he was wishing he hadn't come. The atmosphere in the room was dominated by a boorish group of male teachers, oblivious to the impact they were having on the mood for everyone else. He was about to leave when he noticed a petite, stylishly dressed woman glancing at him. She appeared to be with someone from the group, although she was excluding herself from their banter.

She moved away from them and began to look absent-mindedly through the host's collection of CDs. Every so often she would run her hands upwards through her dark, glossy hair. Cut into a bob, it emphasised her high cheekbones and generous mouth. He guessed she wasn't a teacher—she lacked the 'one notch under hysterical' level of banter characteristic of teachers at parties.

The man who he assumed to be her boyfriend wasn't in her league. He was a teacher at another local school who never stopped moaning about 'the fucking kids and how unteachable they were'. *God knows what she sees in him*, he thought as he held forth yet again.

Robert walked over to her, enjoying the feeling of anticipation and apprehension.

"Hi, I'm Robert. Anything that captures your imagination in the CD collection?"

"Not really, I'm afraid. It's one of those 'Must get all my classic albums on CDs' collections people put together in the 80s. Too light on originality for me. Nice to meet you, Robert, I'm Emily. Are you another one of the Camberwell High posse?"

Robert grimaced in mock embarrassment at the term, clearly aimed at the laddish, heavy drinking group, who apparently thought it was a really cool moniker. *Jesus, teachers can be embarrassing*, he thought.

"God no. Some of them are OK, but I've never understood why they don't realise how ridiculous the hard drinking, laddish act makes them look."

Emily stifled a laugh, enjoying a private joke. He was standing close enough to catch the smell of her scent and take in her striking green eyes. She returned his gaze.

"As one of them invited me, I may be able to throw some light on that. It's probably compensatory activity for some deep insecurity about teaching not being a proper man's job, so they need to show how macho they are. You're a teacher, though, aren't you? So, you'd know better than me about that. Maybe someone with your self-confidence doesn't need those props?"

I think you've just blown it.

"Oh God, I'm sorry, that was out of order."

"It's OK, I'm just teasing. To be honest, I agree with you—the whole thing is just ridiculous posturing."

As she said this, she placed her hand lightly, but deliberately, on his arm. Her wrist and hand, thin and delicate, somehow seemed incongruously fragile on someone so self-assured. Robert remembered something Molly had once said.

"If a woman you've recently met touches your arm 'by accident' in conversation, Robert, it's probably not an accident. She's letting you know she's interested."

They talked easily for over an hour, about work, music, how London was changing. She was a lawyer, and when she told him about the legal cases she took on—people being shafted by their bosses, asylum seekers obstructed by home office bureaucracy—his attention began to wander. He wasn't that interested in solving other people's problems.

At the end of the party, she asked him if he fancied meeting up for a drink.

"What would your boyfriend think about that?"

Emily looked at him, surprised.

"Oh, Dave's not my boyfriend; how on earth could you think that? Not my type at all. We're just old friends from university, and he asked me if I wanted to come to a party."

Robert was taken aback by the sharpness of her response. *Maybe this woman's too high maintenance.*

"Sorry, I made the wrong assumption. Maybe some other time. I'm snowed under with work deadlines at the moment. It's been nice to meet you, though, Emily."

"Sure, I understand. Good luck with the school camp."

By the middle of June, he'd completed all the forward planning for the camp; approval from the council for the itinerary and activities, permission from all the parents, transport booked, and fees collected. He'd allowed two especially challenging boys to sign up, believing that the experience of being part of a sharing community would be good for them. Not all the staff were happy with this; in particular there'd been concerns about one pupil, Tom, a boy with Asperger's syndrome. But Robert had organised a meeting between concerned staff and parents, and they'd been won around.

He increasingly berated himself about his impetuous response to Emily at the end of the party. *OK, she was rather obsessed with her work and responded sharply to your assumption about her boyfriend. But how many striking, sexy, intelligent women have asked you out recently?*

But he was too proud to get her number from the colleague who'd invited him to the party.

The camp was due to start on July 30th[th], which was four weeks away. He was having his first lazy Sunday since the training trip to Wales. Sue had rung and asked him out for a drink that morning, but he'd made an excuse about the camp preparations taking up all of his time.

The phone went. He was going to leave it to go on to answerphone, thinking it could be Sue once again, but he disliked doing that.

"Hello, Robert Mason."

"Hi Robert, it's Emily. We met at the party a couple of weeks ago. I thought we were getting on well until the end, when I think I might have annoyed you."

Robert was immediately aware of a light-headed feeling, a quickening of his pulse. She sounded a little nervous, which was a good sign, he thought.

"Hi, Emily, of course I remember. It's good to hear from you. Sorry if I seemed pissed off, that was juvenile. I was genuinely snowed under with work at the time, but the school camp is pretty much all organised now."

"That's good; it must be a horrendous job pulling all the different aspects together."

"It is, especially the first time."

He paused. *She's done the big thing, ringing you, so don't fuck up again.*

"Would you still like to meet up for a drink in the next few days?"

"That sounds great. I'd love to."

They met in a pub she knew in Farringdon, south of Kings Cross, near her office. He saw her as he walked in, sitting in a booth away from the crush of city workers by the bar, a glass of white wine in her hand. She looked relaxed, provocatively attractive but appearing not to know it. She turned, saw him and smiled broadly. He walked over, reminding himself not to blow it with some inappropriate remark in the first few minutes.

After an hour of non-stop conversation and laughter, Robert knew he had to see her again. The shared attraction was obvious; there was warmth in her eyes when she returned his gaze. Two hours later, Emily looked at her watch for the second time that evening.

"I'm afraid I've got a meeting with a senior partner tomorrow morning to discuss a difficult case I'm handling, so I should be getting back. It's been a lovely evening. I've had a really good time."

"Me too. I had no idea that was the time. Would you like to meet again, in the not too distant future?"

"I would. Is next Saturday too distant?"

"Sounds good. Shall I give you a ring and suggest somewhere near me?"

"Perfect. Just leave a message on the answerphone, where and when."

He missed the last tube and jumped in a taxi. Sitting on the back seat, watching the crowds of drinkers meandering over the pavements, he replayed the last few hours in his head. He couldn't identify exactly what had passed between them so quickly that could explain the strength of his feelings or why he dared to feel it was the same for her.

He'd left a message suggesting they meet in a little Italian restaurant he'd discovered near Newington Green, less than a mile from his flat. Robert had been at their table for over ten minutes, slightly apprehensive that the message hadn't been recorded, when Emily rushed in. She was wearing a dark suit, carrying a large shoulder bag and had clearly come straight from work. She came over, apologising profusely.

"So sorry, I'll explain in a minute, but I've got to freshen up first. Where's the ladies?"

As she sat down, she explained that her boss had insisted they meet at the office to finalise the papers for the case, Saturday or not. They talked about families, work, politics and friends—the kind of conversation that you invest in when you want to know all about somebody. When Emily told him about the cases she took on—workers denied their legal rights, asylum seekers detained indefinitely in terrible conditions—she sensed from Robert's reaction that he wasn't someone for whom politics was that important. But she felt a draw between them, whatever that meant, and his enthusiasm when he talked about teaching endeared her. He gave off an inner strength, a self-confidence, that she found very attractive, which, along with his obvious physical attributes, had helped persuade her to ring him ten days ago.

This morning, she'd decided not to pack her overnight things. However well the evening went, she wasn't going to sleep with him. It was too soon. Looking at him across the table now, she wondered if she'd been too cautious. So, when he said, "Do you fancy coming back to my place?" she surprised herself by declining.

"I'd like to see your place sometime, but I think tonight is too soon. You can walk me to the nearest tube, though."

"Oh Christ, that came out badly. I wasn't suggesting that we sleep together."

Emily smiled, looked him in the eye and said, "Thank goodness for that, the thought had never occurred to me either," and they both laughed.

Robert put his arm round her waist as they left the restaurant to walk to the tube station.

"Just what a gentleman should be doing," she said.

Robert stopped and turned towards her. He felt his heart beating as if this was his first date.

"And what about this?" he said. He smelt the shampoo on her hair as he kissed her, gently and dryly at first, then harder and more urgently. Emily felt his tongue against her teeth, then inside her mouth, warm and slippery. They remained pressed together, on the pavement and oblivious to the world, until someone called out,

"Bloody hell, get a room, you two!"

They broke apart, laughing. Robert murmured,

"Well, I did try," and they laughed again.

Back at her house, relaxing in the bath, Emily reflected on the evening. As she'd gone into the tube station, she'd asked him if he wanted to come over to her place for dinner next weekend if he was free. *That was impulsive, not like me*, she thought. *I've just basically invited him over to sleep with me after two dates. So, where's this going? I've always taken time with previous boyfriends, making sure we're on the same wavelength, politically, ideologically. I believed that was important if we were going to be lovers. This is different. He doesn't fit that image at all; he seems uninterested in issues and causes. Maybe that's been my problem; too keen to find my soulmate clone from the Guardian? When I'm with him, I feel he wants me; he makes me feel desired.*

"It's number 79," Robert called out to the cab driver as he turned into Sansom Street, a week after their second date. He thought back to their kiss on the pavement, Emily suggesting that he come over to her place for dinner; if the evening goes well, we'll probably sleep together. He became aroused at the thought. She was different from anyone else he'd dated before. *Not only funny, bright and sexy, but good for me, in a way that I can't explain yet.*

Her house looked the same as the other narrow two-storey terraced houses in the street, only more cared for. He felt the adrenalin surge as he walked up the path and saw her at the door, smiling broadly. Wearing a tight bottle-green dress, a few inches above the knee and a neckline revealing a hint of cleavage, she looked amazing.

"Welcome to my little house, come on in," she said, kissing him lightly on the lips and taking his bottle of wine. "Wow, Pouilly Fume, thank you."

The green figures on the digital alarm read 2.45. Robert had fallen asleep fifteen minutes ago and was lying on his side with his back to her. She looked at him. He was in great shape; slim and nicely muscled. Half way through the meal, she knew she'd sleep with him. *I know little about him, we've seen each other only three times and it's clear that we engage with the world in different ways—and that would have been a problem for me in the past. But there's something going on between us; for once I'm going to take a risk and see where this goes.*

She'd only had four lovers before, and sex had been disappointing with all of them, in different ways, so she'd been cautious not to raise her expectations.

But they'd taken their time, getting to know each other's bodies with a lack of inhibition she'd not experienced before. Afterwards, as they relaxed, she'd reached down to him as he lay with his head on her stomach, and pulled him up beside her, his face glowing with the smell of her.

"I think you've had some practice with that," she'd said.

He'd fallen asleep in seconds.

A noise in the street woke him, bright sunlight streaming in through the curtains. Robert turned towards her. Seeing she was awake, he leant over and kissed her.

"Good morning. You're a gorgeous sight to wake up to. Have you been awake long?" he said.

"No, not long. I was thinking the same about you, funnily enough. I hope last night felt as good for you as it did for me. I must go to the loo, sorry."

She threw the duvet back and rolled out of bed in one gymnastic movement. It was the first time he'd seen her naked in daylight, and he watched as she walked across the room with an unself-conscious grace. He leant back against the headboard, growing aroused as he heard her pee splashing against the bowl. As she walked back into the bedroom, her gaze took in his long, naked body, penis brazenly, comically, signalling his desire. Emily smiled and sat on his lap, one leg each side of him. This would probably be their last time together before he went away on the school camp next week. She leaned forward and kissed him.

"What do you think we should do with this?" she said, reaching behind her and holding him.

"Do you have any suggestions?"

She leaned forward, took hold of his penis and guided it into her as she lowered herself, contracting her pelvic floor muscles.

Robert gasped.

"Do you like that, sir? Is this good for you?"

"Fucking hell, Emily."

They stayed in bed until early afternoon.

"Can we do that again soon?" he said as they stood at the front door, holding each other. "If that's not too forward."

She had one hand resting against the side of his face, rubbing his stubble. "I'm OK with forward. It was lovely, and I'm sorry we won't be seeing each other for three weeks, so take care of yourself and remember to bring a razor next time. My thighs are still burning."

A week later, Robert was standing next to the coach outside the school, checking that every pupil had brought the right gear. He didn't notice a black Vauxhall Astra pull up across the road or see Emily walk up behind him.

"Good morning, Mr Mason. I've come to check your equipment's all in working order."

Robert whirled around, not quite believing what he'd heard. She stood there, a huge smile on her face, so pleased she'd surprised him.

"Emily! What are you…?"

"I thought I'd come and see you off. You look very commanding. Be safe and have a great time."

He gave her a hug, then chanced a chaste kiss on the mouth. Not chaste enough to prevent whoops of 'Yes, Mister Mason' from some of the pupils.

Long queues on the M4 around the Severn Bridge meant they didn't arrive at the camp site until late afternoon. Robert had arranged for a small group of teachers and sixth formers to travel to the site early, set up the cooking and eating tents, buy food and cook the first evening meal. All the pupils had to do was put up their own tents in the early evening sunshine, then join the queue for food. Around seven o'clock, taking a walk around the site, Robert felt a stronger sense of achievement and satisfaction than he'd ever experienced before. There was a noisy teachers versus pupils football match, groups of girls sitting outside their tents laughing and the most adventurous kids already trying out the canoes on the canal, under Frank's supervision.

He'd made all this happen, nobody else.

A smile crossed his face as he thought of telling Emily about this scene when he got back in twelve days' time.

6

Catastrophe

Robert trod cautiously over the uneven ground, careful of the misleading shadows cast by the torch, boot laces occasionally snagging on the bracken, increasingly aware of the cold slowly seeping through his clothes and boots. *If I'm feeling like this with all this gear on, what's it like for Tom? Assuming he's OK, Sue and I need to agree a story to explain to the others how Tom had managed to slip away unnoticed during her shift. And if he's not OK?* Suddenly, the beam picked out a faded white sign on a fence ahead. As he got closer, he could see part of the fence had collapsed. He read the sign:

"DANGER: KEEP OUT, OLD MINE WORKINGS"

Heartbeat pounding in his chest, he walked gingerly up to the fence. Now that he was next to it, he could see some wooden bars had been dislodged. The dank, peaty smell was overwhelming, as he crawled on his hands and knees to the edge of the collapsed mine shaft and shone his torch down into the blackness. At first, he saw nothing, but the wave of relief that swept over him was instantly snatched away as the torch beam picked out a small, misshapen form on a ledge, fifteen feet below. From the grotesque angle of Tom's limbs, he knew he was seriously injured. Or worse.

In desperation, he began shouting repeatedly at the body below.

"Tom, can you hear me, are you hurt?" But there was no movement or response.

If he's dead, I'm finished, was all he could think.

Gripping the torch between his teeth, he braced his arms and legs against either side of the shaft and started to edge downwards.

After five minutes, he'd only descended half way to where Tom lay. His footholds had given way twice and he'd only saved himself by wedging his fingers into cracks in the rock, while he regained his footing.

What the fuck am I doing? My priority is to tell Sue to contact mountain rescue, not try and play the hero. I can't do anything to help Tom, even if I do get down to him without killing myself. Start thinking straight, Mason.

It was another eight minutes before he managed to clamber back up, panting with exertion as he pulled himself over the over the edge of the shaft. He switched the walkie-talkie to SEND.

"Sue, can you hear me, over?" Robert was struggling to control his voice.

"Loud and clear, Robert. What's wrong?"

"I've found Tom. He's fallen down a mineshaft, looks badly injured and unconscious. Can you contact Frank immediately, tell him to ring the mountain rescue number and tell them we urgently need a rescue party, with ladders, and a doctor? We have a critically injured teenager on the mountain, the grid reference is 310540 East, 221402 North. I will wait here to signal them with my torch. Did you get all that?"

"Oh my God, poor Tom. How seriously is he hurt?"

"I think it's very serious. Please call Frank now, and call me back on the walkie-talkie when they're on their way. 310540 East, 221402 North. OK, Sue?"

"Yes, I've got that."

Robert peered over the edge again, confirming that the climb down to Tom's body was as dangerous as he'd first thought, then lay on the heather. He tried to stay focussed on what needed to be done, making sure he'd covered everything. But another thought kept crowding in; *what if he dies? I'm in charge, I'm responsible, but I was in my tent with Sue, who should have been on duty, when he walked off site.*

His walkie-talkie crackled again.

"Robert, can you hear me?"

"Go ahead, Sue."

"They're sending a helicopter with a medic and two men. Luckily, there was one on a training exercise in the area. They should be with you in ten minutes and will look out for your torch signal. Please God, he's alright, Robert. I was on this camp to support him, yet I was in your tent when I should have been on duty."

"Don't mention that to anyone else, Sue, that's really important. It's not your fault, try to stay calm."

He heard the helicopter in the distance.

"I must go now, I can hear the helicopter. Keep the walkie-talkie next to you; I'll let you know what's happening."

As the helicopter approached, he stood up and waved his torch. The lights underneath the fuselage lit up the landscape, and for the first time Robert could see that it would be possible for them to land on a patch of almost level ground not far from the mine shaft. As the helicopter slowly descended, the noise and downdraft from the rotors became overwhelming, sending loose vegetation in all directions.

As soon as the wheels touched the earth, three men in orange flying suits jumped out, one carrying a large medical bag. They ran over to Robert, who pointed to the mineshaft; he followed them as they cautiously approached the hole. As soon as they saw Tom, one ran back to the helicopter, its blades still turning, and got a lightweight, extendable ladder.

The doctor walked over to Robert, coming straight to the point.

"How long has he been down there?"

"Between thirty minutes and an hour, probably."

The doctor's expression left his surprise in no doubt, but he turned away, walked to the shaft and began to carefully climb down the ladder, which was held in place by his colleagues. As soon as he re-appeared, two minutes later, his expression told Robert that Tom was dead.

"Are you his teacher, sir?"

"I'm one of the teachers on the school camp, yes."

"I'm very sorry to tell you, but he died of the injuries he sustained in the fall, almost certainly a broken neck. At least he wasn't lying down there in agony for the last hour."

A wave of panic swept through him, brought on by the implications of the doctor's words. He began to shake; he had to speak to Sue urgently and agree a cover story.

The doctor mistook his panic for grief.

"I know this is a terrible shock. I'll get a thermal blanket, please wrap it round you and sit down while we retrieve the body. Given the location, it will take around an hour."

Robert watched as the team prepared a harness and ropes to bring Tom's body out of the shaft, his mind focussed on one thing; how to explain Tom leaving the camp unnoticed. He switched on the walkie-talkie.

"Sue, this is Robert, come in, please."

"What's happening, Robert?"

Robert took a deep breath.

"I'm afraid Tom died from a broken neck, falling down the shaft, Sue. The rescue—"

"No, he can't be dead!"

Robert heard Sue's scream, then silence. Seconds later, he heard Brian on the line.

"Robert, it's Brian. Sue's collapsed and we're taking her to her tent. I understand the news is very bad?"

"I'm afraid it is, Brian. The worst. Poor Tom fell down a mineshaft and died from a broken neck. The rescue team is bringing him to the surface now; then they'll take him to the hospital in the helicopter. Once they've taken off, I'll come back to the camp, which will be in a couple of hours, I guess. Has anyone else returned yet?"

"They're all back except Frank, who's on his way. I'll give them the news about Tom. Be careful walking back, Robert."

"I will. I think we should wake the rest of the staff early with a cup of tea and give them the news before telling the kids."

Robert paused momentarily, unable to carry on.

"This is just unbelievable, Brian, so awful. Things like this are only supposed to happen to other people, on the news. But we've all got to stay strong for the kids."

Robert watched the rescue team lift Tom's body out of the shaft. The three middle aged men carried his body to the helicopter with great care, strapped firmly to a stretcher. He walked over as they slid it into the helicopter and looked at Tom. His eyes were closed, and his face showed no obvious injuries. He almost looked peaceful.

He set off for the camp as soon as the helicopter had taken off. One of the rescue team had given him the compass bearing to get back, and he made it there in under thirty minutes.

As soon as he walked into the camp, Sue ran over and threw her arms around him, sobbing.

"I let him down, Robert. Tom was vulnerable, and my role was to support him."

"You mustn't blame yourself, Sue, you're no more responsible than any of us. I hope you haven't told anyone about being in my tent last night?"

"Of course not, but I'm out of my mind with worry that it will come out."

All of the staff were up; Brian and Frank had decided to wake them with a cup of tea and give them the news. Some we're crying, holding onto a friend, others were sitting alone, drinking their tea and staring into the distance.

In the days to come, his colleagues all agreed how well Robert handled everything after the discovery of Tom's body; telling the pupils about Tom's death, supporting staff and students for the rest of their time on the camp site, liaising with the police and rescue services and organising the clearing of the camp.

His phone call to the head teacher, who was luckily not on holiday in a remote part of the world, was the most difficult that he'd ever made. Hatton agreed to contact all the parents and ask the travel company to send a coach to take pupils back the next day, as many were becoming distressed. Parents could drive to Wales and collect their child, if they wished.

They also agreed that Tom's head of year would take on the horrendous job of informing his parents, as she knew them well. They would need to come to Wales to see their son's body, which would remain in the Brecon General Hospital for the autopsy and inquest.

Before the coach arrived to take the pupils back, Robert asked them to gather with the teachers in the centre of the field. He made a short, emotional speech about the injustice of such a young person losing his life so tragically, then asked if anyone else wished to say anything.

Most people were too upset, apart from one boy who'd spent time with Tom on the camp and said he would remember his kindness forever. Teachers and pupils hugged each other, many weeping, as pupils said goodbye and boarded the coach with the three teachers who'd volunteered to go with them. As soon as the coach was out of the field, Robert called the remaining staff together.

"I don't think now is the time to look for reasons how this could have happened—there'll have to be an investigation, and we're all too upset and raw for that at the moment—but if anyone wants to share their thoughts, this seems the right moment."

At first there was silence. In the mid-afternoon sun, Pen y Fan looked majestic. Robert was struck by the cruel contrast between the inspiring beauty and the tragic events of the previous night. Derrick broke the silence,

"What happens now, Robert?"

Robert paused. "Like everyone, I'm only just beginning to come to terms with this, but my guess is that there will be a coroner's inquest. Unless the coroner thinks there's anything suspicious about his death, it should be judged accidental. Any of us could be called as witnesses, but I don't think that will happen, as it's tragically clear how Tom died.

I'll write a report on the events of yesterday evening for the head teacher and governors, so if anyone noticed anything unusual about Tom's behaviour in the last few days, please write it down for me. We know he was upset after the incident with Sam, but was anything else going on? I'm sure that his parents will want to know."

"Who was actually on duty at the time? Did they see anything?" Peter had asked the question on everyone's mind.

Before Robert could answer, Sue broke the silence. Making an effort to control her voice, she said,

"I was. All seemed normal as I went around after taking over from Laurie. When I got to Tom's tent, I could see the flap was wide open, saw he wasn't there, did a quick check of the toilet and food tents then alerted Rob."

Robert was very glad she left it there, as they hadn't had a chance to agree their story. He said, "I suggest we try and pack up all the gear, except the food tent, by this evening, then clear the rest tomorrow morning, load up the Transits and drive back. All OK with that?"

"Would it show disrespect to be seen eating out tonight? I can't face cooking."

"What do people think?" asked Robert.

There was unanimous agreement, so in the evening the staff went several miles into Brecon and ate a very subdued meal in an Indian restaurant. As the staff cleared the camp the following morning, Robert reported to the local police station, as requested, and gave them contact details for himself, the school and Tom's parents. The camp was deserted by one o'clock.

During the clearing up, Robert told Sue his proposal for explaining how Tom had managed to leave unseen. He felt she should say that when she took over on her shift, she'd set off round the tent circle in the opposite direction to the previous teacher, meaning the time that elapsed between checks on Tom grew to over four minutes. Because Tom was one of the few students not sharing a tent, plus the fact that his tent was nearest to the camp perimeter, he was able to slip away unnoticed. She wasn't happy but agreed to discuss it in the car on the way back.

As soon as they drove away from the field, she said she wanted to 'come clean' and tell the truth about the incident. It took him until they crossed the Severn Bridge to convince her that if she did that—and he would obviously have to support her—it would mean the end of their careers, with no way back. As the person in charge, he could face a criminal prosecution. Eventually, she reluctantly agreed to go along with his story.

"I can imagine what the press would make of this if it came out. Which it will. Everyone will assume we were having sex while Tom walked off to his death. I love my job, and you've convinced me it would mean career suicide to own up, not to mention the reaction of my friends and family. My parents would stick by me, but I can just hear some of my so-called friends judging me. People love having someone to blame in these cases. But you need to know that covering this up, when I'm to blame, is very difficult for me. I'm going to need your support, Robert, until the investigation is over."

"Of course, I'll be there to support you. There's no evidence to contradict our version, so as long as we keep to our story, what can they do?"

It was after six o'clock when he dropped Sue at her house, promising to be in touch within the next couple of days if there was any news. They arranged to meet for a chat next week. As he drove back to his flat, his mood deepened further as the consequences of Sue abandoning her shift and Tom's impetuous action sunk in. *What on earth gave Sue the idea that I wanted to screw her? Why did the stupid boy run off like that? Why did he take that particular route? Pointless thinking like this.* He longed to talk everything through with Emily.

He rang her as soon as he'd unloaded the car.

"Hi there, Emily, I'm back in London. I'm afraid there was a terrible accident with one of the kids, and the camp has ended early. I don't suppose you're free this evening, I'd love to see you."

"Oh my God, Rob, why didn't you tell me before? I'm supposed to be seeing Alison for a drink later, but I'll re-arrange. Come over from 7.30. I'll get us something to eat. What happened—how serious was it?"

"As serious as it gets. One of the kids wandered off in the middle of the night, fell down a mineshaft and died. It's been awful, really awful."

There was a long silence down the phone. Robert guessed that, with her lawyer's mind, she was running through the possible implications for him as the camp leader.

"God, that's terrible, Rob, I'm so sorry. I won't ask anything else, just come over as soon as you're ready."

An hour and a half later, he was taking her through the shocking events of that night, which he realised with amazement were barely forty-eight hours ago. He'd thought hard about telling her the truth about the incident and was surprised at the strength of his desire to confess. But he'd only known her for a month, and the consequences, should they split up, could be disastrous.

Every so often, Emily stopped him to clarify a detail, as she sought to assess his level of risk to an accusation of negligence and a disciplinary process.

When he finished, Emily refilled his glass, then began.

"First of all, I hope you've not formally apologised or admitted blame to anyone."

It was clear the question required an answer. He told her he hadn't, but that he did feel responsible on one level. *The strange truth*, he thought, *was that I don't.*

"It's normal for decent people to feel that, Robert, but I'm glad you haven't. The good news, from what you've told me, is that I'm sure the coroner will find that Tom's death was accidental. He or she would have to feel there's something suspicious about his death not to, and there's no evidence for that. I suspect the council will feel duty bound to hold their own disciplinary enquiry, which has a lower burden of proof and could, in theory, find that you and other staff were negligent in some way.

"Even if they do, and I think that would be grossly unfair, that doesn't mean dismissal. They could simply issue a written warning, which then lapses after a year or so. Contact your union lawyer as soon as possible, and don't submit your report—I assume you'll be writing one—until she's read it. I'd like to see it too, if you're happy about that."

He sat there taking this in. She was good; he was going to need her over the next few months. He reached out and took her hand.

"Thanks for setting it out so clearly, that's kind of what I'd thought would happen, but it's good to hear it from you. I'll contact the union tomorrow. How long could this take?"

"That's the question all lawyers hate to be asked, and I'm afraid my answer is 'as long as it takes'. You need to prepare yourself for at least three months from now, assuming that the coroner finds it was an accidental death. The biggest delays are often caused by factions within the council using cases like this to score political points off their opponents, which makes you a pawn in their game. But I promise I'll be here for you all the way."

She leaned over and kissed him.

"You must be shattered. I'll finish cooking, then we'll eat and have an early night. Just relax."

Later, awake in the middle of the night, he wondered again if he should tell her the truth. He realised that if he didn't do it now, and their relationship developed as he hoped it would, this deceit would always be there, between them. But he couldn't take the risk.

Emily phoned work with an invented boiler emergency in the morning and they went through the things he needed to do immediately. It would help his case if he was as open as possible from the start.

Contact the union lawyer;
Arrange to meet the head teacher, brief him, agree a date for his report;
As above, with the Director of Education;
Phone all the staff, check how they are;
Contact Tom's head of year, find out how the parents are coping;
Contact the Brecon police, as a courtesy.

The head teacher had pressed to see him, and they arranged to meet in his office the following morning. Emily warned him that the school and (particularly) the council could try to cover themselves by taking a tough line with him in order to send out the 'right' message to the press. She advised him to take his lawyer with him, but he failed to set that up. As soon as he saw the Director of Education sitting next to the Head behind his desk, he realised, too late, that she'd been right. He wouldn't ignore her advice again.

The Director of Education came to the point from the moment he sat down. He was to be suspended on full pay, pending a formal council enquiry to investigate whether he or any of the staff responsible for the camp were guilty of negligence under the council's code of conduct. As this enquiry couldn't legally begin until the post mortem and coroner's hearing were over, proceedings couldn't start until early September. He should not enter the school premises until the enquiry was over.

"We will make it very clear in our press statement that your suspension is a legal necessity under our code of conduct and is not to be read as an assumption of guilt." The Director paused, then continued.

"I know that this tragedy has hit you personally, the rest of the staff and the pupils on the camp very hard. There will no doubt be calls from some quarters to stop taking children on camps such as this, but they won't be coming from me or this local authority. Young people benefit enormously when staff like you give your time to provide them with this kind of experience."

There was an awkward silence as they all realised that the children's experience on this occasion would probably stay with them for many years, for all the wrong reasons.

"All contact with the head teacher and the council from now on should be made through your union lawyer, so please let Mr Hatton know who that will be as soon as possible. I'm assuming you'll be contacting your union as soon as possible, if you haven't already. Do you have any questions for us, Mr. Mason?"

Robert took Emily's advice and adopted a conciliatory tone.

"I do understand the wider issues involved; while my suspension isn't a surprise, I'm sorry not to be returning to the job in September and hope that the legal process moves quickly. I don't feel that any us on that camp could have done anything more to prevent Tom's actions that night, though I understand that's for the enquiry to decide. I want to keep up to date with any changes in the school, so is it OK to meet colleagues outside of school?"

"Of course," said the Director.

Robert met Sarah Shaw, the union lawyer, the following day. He'd always been indifferent about unions, but now he saw their point. She told him bluntly that she should have accompanied him to his meeting with the head teacher and Director of Education though didn't feel it would have made any difference to the outcome, which was, she said, standard procedure in these cases. He went to see Emily that evening as she'd asked him to come around after he'd seen the lawyer.

"But would you mind bringing a takeaway, there's a great Indian just up the road, I'm just too knackered to cook, sorry."

Just before she'd met Robert, Emily had been encouraged by her firm's partners to begin the training that would enable her to act as an advocate in the higher courts. This was now eating into her time at weekends and leaving her with few free evenings during the week. *Bad timing*, she thought. Robert will have at least three months with comparatively little to do, outside of preparing for the coroner's hearing and the Council's enquiry.

They'd planned to take a week's holiday in Portugal towards the end of August, but she realised it would be a bad idea in the circumstances.

"I hate to say this, because it's probably just what you need, but you can't afford to be out of the country at this time. You could be summonsed to appear before the coroner at short notice. And, however unfair it sounds, it won't look good for you to be seen enjoying yourself at the moment."

"I know you're right, but it seems so unfair on you. You could really do with a break—why don't you go on your own?"

She reached out and took his hand.

"I wouldn't want to without you. But to be honest, this training is taking up so much of my time that I might have had to cry off anyway. Look, my course will be over in three months, around the time when you get the all clear from the enquiry…"

"If I get the all clear," he interrupted.

"No, when. I'm certain, given the circumstances. As I was saying, we can go away then for a few days to celebrate."

They looked at each other, the assumption behind what she'd said clear to both of them. Emily looked uncertain; had she assumed too much?

Robert smiled at her. "That's a fantastic idea. It will give me something to look forward to if things get tough in the next few months."

Emily knew they could.

"OK, before I drink any more wine, I'll take you through the inquest process and the kind of questions you should be expecting. You should soon hear when it will be."

She'd been refreshing her knowledge about inquest procedures since hearing about his incident. They didn't go to bed until she was sure he'd understood everything.

Standing in the bathroom, putting her cap in, Emily couldn't help thinking how surreal this was. *I've slept with this man twice, hardly know what he believes in, inspires him or thinks about all kinds of stuff. I can't even truthfully say I know what he feels about me. But when we're together, it feels right. The last few days seem to have fast-forwarded us into a more intense relationship than I'd thought possible.*

"You look thoughtful," he said as she came out of the bathroom. "Nothing on your mind, I hope?"

"Well, I wouldn't say that exactly," she said, pulling back the duvet, getting into bed and kissing him.

When she came downstairs in the morning, he'd already prepared breakfast: muesli, yoghurt, fruit and coffee.

"I hope this isn't too presumptuous, but I woke early and thought I could at least ease you into your day. Say if I'm overstepping it."

"Robert, you can do this every time! Let's just say I'll tell you if I feel things are going too fast and you must do the same." She put her arms round him, kissing him on his cheek.

Two days later, he heard that the inquest would begin in Brecon crown court in four days; he was to give evidence on the second day. He rang Sue as he promised.

"Robert, I need to see you. Have you been told the hearing starts in four days? I'm down to give evidence on the third day, how about you?"

He felt relieved they weren't giving evidence on the same day.

"They want me there on the second day. I'm glad you rang as we need to go over our story again. I hope you've been in touch with the union lawyer; she'll brief you in detail about what to expect. We could meet somewhere convenient for you this evening."

As he walked into the pub in Camberwell that she'd suggested, he saw her sitting in one of the booths, tearing pieces from a beer mat. *If she shows any sign of wavering, just keep reminding her how much is at stake here. All of this is her fucking fault.*

Robert listened as Sue went through her doubts again.

"I feel this is all wrong, Robert. Tom's parents deserve to know the truth and here we are constructing lies to make things easier for ourselves. All I could think about for the last few days is that once I've lied in front of that panel, I'll have to live with that deceit for the rest of my life."

Robert felt furious, wanting to knock sense into her. But she was clearly in a fragile state and he had to judge his next words carefully. Misjudge it and God knows what she might do.

Finally, he said,

"Sue, I do understand, and don't think I haven't had similar feelings myself. But there's a lot more at stake here than just making things easier for ourselves. If we change our story now and admit blame, they will make an example of us. Who knows what the consequences could be, not just for our careers but for the rest of our lives. We could both face criminal charges. If we just keep to our story, we can still come out of this OK. Telling the truth won't bring Tom back."

They carried on talking for more than an hour. At the end, he'd persuaded her that she had too much to lose by going back on the story now. He had to agree, reluctantly, that she could ring him at any time.

Emily rang to wish him good luck the day before he travelled to Brecon.

"Remember, Tom's family will be there, emotions running high. Stay calm and don't get drawn into an argument; just say that you can't talk to them and walk away. Under no circumstances apologise. That may seem heartless, but it could be turned against you later. Answer the coroner's questions accurately, but don't elaborate and talk about anything you've not been asked about. Most people have a tendency to over-speak in court, and that just leads to further questions. Keep it simple."

"Thanks, Emily, that's really helpful. You're fantastic. I'm staying overnight in case they want to see me on the second day, so I'll ring you at the end of day one."

"Just make sure you behave yourself. I hear those Brecon women have a reputation. I'll be thinking of you, take care, my love."

Two days later, Robert sat in the bar of the Red Dragon Hotel on Brecon High Street, savouring his pint, going over the day's events. He hadn't had a drink in three days and told himself he deserved one. Emily's scene-setting and advice about the coroner's court had been invaluable. Particularly when Tom's elder brother charged up to him, screaming, outside the court.

The image of this short, stocky, red-faced guy rushing up to him remained vividly in his mind.

"How can you live with yourself? We all trusted you to look after Tom, you promised my mum and dad at the parents meeting that safety was your priority. You should be struck off."

Tom's father came up and led his son away, but not before glaring at Robert with a furious look.

Waiting to give evidence two hours later, he'd felt proud of the way he'd managed to regain his composure. *I thought I was going to get hit. I did well to get myself back in control.*

He finished the pint and went to his room to ring Emily.

"Hi there, gorgeous. It went pretty well, I think, and I want to thank you for your brilliant advice. It prevented me getting into a brawl with Tom's brother outside the court when he rushed me. And kept me focussed on 'less is more' when I was answering questions."

"I'm so pleased, though I knew you'd be fine. I've managed my work this week to leave tomorrow afternoon and evening free, so why don't you come 'round for something to eat and tell me about it then?"

"Sounds great, I'll see you around six."

"Where are you now?"

"I'm in my hotel room. I saw a Greek restaurant that looks OK, and I thought I'd eat there later."

"Well, just remember what I said about those Brecon women. I mean it, too."

"Ahh, too late I'm afraid. I'm meeting Bronwyn in the bar in half an hour."

"I'll stick hot needles through her eyes if she tries anything. I can't wait to see you."

"Thanks for everything; your support means so much."

Sitting in the Pearl of the Adriatic, thoughts triggered by their previous conversation, Robert reflected—really for the first time—what the consequences of his suspension, the coroner's hearing and Council enquiry could be for their relationship. When they'd met, one of the things he'd liked was that they were both equally ambitious, successful professionals with promising careers. Ironically, if he'd met her eighteen months before, her self-assurance and success would have overwhelmed him. But not now.

This incident has changed that, for the next few months at least. She'll be building her career and acting as my unofficial legal adviser, while I'll be sitting around reading the *Times Educational Supplement* and preparing for the Council enquiry. *She might start to disrespect me, unconsciously.*

He didn't underestimate the risk. *I've never needed someone as much before. If I'm in the clear when the case is over, I'll re-balance things between us.*

Sitting at her desk, papers from her training programme in front of her, too pre-occupied to work, Emily smiled about Bronwyn. *Of course, I trust him not to cheat*, she thought. *We've only known each other for a few weeks but whenever I find myself thinking ahead, he's part of that picture, sharing my life. If someone had described him to me before we'd met, I'd have said he's not my type, but now it's hard to imagine life without him.*

The next few weeks will be a test for us both. As far as I can judge, he'll be cleared. But what if he isn't? His self-assurance is bound to take a knock. We'll face it if it happens, but I must be careful about this advisor role I'm slipping into. Things are equal between us and that mustn't change. Sitting around without a job, he may start to feel emasculated, whatever that means. Be sensitive, Emily, and it will work out.

Act 2

7

The Reprieve

A warm, light rain was falling, just enough to need an occasional sweep of the wipers, as he parked the Alfa outside her house and looked at the leaden sky. *Typical London light*. She'd given him a key— "It's just sensible, really" —and as he walked down the hallway, Radio 4 in the background, he saw her standing at the cooker. She hadn't heard him come in. He stopped and watched her, simply being in the moment.

In that instant he could imagine spending his life with her.

She sensed his presence and turned, startled.

"God, you gave me a shock. How long have you been standing there?"

"Oh, about ten minutes. You're very sexy when you're cooking."

She stopped stirring, wiped her hands, came over and kissed him.

"So how was Bronwyn?"

"She didn't show up, the bitch."

They took their time over her shell fish paella, then sat together on the sofa with a glass of wine.

"You look exhausted, are you sure you want to go through it now?"

Robert insisted. She let him talk, only interrupting to check that the coroner had followed procedures. When he finished, she thought for a moment, then said, "From everything I've heard, I don't think there's much doubt that the verdict will be accidental death. Nothing in his line of questioning suggests to me that he feels there was neglect involved on your part. I presume that he'll see other teachers who were on duty, so I can't be one hundred percent sure, but it's looking good. How do you feel you came across?"

"Nervous at first, then I relaxed after the first question, which was all about the safety briefings pupils had received. Your comment about the other teachers is relevant, though. There's one that I'm a bit concerned about; she's giving evidence tomorrow and has felt guilty about the accident ever since, so I'm not sure how she'll hold up."

"Who's that?"

"Sue. She was the member of staff responsible for Tom, so she's feeling particularly vulnerable."

They talked past midnight about the likely timetable of events over the next three months, assuming she was right about the inquest verdict. Robert finally raised the issue that was hanging between them.

"Obviously, we're going to be leading different lives for as long as I'm suspended. I'm not going to become a couch potato and I'm determined not to treat you as my 'go to' legal adviser, tempting as that may be. That's what the union lawyer gets paid for. But if you can give me some idea each week when you're not likely to be working, then I could be our events' organiser. Plus, the odd sleepover during the week. How does that sound?"

"It sounds like a scarily well organised way to continue our love affair. Seriously, it makes a lot of sense. I'll look forward to my weekly surprise events."

He fell asleep within seconds of going to bed. Emily looked at him adoringly, then went back to the bathroom and took her cap out.

Robert woke as she came back to the bedroom from her shower, drying her hair with one towel, another wrapped around her. She smiled when she saw he was awake, unwrapping the towel and drying herself under her arms and breasts. He was captivated, as if watching a performance in the theatre. Not just by her physical beauty—that had excited him from the moment he'd seen her—but by how she moved, un-self-consciously, by the smell of her, by the way she nimbly stepped into her knickers. She pulled on her bra, came over and kissed him deeply.

"Well, you weren't much use to a girl last night. Sorry, but I'm rushing in this morning, though I could come over and stay at yours on Friday, if that's OK?"

"God, you don't take any prisoners, do you? I'll check out some venues, cook us something and try to do better on Friday night."

"I'm glad to hear it."

"Emily."

"Yes, sweetheart?"

"You've been fantastic. I don't know how I'd be getting through this without you, you're very special."

She walked quickly to the tube station, his last words turning over in her head. Running down the escalator, she just made the train, a young banker holding the doors for her to jump on as they we're closing. He spent the next three stops smiling at her.

Robert showered and dressed quickly, as he'd agreed that Sue could ring him after her appearance in front of the coroner. As he drove back over the river at London Bridge, past Spitalfields, Moorfields Eye Hospital then onto Newington Green, his anger towards her returned. *This selfish fucking woman, brings turmoil to my life, threatens my career, yet demands I support her. Worst of all, I've no choice. If I show I'm pissed off, she could tip over the edge and threaten to tell all.*

But their conversation went better than he'd thought it would. She felt they'd believed her and assured him that she'd stuck religiously to the script. They agreed to speak again when the coroner announced his findings, which would take a week or so.

He spent Friday afternoon cooking a parmigiana, stocked up with wine, and cleaned his flat fastidiously. He'd always liked cooking that dish, the scent of oregano filling his flat.

He buzzed her up when the entry phone went and waited at the top of the stairs. As she turned the last corner, looking tired, he saw she was carrying a large bag.

"Hi, my love, it's so lovely to see you. Something smells good. I'm sorry, but I've had to bring some work with me as I didn't want to rush off tomorrow. Is that OK?"

"Of course, it is. I'll clear my desk and you can use that. You look tired, what can I get you?"

"Well, as you asked and if it's not too cheeky, I'd love a bath. With a glass of white wine by the side, if I'm really pushing it."

"I'll run it now. I've even got some bubble bath. I've cleared a space in the bedroom wardrobe, so you can use that."

Just as he left the bathroom to tell her the bath was ready, she came out of his bedroom, naked.

"Sorry, I didn't know you were coming out," he stammered, then laughed.

Emily stood there, grinning. "If you're going to apologise every time you see me naked, then this isn't the relationship I hoped it was. I forgot my dressing gown, but I believe you're already well acquainted with my body."

"Your bath awaits you, ma'am. Come here."

Without any shoes on, she was eight inches shorter than his five-feet-eleven and he had to bend his head down as they kissed. His fingers ran down her spine, then between her buttocks, but she pushed him away gently.

"A glass of chilled white wine is all I require for now, thank you."

She wiped the steamed-up mirror and looked around. It was surprisingly clean for a man's bathroom. She got into the hot bath and lay back, her head on the rim. It felt good to lie there, her body almost weightless. *There's a real affinity between us.* None of her previous relationships had clicked like this. *I can't believe how well it's going.*

Robert came in with a glass of bubbly.

"Oh, I could get used to this!"

"Only Cava, I'm afraid, but it's a really dry one."

"Unlike you," she said, splashing water over him, shrieking with laughter.

"Right, that's it!" Taking off his shoes, Robert got into the bath, fully clothed, bath water pouring over the rim.

"You're crazy, you'll ruin your clothes!"

"There's a forfeit that must be paid for abusing the waiters at this hotel. To be revealed later."

She woke before him the following morning, got up quietly and put on his dressing gown, which smelt of bubble bath and shaving gel and came down to the floor on her. She took out her cap and replaced the spermicide. Sitting at the small kitchen table, looking out of the window at the early morning dog walkers, skateboarders and street sleepers in the park below, she tried to make sense of her feelings.

Compared to previous relationships, Emily felt she was going out with a grown up at last, someone who took responsibility for himself and for bringing fun and romance into her life. He was being really strong, dealing with the pressure of the tribunal. She felt cherished, but not in a cloying way. He recognised her need for time by herself.

"I don't suppose you fancy bringing your cup of tea back to bed?" he said as he kissed the back of her neck, interrupting her thoughts. "God, my dressing gown needs a wash, sorry about that."

She turned around. It was her turn to be surprised by his nakedness, as he stood next to her in front of the window. She looked at him, fascinated by the line of dark hair running down his torso, feeling its silkiness as she ran her fingers through it, across his stomach to the bush of hair around his cock. *Men's bodies can be oddly unattractive sometimes. Not this one, though.*

"The dressing gown smells of you, I like it. Go back to bed, I'll make you a cup of tea."

They established a routine, staying together at his place or hers every weekend. It was usually Emily's, as she often had mountains of work to do. Just as they'd agreed, she would ring him at the last minute if she found she was free during the week and he'd surprise her with a film, play or gig somewhere.

Robert felt he was a better person being with her. He'd grown to admire her passion for her work and the causes she believed in. She would be horrified by some of the things he'd done, and he could never tell her. She would finish with him on the spot, a thought that was unbearable. He realised from things she'd said that she admired the calm way he was dealing with the stress of his suspension, but she didn't seem to be aware of the role her support played in that.

As the new school year began in September, he started to obsess about how his colleagues were reacting to the case. He decided to ring Molly as he was sure she would know all the gossip. She was really pleased to hear from him and they arranged to meet the following Tuesday in a wine bar that had recently opened in Stoke Newington.

"So, be honest, what are staff saying about me? Do they blame me for Tom's death?"

"God no, quite the reverse. Everyone who staffed on the camp says you were fantastic. You stayed calm, organised people, did everything you could. They don't understand why you've been suspended; they think it's really unfair."

"And how about the kids that were on the camp? Any of them showing signs of stress or anxiety?"

"Only Sam, Tom's friend, who's gone into himself. I think he'll be OK, though. The pupils I've spoken to have all asked when you're coming back and say you shouldn't blame yourself. Tom's parents wanted him to have the same experiences as the other children and accepted the risks involved. You provided extra supervision during the camp; I don't see how they can find that you're to blame."

"Thanks, Molly, that means a lot. I hope you're right, but 'must find someone to blame' is never far away."

A week after Robert saw Molly, Sarah Shaw called with the good news.

"The coroner has found that Tom's death was accidental, with no case to answer in relation to neglect. You carried out all the proper risk assessments and implemented appropriate supervision arrangements. No caveats at all as far as I can see. Well done, Robert, that's the first big hurdle cleared. Now we prepare for the Council's enquiry. This verdict will make it difficult for anyone on the tribunal who wants to further their political career by making the case a cause celebre."

He celebrated that evening with Emily, even though she was snowed under at work. When he rang her to tell her, she insisted that they had to do something.

"Meet me at six-thirty outside the office and we'll go 'round the corner to The Fox for a quick celebration. I'm so happy for you, Robert; it would have been a travesty if he'd reached any other conclusion."

When he got back to his flat, after a not-so-quick celebration, he rang Sue to make sure she knew the outcome, though as one of the other staff who'd given evidence at the inquest, he assumed she would.

She became immediately confrontational.

"Good of you to tell me. No one else has bothered; I'm clearly very low down on the lawyer's 'to do' list. I feel so alone with all this, Robert. I was expecting more contact and support from you."

He felt contempt for her self-pitying response.

"I'm sorry you feel that, Sue, but I think you're being unfair. There was no news to talk about until a few hours ago and I assumed the union would ring all of those who gave evidence. But when I take the trouble to ring, you give me a bollocking. I think you should contact the lawyer and make the point to her."

"It's not the same, you know that. You've got your lawyer girlfriend to support you, Martin's not interested."

"But you're not suspended! You've got your friends at the school to go to for support. I saw Molly the other day and she said the staff were all behind us."

"But you know I can't talk to them about the one thing that preys on my mind the whole time. I can only do that with you. I just need to talk to you, to see you sometimes, to help stop me going crazy with guilt."

Robert made an effort to stay calm. She was the one to blame for the potentially ruinous situation they found themselves in. Not only had she not acknowledged this but made constant demands on him under the threat of having a breakdown and revealing everything. *Until we're in the clear I don't have a choice, but when this is over, I won't forget her blackmail.*

"Alright, I understand. Let's meet once a week to talk, everything on the table. We'll need to keep in touch about developments with the Council's enquiry, anyway."

"Thanks, Robert. Sorry, but some days I feel that I'm going mad."

Two weeks after he'd heard about the inquest outcome, Sarah rang and gave him details about the council's tribunal hearing.

"It's going to be at the town hall on the 20th October. I expect it will last at least three days and I want to arrange dates for us to meet now, before my diary gets too full. There'll be three councillors and two council officers on the panel. Given the inquest verdict, I don't think you've got much to worry about, but it's best to be prepared. I'll advise you on what to watch out for with the panel—it won't be like the coroner's court."

He didn't want another argument with Sue, so he rang her at work, told her the news and arranged to meet her the following evening. Emily rang soon afterwards.

"I've got a couple of old friends dropping round unexpectedly tomorrow evening. I just wondered if you were free? They'd love to meet you."

"I'm really sorry, I've just agreed to meet Sue Goodall from the camp. You know, the needy one. I'd love to meet them, but this woman is really on the edge."

Emily was annoyed; she'd really wanted him to meet her friends. *I can't wait to put the council enquiry behind us, when Sue is out of our lives. If I didn't know him well, I'd be suspicious, particularly as he told me they'd once had a one-night stand.*

On the 17th October, Robert met Sarah Shaw for the last time before the tribunal.

"Compared to the inquest, the big difference will be the tone of the questions. The coroner just wanted to get at the truth; he wasn't interested in catching you out. The councillors on the panel will be. They will be trying to score points off each other, each hoping to be the one that catches you out, asking the question that trips you up, looking smart. Don't fall into the trap of getting riled; if you don't understand a question because it's too convoluted, ask them to explain it. I will be there to ensure they stick to the agreed procedures for conducting enquiries. Good luck, Robert. It's almost over."

On the morning of the enquiry, he stayed at Emily's—her house was an easier journey to the town hall. She'd told her boss she wouldn't be in until mid-morning so that she could get them breakfast and walk to the tube with him. He hardly ate anything, he was so nervous. Much more than before the inquest.

"Just keep remembering you've done nothing wrong. As I said before the inquest, know when to stop talking. Less is more—if they want more information, they'll ask for it. The more you say, the more opportunity you're giving them to trip you up over some detail. I'll be thinking of you. Ring me at work once it's over."

8

The Tribunal

Robert sat sweating uncomfortably in the overheated, windowless corridor, staring at the committee room door, willing it to open. The pervasive smell of floor polish was making him nauseous. If the clerk to the enquiry didn't emerge in the next minute, he would have to go to the toilet for the third time this morning. But leaving his place, even for a few minutes, was out of the question; he had to stay put until called to give evidence.

The feeling of hot, liquid turbulence inside him eased slightly. Pointlessly, he found himself going over the events that had led him to these austere surroundings, his career in the balance. He'd been re-assured somewhat during his meetings with Sue over the last three weeks, as they'd rehearsed their story about the events on that night. The inquest outcome seemed to have increased her confidence about performing in front of a panel of inquisitors without fluffing her lines. But it was clear that she was still conflicted about the morality of their deceit, and he couldn't be sure she wouldn't crack under the enquiry panel's forensic questioning.

He'd initially assumed the council's enquiry would be less harrowing than the inquest, but it felt worse. The inquest verdict—accidental death—had angered the parents as it seemed to absolve those in charge of any blame. But he'd learned that some questions which had been superficially addressed at the inquest would now be dealt with in a more adversarial way. He must remember Emily's advice: don't over-answer the questions, focus on what you want to say and no more.

His thoughts were interrupted as the clerk to the hearing opened the door.

"Mr Mason, so sorry to keep you waiting. The panel is ready for you now."

Surprised by the clerk's appearance, Robert hurriedly gathered up his papers and briefcase and followed him through the door.

Walking towards the boardroom table with an outward confidence he didn't feel, Robert hoped he was making a good first impression on the five panel members; Emily had helped him decide on the most appropriate suit, shirt and tie to wear. Sarah Shaw sat to one side. They'd agreed yesterday that she would only intervene if the panel failed to observe due process.

"Please take a seat, Mr Mason," said the Chair, indicating the vacant seat at the table facing the panel.

Robert approached them. He'd been advised to introduce himself confidently to each person in turn, but as he extended his hand to the woman on the far left, the Chair interrupted him.

"If you could please just take a seat, Mr Mason, we're quite able to introduce ourselves."

Robert sat down, feeling awkward and embarrassed. *What an obnoxious twat*, he thought, *why humiliate me like that?* Memories of his father's regular put-downs were triggered. He looked at the Chair and the rest of the panel, so sure of themselves; how dare they presume to judge him?

They introduced themselves one by one, but Robert's thoughts were so scrambled he'd forgotten their names by the time the Chair spoke again.

"I'd like to begin by explaining the panel's role. Our job is to consider the incident that took place on the night of 5th August 1994, and decide whether negligence by staff, including you, contributed to the tragic outcome. We'll be taking evidence from teachers on duty and from members of the emergency services who attended the scene. Once we have gathered all the relevant evidence, we will decide, on the balance of probabilities, whether any of the staff in charge that night were negligent. Following our decision, we will make recommendations to the General Teaching Council, which could potentially include dismissal. Do you have any questions at this stage?"

"Not a question as such, but I would like to take this opportunity to express my sincere condolences to Tom's family and will do everything to ensure they're given a full account of events that night."

Without replying, the Chair looked impassively at Robert, then began.

"At exactly what point did you realise that one of the young people for whom you had ultimate responsibility had gone missing in the Brecon Beacons at an altitude of 230 metres, with light rain falling and a temperature around six degrees centigrade?"

The image of Tom's twisted body flashed into his mind and Robert was acutely aware that the course of his life could change irreversibly in the next two hours. He began to sweat and felt physically sick but knew he must compose himself quickly and regain control.

"Well, Mr Mason? The question surely doesn't require that much thought, does it? You must have gone over the events of that night many times in the last few months?"

The question came from the unsmiling woman on the left, who had clearly decided to compete with the Chair to be the most adversarial panellist. Leaning forward and looking at the Chair, Robert began.

"It was around 11.30pm when Sue Goodall, the Head of Learning Support, woke me to report that Tom's tent was empty. I got up and dressed at once, then Sue and I woke several other staff members and checked all tents and the campsite area thoroughly. It soon became clear—it wasn't a huge site—that Tom wasn't in the immediate area, so I decided that six of us should spread out and cover a wider radius around the camp. I also sent someone to the nearest public phone to alert Brecon Beacons Mountain Rescue as there was no other way of contacting them."

Robert waited for the next question, looking at each member of the panel in turn. It came from the smartly dressed man in his thirties to the immediate left of the Chair.

"Please take us through what happened after that, Mr Mason, in as much detail as possible, leaving nothing out however insignificant it may appear. We have as much time as it takes."

Robert felt surer of his ground now. Painful though the memories of the search and its horrible ending were, he could recount them without lies or fabrications. Unlike his account of the time leading up to the moment when Sue had come running frantically back to his tent five minutes after she'd left, her face flushed in the torchlight.

He spoke for well over an hour, with a few interruptions from the panel for clarification. It was particularly uncomfortable recounting the moment when he'd cautiously peered into the mineshaft and seen Tom's body, grotesquely contorted and lodged four metres down on a ledge. But he controlled his emotions and came through OK.

"Thank you for taking your time and going through the events in such detail, Mr Mason," said the Chair when he finished. "I have only one more question. We will of course be asking Ms Goodall when we see her tomorrow, but can you explain why it was that Tom was able to get dressed and leave the camp undetected, in spite of all the checks you'd put in place?"

Although he and Sue had repeatedly rehearsed their story on this crucial period, Robert's stomach tightened at the thought of repeating it. Up to this point, he'd not perjured himself to the panel, but once he began there would be no going back. His lie would be on record, for ever.

"With hindsight, I can now see that while I was convinced the rota covered every reasonable eventuality with regard to students going off site, there was a window for a determined person to slip out undetected."

Robert paused to clear his mind of anything save his memorised version of events.

"Please go on, Mr Mason," said the Chair.

"As I recorded in my written statement, every member of staff on duty that evening had to regularly check every tent in turn, once the students were in their sleeping bags. They were told not to return to their own tent at the end of their shift until they'd handed over to the next colleague on the rota, who would carry on checking from that point. This way, the time between checking on each student should have been little over a minute and a half—the time it took to go 'round the circle of tents. However, when Ms Goodall took over her shift, she set off round the circle in the opposite direction to the previous teacher, meaning the time that elapsed between checks on Tom was over four minutes. Because Tom was one of the few students not sharing a tent, added to the fact that his tent was nearest to the camp perimeter, he was able to slip away unnoticed."

Robert paused and waited for the follow-up questions that would unravel his story, but they never came. To his surprise, he was told he could leave after a few more routine questions.

"Do you have any questions for us?" said the Chair.

"Thank you, just one. When am I likely to learn my fate?" He realised at once that his turn of phrase was unwise, but glancing across at Sarah Shaw, her deadpan expression gave nothing away.

"Your fate, to use your rather unfortunate phrase, won't be decided until we've heard from all of our witnesses and taken advice from Mountain Leadership professionals. Until then, you remain suspended from work on full pay, as you know. Please don't speak to anyone else about these proceedings, particularly if they were involved in any way in the incident."

Robert gathered up his notes, thanked the Chair and the panel for giving him a fair hearing and left the room. It was mid-afternoon as he left the Council Offices and he decided to walk along the South Bank, in spite of his mental exhaustion. He hoped the walk would clear his head, but he couldn't stop their questions and his responses going around in his mind.

He saw a phone box and rang Emily.

"Hi there, you. Well, I'm out at last and I think it went OK, but I'm totally shattered."

"How long have you been out? Has it only just ended?"

"I needed some time to clear my head. It was pretty gruelling; I felt like I was in there for hours. Now I just wait, I guess."

"Would you like to come over? We could get a takeaway."

"That's a lovely idea, but I'm feeling so exhausted that I think I'll go back home, have a drink and go to bed. You've been completely fantastic, Emily, there for me all the way. I love you very much."

"I love you too, Robert. Remember Angus and Maria are coming over on Saturday. I hope you're still up for that."

"Absolutely. I thought I'd come around seven on Friday; anything you'd like me to bring?"

"I don't think so. I'll let you know if I think of anything. I can't wait to see you, take care, my love."

"Bye, gorgeous. Sleep well."

Robert would have loved go to Emily's this evening, but he felt he had to ring Sue and brief her about his interview. He didn't want to do that at Emily's as he'd noticed she was getting irritated by the number of times they'd cancelled because he was seeing Sue.

It was seven o'clock by the time he got home and rang Sue, after stopping at the Admiral. Yet again, she started having a go at him.

"I don't believe that you couldn't have rung me before now. Just to remind you, I'm about to lie to a disciplinary board about my role in the death of a young boy, in order to save our careers."

"Come on, Sue, this isn't just about you. Before I spoke to anyone, I needed to wind down and give myself space to clear my mind. Are you in the mood to listen, because I'm just not ready for any more abuse?"

He was half expecting her to hang up, but she apologised and asked him to carry on. Robert knew it was a good idea to brief her in detail on both the panel's questions and his responses. She listened carefully, without referring to her previous concerns, as he went through the advice that Emily had given him about not 'over speaking'.

"Sue, if we just keep to our story, we can still get our lives back. Good luck tomorrow; give me a ring afterwards if you want to."

Robert sat at the kitchen window, looking out over the park, which was always busy at this time of day. Figures walking home from work moved in and out of the dim light cast by the widely spaced street lamps, hurrying in the fine rain that had started. He thought about the conversation he'd just had. *Sue had said the right things and seemed to be on top of the story, but will she hold up to some of the aggressive questioning I've just received? This has been my worry all along, because she's always struggled to justify the deceit, morally. Her wobble earlier was just one more example.*

At nine o'clock the next morning, his lawyer rang.

"I think you handled a difficult panel very well. Some councillors on those panels think they're part of the grand inquisition. The main thing was that you came across sincerely and didn't make any mistakes. Well done. Now, we just have to wait."

Sue rang around mid-afternoon. She began speaking before he had a chance to say "Hello."

"Don't ask," she said, "I've got no idea how it went, really. I mean, I stuck to the story and didn't have any wobbles, but I couldn't really tell from their responses whether they believed me or not. I can't say it was pleasant, especially when the Chair was asking the questions."

"Well done, it sounds like you did well. The next week, waiting, is going to be the worst part. Is Martin there for you?"

"Don't be fucking stupid, Robert. Apart from my friends at school—and you know the limits of their support—you're all I've got. Sorry to put it like that, but it's true."

A few days later, on Saturday afternoon, he was lying on Emily's sofa with her head on his shoulder, absorbing the smell of her recently-washed hair as she leant against him. She'd brought little work home this weekend, for a change, and they'd stayed in bed until midday, lost in their shared desire.

With his mind on the outcome of the tribunal, he wasn't looking forward to making small talk with Angus and Maria. Both lawyers, Emily had known them separately at university, before they became an item. He'd only met them once and was a little anxious.

"What do you think, should I be upfront with them about my situation?"

"With those two, I think you should, definitely. They're not judgemental and might have something useful to say, you never know. You've got nothing to be defensive about."

The evening went well. Angus and Maria were great fun, just what Robert needed to help him forget the enquiry. He could imagine they'd see a lot of them in the future, unlike most of his friends and their partners. If they had a future.

Lying next to him, Emily seemed to have read his thoughts.

"That was a great evening, it worked really well. I've never seen Maria in such good form. She was clearly flirting with you, I'm going to have to watch that. How are you feeling about the next week?"

"Like I need to go somewhere for a few days to take my mind off it. I thought I might throw my camping gear in the car and drive down to the Lizard, before the weather breaks—there's a beautiful camp site there, which should still be open. And I think you could do with a break from supporting me for a while. I'll check if the site is still open in the morning."

She kissed him on the cheek, his stubble prickling her lips.

"I think it's great if you want to go to the Lizard for a few days, though I'll miss you. But don't do it to give me a break—I'm there for you, whatever. I love you."

He'd forgotten how beautiful—and windy—the Lizard was. His ridge tent was designed to be pitched in a gale; he put it up quickly and soon had a chilli con carne going on the stove. He loved the sense of freedom and self-reliance that camping gave him, particularly on a deserted campsite. That night, as he lay in the tent, listening to the taught flysheet ballooning back and forth in the gale, he thought about his options, if the tribunal found against him. That would depend on the penalty imposed by the General Teaching Council, which could go all the way to a teaching ban. Unlikely, but possible. He also dreamt of the opportunities that would open up if he was cleared. A life that he could imagine spending with Emily. But if he was struck off, would she stay with him?

The next day, as he walked over to Mullion cove, down to Bass Point, the lifeboat station and back to the campsite, he turned over the events surrounding Tom's accident in his mind, thinking through countless 'if only' scenarios. He'd never been able to lose the feeling that what had happened to him was too harsh and unfair in some way. He knew most people would feel that his situation deserved little sympathy in comparison with the pain that Tom's parents must be going through every day, but he struggled to feel guilty about this.

On that night, he'd had to face for the first time the realisation that guilt and remorse weren't emotions that came naturally to him, even in these extreme circumstances. The shameful truth was that his actions had been driven solely by the need to limit, or even escape, any blame for the tragedy. And he'd achieved a certain equanimity—more or less—with that realisation.

He envied people like Emily who tried, and succeeded, most of the time, to live according to sincerely held beliefs and values. It wasn't that he didn't have any, but their purpose was to provide an adaptable, day-to-day template, not to overrule self-interest.

After three days, he'd covered all of the Lizard that was worth exploring and drove back to London. He was expecting to hear the outcome any day.

During Robert's absence, Emily had time to reflect on their relationship and her deepening feelings for him. In the last few weeks, as the intense emotions around the coroner's hearing and tribunal brought them closer, she'd realised that this relationship could be 'the one'. They shared the same 'make every day count' outlook on life, an eclectic taste in music from Joan Armatrading to Bruce Springsteen via Bob Marley and a similarly inappropriate sense of humour. She wasn't sure what his politics were (or even if he really had any), but he was intelligent, funny and never dull. He was strong and determined but didn't try to dominate her.

She couldn't truthfully say that she really understood him yet, knew what inspired him or kept him awake at night (current crisis excepted). But she was certain of the sincerity of his feelings for her. Whenever her friends asked her about their relationship, she would say she loved him and thought he felt the same.

She was at her desk, working her way through the papers on her latest case, when her phone rang. They'd spoken twice, briefly, since he'd got back a couple of days ago, but she sensed this was him, ringing to tell her the outcome. She felt her heartbeat increasing as she picked up the receiver.

"Hi there, you." His voice gave little away. There was a pause that seemed to go on for ever.

"No negligence, no health and safety breeches, all risk assessments correctly carried out. I've got my life back, Emily. We've got our lives back—thank you for everything."

"Oh, Robert, that's fantastic, I'm so relieved and happy for you. Anything else would have been outrageous, but we couldn't be sure until the judgement."

"What are you doing tonight?"

"Celebrating with you, I hope!"

They arranged to meet at 7.30 in the usual bar around the corner from her office.

After Emily put the phone down, she started to think about the advice she needed to give him about what happens from here—it wasn't over yet.

He rang Sue. Their lawyer had already told her, and they had a relaxed, happy conversation for once, with no anxious outbursts about the morality of what she'd done. He set off to meet Emily as soon as he put the phone down.

"So, you're saying that I need to watch out for any sign of discrimination against me when I return so that I can counter it straightaway? I thought the tribunal's judgement would be the final word on the matter?"

Champagne glass in hand, Robert was responding to Emily's cautionary advice that the school might try to make things difficult for him when he returned.

"Legally, of course that's right. But I've known of cases—not unusual—where an employee returns to work to find a number of adverse changes have been made to her role, to try and make her leave. For example, the head teacher might try and change your timetable, reduce your responsibilities or replace your line manager with someone more adversarial. I'm not saying it will happen, just be aware and insist you get your old role back."

"I'm glad you warned me. I've arranged to see the Head and Chair of Governors tomorrow in school and wasn't going to ask Sarah Shaw to come along. I'll ring her first thing tomorrow; if she can't make it, I'll re-arrange."

Luckily Sarah was able to cancel something. She couldn't believe he was being so naïve, again, to go in alone after all he'd been through. During the meeting, the Chair of Governors tried to propose a reduction in his duties "just until you settle in again." Sarah bluntly read out the Local Authority's policy relating to his case, and no more was heard on the matter.

That evening he rang Molly and gave her the news, which she'd already heard, of course.

"Is it all round the staff already, then?" he asked.

"Just about everyone knows now and we're all really pleased with the outcome—and I mean all. When are you coming back?"

"I start on Monday, though I'll be in school over the weekend to prepare for next week. The last few months have been really awful, Molly, and I can't remember ever looking forward to going back to work this much."

"Brilliant, though give it a couple of months and I expect you'll be as jaded as the rest of us. Let me take you out for a drink on Monday."

Robert spent the weekend on his own, catching up on paperwork and pupils' reports. Emily was away at a conference in Nottingham.

9

Deceit

When Robert walked into the staffroom on Monday morning, colleagues greeted him with a spontaneous round of applause. Hatton made a point of welcoming him, saying how pleased he was to have his Head of Year back in school. During the two weeks before the November half term, Robert was determined to make a positive impression around the school. If there were any sarcastic comments from pupils, he wouldn't rise to them.

That evening, he met Molly at a wine bar that had just opened around the corner from his flat.

"It's so good to see you back, Robert. I've missed you! How have the last few weeks been, honestly?"

"Like a roller coaster. I know it's a cliché, but I don't think I've ever experienced so many emotional highs and lows before, and don't want to again. Emily helped me get through it. I really think I could have gone under without her support."

"I hope you knew that you could have always come to me. I've been there for you in the past."

"I do know that. In this case, though, I thought it would put you in a difficult position. But thank you."

They talked easily about changes at the school, the Head's attempt to reduce his responsibilities and Molly's ('non-existent!') love life.

"I'm the wrong side of thirty and just not interested in casual flings anymore, but that's all the blokes I meet seem to want. What's the matter with you lot? It's not as if I look like the back of a bus."

"You're gorgeous and you know it, so stop fishing for compliments. Maybe you shouldn't be so resistant to a fling; based on personal experience, once they've spent a night with you, they won't be able to keep away."

He grinned at her across the little table, triggering a memory for both of them and a broad smile from Molly.

"Yes, our first night was pretty amazing, wasn't it? Time to change the subject, I think. I'm starving. Is there anywhere cheap to eat around here?"

"There's an Indian 'round the corner that I've not tried before, we could give that a go."

"Sounds good."

Their curries were awful; her chicken dhansak was swamped with lentils and his lamb dopiaza reeked of onions.

"What a disappointment! I won't be coming again in a hurry. I've got some decent wine in the fridge back at my place, if you fancy cleansing your palette?"

"Lovely, let's go."

One hour and a bottle of wine later, sitting next to Molly on the sofa, inhibitions on hold, Robert put his glass down and looked at her.

"I really like you, Molly. You've been such a great friend. And more."

"I really like you too, Robert." She laughed, not sure if this was going where she thought it was, and not sure if she wanted it to stop.

As his mouth closed against hers, she felt his hand sliding along her stockinged thigh. Returning his kiss, she abruptly pulled his hand from between her legs and turned her head away, looking over his shoulder, horrified.

"Don't stop on my account, I can see you're having a really good time. Please carry on, while I collect my things from the bedroom. I don't think I'll be needing them here anymore."

Emily's voice was ice cold, eerily stripped of emotion.

She walked out of the lounge, throwing a bunch of flowers on the floor and was pulling her clothes out of the bedroom wardrobe as Robert walked in.

"Emily, I'm so sorry, it's not what you think. We were…"

She burst into near-hysterical laughter, continuing to stuff clothes in her bag.

"Stop now, before you make an even bigger prick of yourself. It is exactly what I think it is. My boyfriend, with whom I stupidly believed I had something special, was about to screw his old flame. I came 'round this evening to surprise you, after your first day back. I'd booked a table at an Italian restaurant in Newington Green. You may remember it from our second date. Thank God I found out in time. If I've forgotten any jewellery, please send it on. Have a good life, Robert. Don't get in touch."

She walked out, throwing his keys on the telephone table, glancing at Molly, who was already putting her jacket on. She couldn't meet Emily's eyes, which were beginning to water.

For the next few weeks, Robert was an emotional mess. He just existed, concentrating on carrying out his responsibilities at school without making serious mistakes. But he felt no joy or enthusiasm—for the job, or life in general. His nihilistic state reminded him of the time at the end of his first year in teaching, before he met Jane. He wanted desperately to contact Emily but knew this would be counter-productive. His depressed mood was broken only by bursts of anger with himself, for being such a fool.

Molly felt terribly guilty. She hadn't initiated things but had done little to stop it. She'd left his flat less than fifteen minutes after Emily, stopping only to say he should let her know if there was anything she could do to help with a reconciliation. They'd hardly spoken to each other at work, but on his second week back, she approached him in the staff room, holding a copy of the local paper. She looked troubled.

"I think you should see this so that you're prepared. Mr Garner, Tom's dad, has sent a letter to the local paper; basically, he's saying it's a disgrace that you're back in school and that the outcome of the inquest was a travesty.

It's horrible, I know, but I think it's best not to respond, let him get it off his chest and wait for it to blow over."

Robert felt physically sick, momentarily. *Will I ever be free of this? What's to stop him carrying on, turning it into a campaign? It's like he's pursuing a vendetta against me.*

He went to see Hatton, who re-assured him that it would soon be yesterday's news, and that the father was unlikely to carry on, now he'd made his point.

"If he complained to the school, I will tell him that the matter is now closed. The enquiry cleared you of any negligence and the governors have the fullest confidence in you."

Robert was longing to ask Emily's advice about how to deal with Garner's letter, but that was out of the question. It was a reminder, if he needed one, of how much he'd relied on her for advice and support in the past. Molly advised him to contact the union immediately and insist that Hatton write a response to the paper, stating that the school is supporting him one hundred percent.

Hatton agreed to write that week, insisting they publish his reply in full. He said he'd keep him in the loop, and not to worry. Sarah Shaw asked him to send her copies of any future correspondence, so that she could monitor developments. Her advice was to do nothing at present.

It was difficult to know whether the school's robust rebuttal of Garner's letter wound him up even more, but over the next two weeks, his campaign against Robert escalated. He visited the school, demanding to see the head teacher and Robert as well, which Robert thought might be worth considering until Sarah and Hatton both told him it was a very bad idea. A member of the local Labour party, he lobbied Councillors and his MP to re-open the inquest.

Tom's brother, who'd tried to assault Robert outside the court in Brecon, began standing outside the school entrance every evening, staring at Robert when he drove out. Robert could see that Hatton and the Chair of governors were getting nervous about the impact of the relentless bad publicity on the school's reputation. He was now in a second fight to save his career, this time a very personal one. And he was on his own.

It was clear that Tom's father wouldn't respond to any of the usual, legal restraints; Robert would have to explore every possible way to stop him, both legal and illegal. It could get very unpleasant.

As a Head of Year, he'd established a good relationship with the sergeant in charge of the team responsible for policing around the school. He asked him, informally, if he knew any ex-colleagues who were now working as private investigators. After questioning Robert at length about his motives, he gave him a name.

Two days later, Robert met ex-detective sergeant Paul Cox in a coffee bar, near Paul's house.

"What kind of research do you want me to carry out on this as-yet unnamed individual? What do you intend to do with it?"

"Putting it bluntly, I want to find out if he's got any secrets that he would prefer remained that way. I need to get some leverage with this guy; I'm not a blackmailer."

"I'm glad to hear it. You need to set a budget at the start—people can get hooked and spend a fortune before they realise it. I charge £70 a day plus expenses."

Robert had recently been left £500 in his grandmother's will.

"I can pay for up to five days, if that's needed. How do we keep in touch about progress?"

"My office is staffed in the morning, and you can leave messages on the answerphone after that. I ring in frequently, so leave me a number if you need me to get back to you. How much information have you got on this guy?"

Robert handed over details of Tom's father's address, family and occupation, all available from the school's records.

"Ring the office in a couple of days. Is there any way I can contact you if I find anything before then?"

"Sure, leave me a message on my home number, but don't give any details over the phone."

Robert had thought hard before going down this route. It was risky, but he had to re-balance the scales in his favour and give himself leverage. If he didn't act now, he could see the steady drip of accusations against him leading to him having to quit.

Paul had nothing specific to report when he rang two days later, though he did say, enigmatically, that he was following up something that could give Robert the leverage he needed.

The next day, Robert got another message from Paul.

"Twice so far, I've followed Garner to the Wansted Flats area and observed him meeting up with another man for sex. These days, evidence of blokes making out with each would be laughed off. It's not a crime. But for Garner's wife and son, it's a sin. A terrible sin. I've found out that they're born-again evangelical Christians, and all hell would break loose if his family knew about this. I managed to take a couple of pictures, but they're not clear. I've bought a much longer lens—don't worry, I needed one anyway—so I'm sure I can get something explicit and conclusive in the next couple of days."

"What are the risks?"

"None for you. Shall I carry on with this?"

Robert didn't need to think about it. "OK, set it up as soon as you can."

Driving back to his flat in the rain, through a depressingly neglected part of Homerton in east London, Robert felt sick with himself. His mood had sunk dramatically in the last few weeks from the break up with Emily, the stress of the vendetta against him, and now the sordid things he was doing to get leverage on Garner.

All he could do now was wait for news from Cox.

Robert received a message the following Friday, telling him to meet him on the Grand Union canal towpath, under St Pancras Way.

"I've got something I think you'll find useful for your research."

He parked his car in a well-trafficked road, under a street light, near Camden Market, then walked 200 metres along the towpath. Robert rarely felt edgy in London, but this area made him uneasy. The thought that he was being set up, to be jumped and thrown in the water, crossed his mind as he approached the bridge over the canal. Three skinny young men stood in a huddle, on this side of the bridge. Probably in their early twenties but looking older, almost certainly users and drug dealers. There was no sign of Paul Cox.

"Want to do some business?" He passed them, not too fast, not too slow. As he got to the other side of the bridge, he saw Paul, standing on a grass verge by the towpath.

"Hi. Let's go to my car. You can look at the pictures in private."

Robert didn't know what to expect as Cox handed him the photos. Garner was clearly identifiable in all of them, as one of the two men involved. Some showed them kissing in the front of a van, others had been taken in a copse of large bushes and showed various sexual activities. Robert reflected on the time that he'd had sex with a girlfriend outdoors, thinking they were hidden and unobserved. *That's all Garner's doing, and just because of that, I'm about to threaten to ruin his life.*

Don't think about it, Robert. He's trying to do the same to you.

He turned to Cox.

"Do you have any advice on how to confront him with this evidence? Remember, I don't want money. I just need to convince him of the consequences if he continues his vendetta against me."

"The golden rule is, don't incriminate yourself in any communication you have with him. Don't attach anything that links you to the pictures when you send them, for example. And make sure that no one else can find the package, if you're doing a dead drop.

With expenses, you owe me £310. I've made two copies of everything; I'll keep one, you can have the other, plus these originals. Good luck."

Robert paid, took the pictures and said goodbye. Now he had to work out how to get them to Garner, without incriminating himself. The first part of the operation was relatively simple. He'd been told by Cox that Garner had a secure builder's yard, with locked double doors. One door had a letter box with a cage behind it, to catch the post. He could put the pictures in there, just before Tom's father opened the yard up in the morning so that no one else would see it.

That left the problem of arranging a safe place to meet.

He remembered a conversation he'd once had with Emily. One of her clients had been so concerned about being assaulted or secretly recorded during a meeting with a gangster, he'd insisted that it took place in a swimming pool.

Robert dropped the package with the prints and a typed message through the letterbox at 6 a.m. on Monday morning, then waited in his car, fifty metres away. The message read: 'If you don't want anyone else to see these, meet me in the shallow end at Kentish Town swimming pool at 10 am this Wednesday.' As soon as he saw Garner arrive, he slowly drove off; as he glanced in his rear-view mirror, he saw an agitated figure storming out of the yard.

Two days later, as he waited chest deep in water, shivering at the edge of the pool, Robert couldn't believe Tom's accident had brought him to this. The situation was surreal. Standing in a public swimming pool, beside the gutter with its detritus of plasters, human hair and God knows what else, waiting to be confronted by a man who hated him. A man who would do him serious harm, if he thought he could get away with it.

Now that he was here, he was acutely aware of the risk he was taking. Yet he was in control of his fear, and that felt empowering—thrilling, even. He had to remember, when the conversation began, that he held all the best cards. The risks for Garner of calling his bluff were enormous. From the information Cox had given him, if the pictures were released, his wife and son would disown him, and his family would fall apart.

Ten minutes after the meeting time, as he was starting to get anxious, he saw Tom's father walking in from the men's changing room. He obviously wasn't a regular swimmer, as he cut a comical figure in a pair of borrowed briefs, two sizes too small for his bulging midriff. Robert stifled a smile. No chance of him hiding anything in there. Surprisingly, he looked more anxious than angry. He saw Robert, went to the nearest steps, awkwardly lowered himself into the water and waded over. Now that he was close, Robert noticed how much he'd aged since he'd seen him outside the court in Brecon. *Poor bastard. Losing a son is bad enough, now he's facing the prospect of exposure. But I can't allow myself to feel sympathy; he'd ruin my life and enjoy doing it, if he could.*

"I knew it had to be you behind this, you cunt. God knows how you did it. Tell me what you want; I don't want to be here one minute longer than I have to."

"I want my life back, Mr Garner. I was cleared by the coroner and the tribunal of any responsibility for Tom's death, which I think about every day. I know there's nothing I could have done to prevent what happened so my conscience is clear. I'm sorry you can't accept that, I can't imagine what it's like to—"

"Save all that bullshit for your teacher mates and the council who backed you up. You've got no fucking idea what my family have gone through since Tom died, so get to the point and tell me what you want. I feel sick just being next to you."

"Your campaign against me has to stop now. That applies to every member of your family, especially your son, and includes any action that's aimed at publicising the case, harassment, criticising the verdicts or intimidating me outside the school. From next Monday, if any of it carries on, then I release the pictures. No second chances. Do you understand, and do you agree?"

"I don't have any choice, do I? How do I know you won't release them anyway?"

"That would be stupid. You and your family would then have no reason not to carry on with your campaign against

124

me, plus you'd no doubt say I was blackmailing you, though I've made very sure there's nothing to link me to the photos. As long as I don't suffer an unexplained death in unusual circumstances—in which case they will be sent to the police—you have my word your secret life will stay that way."

They'd both begun to shiver in the tepid water.

"I don't know how I'm going to get my son to lay off. He hates you even more than I do."

"You'll have to find a way to keep him quiet. I'm not playing around here, Mr Garner."

"Don't worry, I will. Is that it? Don't you want money?"

"Christ, you really have a low opinion of me. Of course I don't want money. All this is just about getting my life back."

Garner looked at him.

"That option closed for me the day my son died."

With that, he walked to the steps, hauled himself out and left the pool.

Robert swam thirty lengths to warm up; *Enough time for Garner to get dressed and leave.*

He'd phoned in sick earlier that morning and felt oddly subdued as he drove back to Clapton, even though he'd apparently achieved what he'd set out to do. Of course, it could still go wrong if the son didn't play ball, but he didn't think that would happen. Garner was clearly desperate to stop these images becoming public and would make sure his son complied. As he walked into the flat, he saw there was a message on the answerphone.

"Hello, Robert, it's Emily. I got a call from your sofa sweetheart yesterday. Life is full of surprises. I don't know how she got my number, but she rang to tell me she's worried about you. She said the boy's family have been conducting a campaign to get you sacked. Is that right? That must be horrible. She also apologised, though I'm afraid I didn't accept. Anyway, if there's anything about the legal implications you need to discuss, I'm here to help. Please don't read any more into this. It's so sad you messed things up, Robert. You're such an idiot."

What the hell is Molly playing at? I can't discuss Garner with Emily now. I couldn't possibly tell her what I've done. I've just got to wait and see if it works out. But I could ring her under a pretext and see if there's a chance of a reconciliation, even though she's ruling that out.

He missed Emily desperately. *I can't sit here staring at the phone and I can't go back to school. I'm supposed to be sick. I might as well go the Admiral.*

10

Redemption

Emily had thought very hard before phoning Robert; she'd felt bitterly upset and betrayed when she'd seen him with Molly. She'd started to believe their relationship could be the one and was still distressed about it ending in that way. Had she been fooling herself about his feelings? Just three weeks ago, she'd told a friend that she loved Robert and that she thought he loved her. *Am I that desperate to find a man? Trust yourself, Emily, don't go down that road. You know there was something good between you, and he felt it too. Unfortunately, that wasn't enough. Like most men, when an opportunity arose, he thought with his prick.*

A couple of people glanced in his direction as he walked into the Admiral. He ordered a pint and sat down in the corner.

The pub was half full with a mix of locals and students with nowhere else to go on a Wednesday afternoon in November.

"Not seen you in here before, have I?" said a woman who'd moved her chair round next to his to make space for another couple. She was late thirties, had taken trouble with her appearance, but clearly hadn't had Robert's comfortable life. She was smiling, appraising him.

"I've been in a couple of times. I only moved into a place up the road a few months ago. I like it; it's got a good vibe."

"Yeah, we get a good crowd in here. I'm Wendy, and your name's—"

"Robert. Good to meet you, Wendy. Do you live nearby?"

He immediately regretted the question. Robert wasn't vain, but enough women had volunteered compliments about his looks in the past for him to accept unwanted advances as the downside. "Welcome to my world," Emily had responded, when he'd told her about it.

Just as he feared, Wendy took his question as a hint. He spent the next ten minutes pretending not to pick up the stream of innuendos in her conversation. He parried them until he left, saying, "I'd better get back, my wife has cooked something special and I promised I wouldn't be late. Nice talking to you, Wendy."

He took the long route back around the park. Years ago, he might have gone back to Wendy's place and fucked her, just because the opportunity had presented itself. She was reasonably attractive; they'd have had a good time. Maybe he'd have stayed over, then left without thinking about her ever again. Now, it hadn't crossed his mind. He thought about Emily, how his feelings for her had grown into something meaningful, become part of his unconscious. And he'd blown it for the thrill of illicit sex with Molly. He could be so weak.

He rang Emily as soon as he got back to the flat.

"Hello, Robert." He remembered that her phone showed the caller's name and number.

"I got your message on the answerphone. It was lovely of you to offer, given the circumstances, but I think things may be settling down with the Garners so it's probably OK."

"I'm glad to hear that Robert, it sounded awful from what Molly was saying."

"I'm sorry she rang you, I had nothing to do with that. It must have been a surprise."

"You could say that. Suddenly, I found myself chatting to the woman I last saw snogging my boyfriend. I had this image in my head of her startled face with your hand between her legs. So, Molly, what shall we talk about, I thought?"

"I regret what happened that evening more than anything I've ever done. We were good together, you and I, and it was getting better and better. You'd stood by me and supported me. There's no excuse, but I'm desperately sorry I hurt you."

"Let's say I believe you, Robert. But I just can't understand why you did what you did. At what point during that evening did our relationship, and your feelings for me, cease to matter? Please don't say you both got carried away. We've all got agency, Robert. You could have changed the course of events at any point. You chose not to, and that really hurt me. It still does."

Listening to her, to the lack of hostility in her voice, Robert sensed an opportunity. It was a risk, but he knew he'd regret it if he didn't take it.

"Could we meet for a coffee sometime? I can't stand the thought that our final memory is that scene in my flat."

"What would be the point, Robert?"

"That I might persuade you to give me, and us, a second chance."

Robert held his breath as he waited for her answer. The silence seemed unending.

"If you try to schmooze me, there's no point. We had something good. For me, a big part of that was knowing we trusted each other, in every way. You betrayed that trust, and I don't know if I can get it back. Unless you're prepared to be brutally honest about your actions that evening, forget it."

"If that's a qualified 'yes', then how about this Saturday around eleven o'clock?"

Again, there was silence down the line.

"Let's meet in Macari's, around the corner from my place. I think you know it. I can only stay an hour; my work is mad at the moment."

"I'll see you then."

I hope you know what you're doing Emily. There's no point, unless you're prepared for the possibility of starting with him again.

Emily looked at the clock behind the counter. It was twelve thirty, and they'd been talking without a break since ten past eleven. She'd decided to let him speak and leave at the first hint that he was justifying or excusing his actions. But he'd been brutally honest with her.

"Yes, we probably would have ended up in bed if you hadn't turned up. We'd both had something to drink, but I was sober enough to know what I was doing. Molly didn't lead me on; we had a relationship three years ago and still flirt with each other, but nothing more than that. I can't justify it. For a few moments before you walked in, lust took over and I stopped thinking about you, or us. I was physically sick after Molly left, which was ten minutes after you. I knew I'd blown everything and had just lost the best thing that ever happened to me."

"Thank you for not trying to justify what you did. It means a lot. But I'm left wondering what "lust taking over" means for the future? If I put myself in the situation you were in that evening, I know that I would never have cheated on you. Rationally, I understand that I've got to believe you when you promise to never cheat again, or there's no point starting over. Emotionally, I don't know that I can. I need time to think, Robert. You'll have to wait. Don't call me, I'll call you."

"I wouldn't ever cheat on you again."

As she walked home, Emily tried to make sense of her feelings. The chemistry between them was there, almost from the moment they'd sat down. His combination of strength and vulnerability had aroused and reassured her, as it had from the second time they'd met. She'd longed to reach out and touch him, for him to touch her, but she was glad she hadn't. Realistically, of course there was a risk he'd cheat again. But she had a chance to try and re-build their relationship, if she wanted to take that risk.

If she did go back with him, she'd have to tell him about the decision she'd made a couple of months ago; he had the right to know. But that could wait.

She'd leave it a few days to finally decide.

By Wednesday the following week, Robert was down to three hours' sleep a night. As soon as he'd walked into the café and seen her, his stomach churned at the enormity of what he'd thrown away, and the thought that so much depended on this conversation. *The only thing she'll respect is honesty, it's your only chance.*

Now, three days later, he wasn't sure. His brain couldn't process anything for longer than two minutes before being consumed by the thought of a second rejection.

That evening, as he was going through the motions of marking a pile of Physics homework, the phone rang. Heart pounding, he picked up the handset.

"Hello, Robert. How are you?"

"I could say fine, but the truth is that I'm an emotional wreck. How are you?"

"I'm well, thank you. After much heart searching, I've decided to put the events of three weeks ago behind us, and try again. If you want to, obviously. There's only one condition. This time, our relationship must be based one hundred per cent on openness and trust on both sides. No deceit, ever again."

Near to fainting from a lack of oxygen, Robert resumed breathing and sat down. He was close to tears.

"I will never let you down again, Emily. I'm so happy. What do we do now?"

"Why don't you come over here this Saturday, around lunchtime? I'll make a light lunch and we'll start to get re-acquainted."

"I'll see you then."

Emily's determination to avoid jumping straight into bed lasted as long as it took for them to walk from the front door to the kitchen. She pointed to the cold buffet on the table.

"I've made a light lunch, I didn't—"

She was cut off mid-sentence as Robert threw his arms around her. She held him tight, returning his kiss, then led him upstairs.

Later, sitting around the table in their dressing gowns—he'd left his at her house—they snacked hungrily on the cheeses, Italian ham and quiche she'd got together.

Emily reached across the table and took his hand.

"I think we knew sex wasn't going to be a problem. But I want us to be honest with each other from the start, Robert. Re-building this relationship is going to take patience and understanding, from both of us. I'm still raw about what you did. I'll probably never understand it, so please remember that. I'll need time; we'll both need time. But I promise I won't hark back to you and Molly or make digs and comments. We start afresh from now and should be prepared for some difficult moments. But I want this to work."

"Thank you for saying that. I'm not sure I deserve it."

"There is something I need to say before we go any further. I should have told you before, but it didn't seem right while you were involved in the enquiry. The first time we slept together, I left my cap inside the next morning, instead of replacing the spermicide. I thought I was into the safe period of my cycle. By the time you came back from the camp, my period was already late, which it never is, and my pregnancy test was positive. I thought very hard about telling you, but we'd just met; you had Tom's death to deal with and I wasn't ready to have a baby. I was only four weeks pregnant, so my clinic prescribed the abortion pill. I've always regretted not telling you; you wouldn't have changed my mind, but you had the right to know."

Robert took in what she'd just said. He didn't feel angry, but he was surprised to find that the thought of being a father was a curiously happy one.

"I'm sorry you went through that on your own. I wish you'd told me, so I could have been there for you when you needed it. What you've just said doesn't change my feelings at all; it was your decision to make."

Robert sat there, looking at her, thinking about the things he'd done that he could never tell her; the real story about Tom's death, exposing the pictures of the drunk teachers, getting Jane sacked, blackmailing Garner. Their reconciliation would be over before it had started.

"That's a lovely thing to say. I did feel sad for some time afterwards. I've always wanted to have children, and like many women in that situation, I found that ending the life starting inside me came with a bigger emotional cost than

I'd imagined. It would be much harder a second time, so I'm going to be more conscientious with the cap. We're clearly very fertile, getting pregnant the first time we slept together."

There was a comfortable silence between them, as they each took in the significance of this last exchange. They'd just had their first conversation about having children together.

Emily decided it was probably as far as they should go for now.

"Changing the subject, how have things been at work since you returned? Has that family stopped harassing you?"

"It's been really busy. It looks like things got slack with my Year group during my suspension; a number of kids got out of line and that's taking time to turn 'round. There's good news about the harassment, though. Hatton told me that Tom's father has been in touch with him and sounded much more conciliatory. He's coming to see him on Monday, so it could be that his campaign is about to end. I'm not getting my hopes up, though."

Another lie, he thought.

"If he's giving up, that would be wonderful. What he did was outrageous." She paused. "I've heard some good news, too, since I last saw you. As you know, I've been studying for that advocacy assessment, and on Tuesday I took it and passed. I've now got higher rights of audience and can represent my clients in a higher court, if I need to, which is something I've always wanted."

"Congratulations, that's fantastic, Emily! I'm so proud of you, I really am."

He felt good he had it in him to be genuinely pleased for her.

The following week, it became clear that his blackmail had worked. There were no more letters to governors, to councillors or the newspaper. Garner's son stopped hanging around outside school and no one mentioned the camp or Tom's death. It was amazing how quickly the school, the staff and the pupils appeared to have moved on.

He hadn't had an opportunity to speak with Molly since her phone call to Emily, so he sought her out in the art room at the end of the day.

"I should be angry with you for interfering, but given the way things have worked out, I wanted to come and give you a hug."

"Best to leave out the bodily contact for now, Robert, but if you're telling me that you two are back together, and my call might have played a part in that, then I'm pleased. I can begin to feel less guilty, at last. What were we thinking?"

"I don't think we were. Thank you for calling her. How did it go?"

"Not as badly as I feared. I was dreading it, as you can imagine. I was almost hoping she'd slam the phone down, at least that would get it over with. She did make me feel a complete shit, telling me how she's never understood how one woman can sabotage another's relationship. Then she took a step back, asked how you were, seemed really upset and promised she'd ring you. Somehow, as women do when they've cleared the air, we carried on talking for over half an hour. She asked me about the time we'd gone out, what you were like with the pupils—all kinds of stuff. I liked her, Robert. Don't mess her about again."

"I'm planning not to. Thanks again, Molly."

Emily and Robert's only commitment for the approaching holiday was Angus and Maria's New Year's Eve party. Their relationship was getting back to its previous closeness, but occasionally, a slight awkwardness—the legacy of Robert's infidelity—arose between them. *We need a distraction to help break the cycle*, she thought.

He'd been invited to spend the Christmas festivities with his mother and her husband, who he couldn't stand, and wasn't intending to go. Emily tried to change his mind.

"Look, you've said we're both invited, you know your mother would love to see you and check out the new woman in your life, who she's presumably heard little about from you. Plus, you haven't seen her for months and you can't avoid them forever. I promise I will turn on my immense charm with her husband and keep him out of your way as much as possible. I'd like to meet your mother, so maybe you could at least do this for me. It can't be that bad."

"You don't know what you're saying. I went last year and hated it. Mike, her husband, just tried to wind me up about how crap schools and kids are now compared to his day. Inevitably, I lost it and we had a big row. Maybe it's hard for you to understand. You said you've always had a good relationship with your mum and the Australian bloke she married after her divorce, when you were nineteen. You get on fine with both of them when they come over to visit you and your brother, which is about once a year. And your dad's now up in Scotland. So, you don't know what it's like for me."

"Don't make assumptions on the basis of the limited amount I've told you about my family, Robert. I would have happily told you more, but I can see you glazing over whenever the subject of families comes up. It could be a laugh. I'd like to go. Please?"

"Wonderful. I realise when you're in a serious relationship with someone, there's an expectation that seeing their parents might be part of the deal, but I hadn't realised that I'd be expected to see mine more often, too. Alright, we'll go. But I'm telling you it's going to be one of the worst Christmases you've had. Nightmare on Lymington High Street. I'm definitely only staying one night, and there's only one spare room with a single bed so we won't get much sleep."

"Thank you. I'm sure that we'll make it work in a single bed; my boyfriend at university and I slept in one for four months. Just think about staying two nights—that would mean we can go down late on Christmas Eve, not have to worry about drinking too much on Christmas day and leave Boxing Day morning. I promise I will keep your step dad off your back."

"Remind me, next time we disagree, that you're too good at this and I might as well concede from the start. I'm going to hold you to your promise to keep Mussolini Mike off my case. Shit, now I've got to get them presents."

"No, you don't. Tell me a bit about them and I'll get something, as a thank you."

His mother was overjoyed when he rang to tell her that they were coming down for Christmas and Boxing Day, 'assuming the offer is still open'. So much so, he even felt a little guilty about being down on her before. It was Mike he couldn't stand—it will be interesting to see how Emily deals with him.

They set off for the drive to Dorset in her Astra around midday on Christmas Eve. The Alfa had clutch problems and Robert wasn't prepared to risk it on a long journey. He preferred to drive, but he rated Emily's driving and could relax with her. As he'd pulled up outside her house, he was shocked at the number of bags that she was piling into the Astra.

"We're going for two nights, not moving in. What have you got in there?" he said, as he pulled his one cabin-size case out of the Alfa's hatch.

"I wanted to be generous with presents, Robert, including yours. Plus, a woman needs several outfits for a two-day break. Plus, I wasn't sure what clothes I'd feel right in until I got there. What are you, the clothes police?"

He smiled. "Presents? Oh shit, I didn't think we were bothering to buy each other presents."

The traffic was nose-to-tail on the M3 and M27, only thinning out once they reached the road through the New Forest, but they'd bought a stack of CDs for a sing along; Springsteen, Oasis, Clapton, Queen and the rest. The winner was the one who made the fewest mistakes with the lyrics. As Emily pulled up outside his mother's house, she declared him the winner.

"Not fair, though, you've had all those weeks on the naughty step doing nothing except listening to music," she grinned.

"You bitch, that was below the belt."

They were kissing in the front of the car when Emily saw his mother, over his shoulder, coming down the path. She broke away, nudging him, trying to remember his mum's name.

"Great, so for the next two days, I have to remember not to show any signs of physical attraction," he said.

"That'll be interesting in the single bed."

They got out and walked round to greet her.

"Hi, Mum, sorry it's been so long. I'd like you to meet Emily."

As his mother came forward, beaming, Emily held out her hand.

"It's lovely to meet you, Janice, and thank you so much for inviting me. What a lovely house."

"I'm so pleased to meet you at last, Emily. I wish I could say that Robert has told me all about you, but of course he hasn't. I'm looking forward to getting to know you. Come on in, we'll help you with the bags in a minute."

So far so, not so bad, thought Robert, as the three of them walked up the path. He saw Mike coming out of the front door towards them, his eyes on Emily.

"Hello, Mike, it's good to see you. Emily, meet Mike; Mike, meet Emily."

"Hello, Robert, nice of you to come at last. Lovely to see you, Emily. Gosh, isn't she a beauty, Robert, I hope you keep her on a tight rein."

Robert held his breath, waiting for her response as she shook his outreached hand.

"Hello, Mike, good to meet you. That's a first for me, being greeted like a horse. I can see I'll have to brush up on my equestrian skills."

Janice looked embarrassed and Robert waited, fascinated to see how Mike would react. He was enjoying Mike's dilemma. He'd probably never had a woman challenge his crude sexism before and his instinct would be to come back even more inappropriately. But as the host, that would be setting an unacceptable example.

"Sorry, didn't mean to cause offence; I'm a bit old school. Let's go in."

His mother had arranged the lounge with four matching brocade armchairs around the coffee table with a magazine rack underneath. Robert, Emily and Mike made awkward small talk about the traffic on the journey, while Janice got the tea and cakes together. *If this is a taste of things to come, then the next 48 hours are going to be excruciating*, thought Robert.

"So, where did you two meet?" said Janice once she'd poured out the tea and joined them.

"Robert chatted me up at a party and I was, of course, swept off my feet by his looks, wit and intelligence. We saw each other socially a couple of times and began going out soon afterwards, which was nearly six months ago. Your son's a lovely guy, Janice. I'm very fond of him. His career's really taking off, you must be proud of him."

Mike gave an unmistakable snort under his breath, which the other three chose to ignore.

"We are proud of him, aren't we, Mike?" said Janice, with no response. Robert threw Emily a glance. *Christ, Emily, go easy on the 'proud of him' stuff.*

"So, what do you do, Emily? Are you a teacher like Robert?"

"No, I couldn't do his job, Janice. I'm a lawyer, a solicitor to be precise. I represent clients who've been unfairly dismissed, bullied in the workplace, exposed to asbestos; that kind of thing."

Robert smiled. *You go for it girl. Wind the bastard up. He no doubt thinks that there should be no such thing as protection in the workplace for the idle working classes.*

"But don't you think all this health and safety stuff has gone way too far, Emily? I mean, isn't that why jobs like mining are so well paid? There will always be a risk, so the job carries big rewards. Workers these days expect it all ways, don't you think? A good salary and no risk."

Right on cue, Mike, thought Robert.

"I'm afraid I can't agree with your analysis of industrial relations in the 90s, Mike. But let's say you're right and that is their expectation; what's wrong with expecting your employer to make sure your workplace is as safe as possible, no matter how much you earn? For example, I understand you were a company director, but I'd expect to represent you if a poorly fixed bookshelf fell on you at work."

This is getting good, he thought. But Janice intervened, to make sure Mike didn't lose it.

"I'm sure you two will have the chance to continue this discussion tomorrow, but let me tell you how we've planned the next two days. We thought we'd eat at the local pub this evening, then tomorrow have a leisurely morning followed by Christmas dinner here, a walk in the afternoon and see how we feel tomorrow evening. We've been invited round to a neighbour's party, but we don't have to go, obviously."

"That sounds perfect, Janice."

"I wasn't sure what to do about your sleeping arrangements, you two." Janice was blushing slightly, and Robert realised he'd never slept here with a girlfriend before.

"Robert's room only has a single bed, so we borrowed an inflatable single mattress that will just fit on the floor. I hope that's OK?"

"I'm sure that will be fine, Janice, thank you."

Lying pressed against each other on his single bed, they couldn't stop giggling. There was only one bathroom, so they waited for Mike and Janice to use it first. He'd immediately put the inflatable mattress against the wall to create more space before getting into his old bed with Emily.

"This is going to be an interesting night; it takes me back to being with Alex at uni. We couldn't leave each other alone," she said.

"Thank you for sharing that with me. How do you think it's going?"

"Honestly? I like your mum; she seems to be a good person with a generous heart, and she's making me feel very welcome. Mike's an arse, though. Gratuitously unpleasant, I hate that. What does she see in him; he clearly bullies her?"

"Now you know why I couldn't face coming down. You've dealt with him brilliantly; cutting, but just this side of rude. Your response to his comment when he met you was a classic. I bet he's never been challenged like that by a woman before; he only mixes with people like him. Anyway, do you think we're going to get any sleep like this, or should I put the mattress back on the floor?"

"Maybe I should sleep on the inflatable for tonight."

Christmas day passed without incident, excitement, or anything resembling intelligent conversation. They exchanged presents mid-morning before Janice started cooking the Christmas dinner. Emily and Robert both felt stupidly nervous as they opened their presents in front of each other, but he was thrilled with his brown leather bomber jacket and Alfa Romeo car manual—her little joke—and Emily loved her hand made silver ring, bracelet and earrings.

After lunch, they all went for a walk around the harbour. Until he moved to Scotland, Emily's father would sometimes take her out on his small sailing yacht. She loved being out on the water, moved along silently by wind alone.

"I can see why you moved down here, Mike. My dad used to have a small yacht and I loved going out sailing with him. Something very elemental about feeling the wind pushing the boat through the water."

"Oh, I'm surprised to hear that. I wouldn't have thought sailing would be your sort of thing—wet, cold and uncomfortable, not good for the hairdo."

"You don't know anything about me, Mike. Do you make these comments to wind people up or not realise how offensive and sexist they are?"

"I think you need to lighten up, Emily, I'm just joking around. You lot need to get a sense of humour."

"I assume by 'you lot' you mean feminists. That's the classic comment some men make when a woman tells them they find those stereotypes demeaning. All I can do is tell you that I find it offensive and ask you to stop. I can't make you, it's up to you."

Emily walked over to Janice.

"How smart is this party tonight, Janice? I'm still deciding what to wear."

"Me too. Most people tend to dress up and not down. There aren't too many occasions in the year to glam up around here so most of us will make an effort."

"Good. I packed with that in mind, though I've no idea what Robert's going to wear."

Robert had warned Emily that they would be the youngest people there and to be prepared for more men like Mike, only drunker. Emily decided to wear the smartest thing she'd brought: a clinging bottle-green seersucker dress with black tights and high heels.

"The party is promising to be more interesting already," said Robert when he saw her in the bedroom. "I can't wait to watch everyone's face as you walk in."

"I just fancied going for it and wearing something sexy. I wanted to look good for you."

"Mission accomplished."

The level of background chatter dipped noticeably when the four of them walked into the massive lounge as various groups around the room paused their conversations to look at the new arrivals. Specifically, to look at Emily.

The hostess walked over to them.

"Janice, Mike, Robert, lovely to see you; come on in. You must be Emily; we're so glad you came. You look stunning, my dear. What can I get you all to drink?"

Robert and Emily circulated among the hosts' middle-aged, middle-class friends, having one pleasant but meaningless conversation after another.

"Almost every man here seems to have the same wardrobe, topics of conversation and haircut," said Emily, as Robert went to get more drinks in the kitchen.

Three middle-aged men, who Emily had caught looking her way and talking about her, immediately walked over to introduce themselves. They'd clearly been drinking. *Here comes the Lymington fast set*, she thought.

"High there, you've certainly dolled yourself up for the party. You're not from here, are you?"

"No, I live in London. I'm Emily, visiting my boyfriend's parents for Christmas—that's Mike and Janice, over there. Are you all from Lymington?"

"Sure, Lymington born and bred. What is it you do, Emily? Are you a teacher like Robert?"

So, they knew who I was all along. Everyone seems to know all about everyone else. No wonder Robert finds it so claustrophobic here.

"No, I'm a lawyer. And what do you all do."

"Oh, various boring jobs. Honest jobs, though. We don't rip people off like lawyers with their huge fees. I'm afraid we don't like lawyers much, do we guys? Particularly ones who dress up like tarts."

Emily looked at the speaker who was smirking at her, pleased with himself, enjoying his crude power. The other two were watching her, waiting to see what she'd do.

She felt as if she'd been assaulted. *Where does this hatred for women come from? Saying nothing isn't an option, even if I cause a scene.* She reached over, took a knife and tapped it hard several times against her glass. Everyone quickly fell silent, thinking that the host was about to say something. The three men looked at each other, concerned.

She began to speak, clearly and calmly.

"I'm so sorry to interrupt the party, but I thought you'd all be interested in hearing about the conversation I've just had with these three gentlemen. Hearing that I was a lawyer, they thought it amusing to tell me that they don't like lawyers, particularly ones that dress like tarts. I've met hundreds of people in my work, from all kinds of backgrounds, but until I came to Lymington, as Mike and Janice's guest, no one has ever felt it was OK to speak to me like that. Thank you for listening."

Robert had heard the tinkling wine glass and come back into the lounge just as Emily began. He'd stood rooted to the spot, exultant and proud.

"You cow, it was just a joke, why have you made such a big thing of it?"

Robert strode over, but Emily stuck out her hand for him to hold.

"Because until women start calling out horrible, misogynistic behaviour like yours, you will just carry on doing it."

In the silence, to her surprise, she heard a couple of women whoop "Yes!" People began talking again, quietly at

142

first, then animatedly. As she watched the men leave the party, her heart sank as she noticed some guests looking at her disapprovingly. Then two middle-aged women approached her.

"Those three characters have been getting away with that stuff for years. Thank you, that's made our day."

"It's easier for me; I don't have to see them again. But if it's helped, that's great."

She turned to Robert. "I'd like to go in a minute if that's OK. I'm still a bit shaken. Do you mind?"

"Of course not. You were brilliant—the look on that guys face! I'll let Mum know we're leaving, and we'll go."

"I just want to apologise to the host first, Robert. There she is."

"I'm sorry for causing a scene at your party, but I was so shocked I felt had to say something. Thank you for inviting me."

"Well, I must admit I was taken aback when you were speaking. But there's no need to apologise. I didn't want to invite those idiots, but my husband insisted, and we'll have words later. Those three have had it coming, and please don't worry. People will be talking about our party until next Christmas—you two must come next year!"

Ten minutes later, they were back at his mum's house.

"What can I get you? Turkey sandwich?"

Emily laughed. "A large gin and tonic please, ice and lemon. Did your mum say anything when you said we were going?"

"She did. Her words were: 'Whatever you do, don't let that girl go'. In the circumstances, I didn't correct her use of the word girl."

"Good. Enough about Lymington's sexism for one day. Can you believe those guys—I thought that stuff had died out years ago."

They carried on talking about the party, then went to bed and made love, hilariously, on the inflatable mattress, bouncing around until it was half deflated.

"So, what did you think of your mum's advice?"

They were lying on the now-completely deflated mattress, facing each other. Emily was looking into his eyes, stroking the hair above his ear.

"What advice?"

"About not letting me go?"

"Some of the wisest advice she's ever given me. But she needn't worry. After coming close to losing the best thing that's happened to me, I have no intention of letting you go. Ever. I love you."

"Ever is a rather long time, Robert. Are you sure you mean that?"

"I love you, Emily. I've never meant anything as much."

"That's lucky, because I realised about two months ago that I loved you but was too scared to say it. Then you went and fucked everything up, and I was frightened those feelings wouldn't ever return. But they are, slowly."

They kissed each other.

"If I'm going to get any sleep, I think I'd better pump up this mattress."

As they drove away the next morning, Robert waved his mum goodbye, then turned to Emily.

"Can you believe Mike at breakfast? He's such an arsehole. 'Well, you two didn't get much sleep last night. I'll have to get my puncture repair kit and fix the poor old air bed. It hasn't seen action like that in years.' My mum didn't know where to look. After the last two days, what do you think now?"

Emily knew Robert was talking about Mike but chose to misinterpret his question.

"What do I think now? I think if we're as committed to each other as we said last night, then we should have a serious discussion about living together."

11

Co-habiting

Emily and Robert didn't waste any time sorting out the practicalities of moving his stuff—clothes, books and furniture—over to Emily's house, and moving furniture she didn't need to his flat to create extra space. Emily was surprisingly unsentimental about getting rid of her things.

"I'm starting as I mean to go on. Some of my friends have tried living with their girlfriends or boyfriends; the relationships that failed were those where one or both partners expected that their life could continue unchanged, without adapting or compromising. So that means me giving up my space for you."

After they'd carried the last pieces of furniture up to his flat, they celebrated what Emily called 'this adventure with the man I love' at a local brasserie.

"I couldn't be happier, Robert. I'm a realist and I know it's going to take compromise to make this work. Tell me what really winds you up, and I'll try not to do it."

"Top of my list would be untidiness, like leaving clothes all over the floor, but I think you already know that. Once, after I'd slept with someone for the first time, I went 'round the bedroom picking up her underwear from the floor. She came back to find me with her knickers in my hand."

"I want to find out all about you, but there's such a thing as too much information."

Robert had to leave the house earlier now, to beat the rush hour and make the journey from Peckham to Hackney with time to spare. He'd not seen much of Sue since before the Christmas break; their last real conversation was in

November, when he was dealing with the harassment from Garner. Three weeks into the 1995 spring term, he went to her office at the start of the day, hoping to see her. He thought he should check on her state of mind.

She was at her desk, looking far less stressed. Relaxed, even.

"Hi, how was Christmas and New Year? Broken any resolutions yet?"

"Hello, stranger, how are you? Well, I made just one, which was to put the events of last summer's school camp behind me, once and for all. That lasted until approximately five minutes past midnight on the first of January 1995, when Martin said how great it would be if I could put all that school camp stuff behind me."

"You're joking? What an idiot. Sorry, he's your boyfriend, I shouldn't say that."

"No, you can, he's not any more. You're obviously not hooked into the school gossip. I've been with Tim since two weeks ago."

"Tim, the head of History? He was on the camp!"

"Nothing happened then, obviously, as I was still trying to get you into bed. But we did get to know each other, and things have been developing ever since. He's left his wife and we've moved in together. So far, so good."

"I'm really pleased for you, Sue. I remember you spent the whole of our journey to Wales telling me how unhappy you were living with Martin. How are you coping with the memories of the camp; are you still troubled about Tom, if you don't mind me raising it?"

"Most days I don't think about it anymore, or if I do, it rarely upsets me. Every so often though, when I least expect it, I get depressed, disgusted with myself for what I did. Tim always notices, but I can't tell him about it, so I might go for therapy in the future if the low moods continue. How about you? It must have been awful when Tom's family were harassing you—has that stopped now?"

"Yes, thank goodness. I guess they realised the school and the council weren't going to budge and decided to move on with their lives. It was horrible at the time, but Emily has been there to support me, whenever I felt like chucking the job in. I moved into her place in the New Year. So far so good. You know you can always talk to me about the camp, if it would help."

As soon as he'd uttered the words, Robert regretted it. *What's the matter with me, I don't owe her anything?*

"That's good of you to offer, but I think talking to you would only increase the chances of my getting depressed. Sorry, that sounds hard, it's not meant to."

"That's OK, I understand. I hope things work out for you and Tim, he's a good bloke. I'll see you around, Sue, take care."

"You too."

They didn't speak about the incident again, as long as they worked at the school.

Robert and Emily had agreed at the start that living together didn't mean being inseparable, and they were both determined to maintain a degree of independence. As spring went into summer, and their lives became increasingly woven together, they dealt with the frustration of compromise with humour and patience.

Emily adjusted to Robert's tidiness issue quicker than she thought she would but found it hard to share her physical space with someone who took up so much room. Robert struggled to adjust to living with someone who could suddenly, and passionately, express her feelings about the state of the world and expect empathy from her partner.

They were both working harder than ever, particularly Emily. The eighties culture of macho management and reduced union representation, which had continued into the nineties, meant that Emily was taking on an increasing number of cases involving workplace bullying and health and safety corner-cutting. She would come back late at night and slip into bed beside him, waking him up as she shaped her body around his.

The happiness they experienced from being with each other, from the level of intimacy that neither had experienced before, remained undiminished.

"Robert, this is an accident waiting to happen."

They were discussing whether she should stop using the cap and go on the pill.

"We could carry on and accept the risk. Would it be so terrible if you got pregnant now?"

"It wouldn't be terrible, we both want children, but the timing wouldn't be great. There are always the side effects to consider, such as my boobs getting bigger."

"You say that as if it's a bad thing."

They loved having friends over for dinner parties. Angus and Maria came around soon after Robert moved in, and the four of them had a hilarious, inebriated evening. Maria's flirting with Robert was blatant and impossible to ignore, but Emily didn't let it get to her.

The four of them were sitting in the lounge, eating cheese and biscuits, when Angus jumped into a gap in the conversation.

"It's brilliant to see Emily so happy, Robert. Maria and I used to despair in the past after we'd met her previous boyfriends. God, Emily, you didn't half pick them. The last one especially."

"Thank you, Angus. Is this open season on all my previous relationships?"

"What's your secret, Robert? What have *you* got that the others lacked?" Maria asked, shamelessly. Emily took her on.

"I'll loan him out to you if Angus is OK with that."

"More than happy, as long as I can join in," replied Angus.

So, the banter went on.

"That was a great evening," said Robert as he loaded the dishwasher. "The four of us get on so well."

"Yes, though I think Maria would like you two to get on even better. God, she doesn't even try to hide it anymore. I feel sorry for Angus."

Four months after Robert moved in, piles of their work papers had accumulated around the lounge and study. For two people who often worked at home, the lack of space was getting to them.

One evening, frustrated after taking half an hour to find her papers from one of the many piles, Emily decided to confront the issue.

"We're both earning good money now. I could sell this house, you could sell your flat and with a joint mortgage, we could buy a bigger place together. We both believe this is for keeps and we could really use more space. I'm ready to take the plunge, Robert. What do you say?"

Robert knew this would be the end of his potential escape route—his flat, which had been let to a colleague. He hesitated for a fraction of a second, then said, "When do we start looking?"

They put their homes on the market in June and began looking for three-bedroom houses that needed improving. Neither of them questioned the decision to buy such a big house; they left it unsaid.

Robert's flat sold almost immediately—his area of Hackney had suddenly become more desirable—which made it easier to get an offer accepted on a three-storey, end of terrace Victorian house in Brixton. Emily's house sold three weeks later. Their new place was in need of a lot of work, and they'd agreed that their summer holiday this year would be spent sanding floors, ripping out the old kitchen and bathroom and supervising work to get the house looking right.

A week before her three-week's leave was due to start, Emily was at a conference about the increasing abuse of disciplinary procedures by employers. Over lunch, she found herself sharing a table with some lawyers from one of the teaching unions. Their conversation had turned to the problem of representing clients who you suspect are hiding something. Without mentioning any names or details, one of them gave an example of a disciplinary case she'd been involved in, nearly a year ago, involving an incident on a school camp. "I never really believed the guy."

As soon as they'd completed on the purchase of their new house, they moved into the building site that was to be their home. With most of their stuff in storage, they slept on a mattress on the floor for six weeks; once the builders and plasterers finished one room, they'd paint it. Emily had a real flair for judging the colours that would work best in each of the rooms, depending on size, height and the orientation of the windows. They used the local swimming pool for showers until the bathroom was installed and ate in local cafes and Italian restaurants. They'd never felt so close. Or so overweight.

Once they were back at work in September, any remaining jobs were fitted into every minute of spare time they had, moving from one room to another. By December, the house was as finished as it would ever be. Emily rarely thought anymore about the conversation she'd overheard three months ago, and the coincidences between the case being discussed and the one Robert had been involved in.

12

An Inspector Calls

"Christ, it's fucking cold. I knew we should have got a bigger mortgage and replaced the old doors and windows. The kitchen patio doors have got gaps bigger than my hand."

Robert had just walked into the bedroom carrying their cups of tea. It was the start of their Saturday morning routine; he'd go down two flights to the kitchen to make the tea, collect *The Guardian* from the mat and take the paper and tea up to the bedroom. They'd take time to catch up on each other's week, swap bits of the newspaper and read out anything that amused or outraged them. There was enough to keep them going all day; 'cash for questions', allegations of sleaze and infidelity against Tory MPs, the increasingly desperate attacks on New Labour and Tony Blair. Several sections of the paper always remained unread.

Putting the colour supplement down, Emily moved her hand under the duvet.

"Have I ever told you that you're one of the sexiest men in Brixton? And there's a lot of competition out there, believe me. I was walking back from the tube yesterday and saw this guy standing on the corner, tall, deep brown eyes…"

Robert felt himself growing in her hand.

"Yes, Emily, I get the idea. But he's not here, so you'll have to make do with me."

His hand moved from her breast, fingertips sliding over her ribs, following the curve of her waist, the swell of her belly and into the mound of soft, fuzzy hair.

Her body quivered. "Maybe you are the sexiest man in Brixton."

Half an hour later, Emily lay looking at the stubbly face that had caught her eye, across the room, eighteen months ago. She kissed him, tasting herself. *Everything is going so well between us. He's even developing a social conscience at last. From a low base, admittedly.*

"If we ever get too bored with each other to do that, let's promise we'll call it a day."

"OK, it's a deal. Though you have to understand that the performance and reliability of men's reproductive equipment inevitably deteriorates with age—a bit like the Alfa Romeo, really."

"Not as soon as the Alfa, surely?"

"In about forty years, or thereabouts."

"So, I could be stuck with you for a long time?"

"I'm afraid so."

Two months later, at the end of a particularly frantic Friday afternoon, one of the partner's in Emily's practice asked to see her before she left.

"Hi, Jonathan, you wanted to see me?"

"Yes, thanks, Emily, I've got good news. The partners agreed at our last meeting that we want to offer you a partnership within the practice as soon as a vacancy arises, which should be within the next three months. We all think very highly of your work. The growing reputation of the industrial relations side of our practice has been almost totally down to you. What do you think?"

"That's amazing, Jonathan. I wasn't expecting anything like that. Wow! Thank you."

Forty minutes later, Emily rushed through the front door, ran through to the kitchen, took the last bottle of Cava out of the fridge, filled two large glasses and took them through to the lounge where Robert was watching a match he'd taped.

"Grab hold of this, we're celebrating!"

As Emily poured out her news, hardly pausing to draw breath, Robert listened with mixed emotions. It was a strange feeling. He was genuinely thrilled for her, saying the right things. But something else was there, under the surface, another feeling that he didn't want to deal with. Feelings that he hoped were in the past, as if they belonged to someone else.

She's doing so well, astonishingly well. A partner! I'm still just a middle manager in the school I started in six years ago with no opportunities for promotion coming up. I should be unambiguously pleased for her. But there's no point deceiving myself that I'm someone I'm not. It will matter a lot if she's more successful. Over time, it could eat away, destroying what we've got together. I need to re-balance this and take a step up, soon.

At the start of the 1996 summer term, Robert was asked to cover an English lesson for the deputy head, who'd been summoned to Hatton's office at short notice, with the rest of the senior team. As he walked around the classroom, talking with those pupils he knew would benefit from personal attention, he realised it probably meant one of two things. A visit by someone very important or an Ofsted inspection. The following day, Hatton called an emergency staff meeting.

"I received a call from Ofsted yesterday, informing me that the school will be inspected in four weeks' time. They assured me we'd been selected at random, but they always say that. Inspectors can be inconsistent. I'm sure we all know colleagues from other schools that have done badly, either because of a minor incident or piece of rogue data. A judgement of serious weaknesses, which of course we don't have, would have major consequences for all of us. We're a good school, verging on outstanding, and we've got four weeks to prepare and prove it."

Robert was swept up in the mixture of anxiety, paranoia and paperwork that followed the announcement. As the head of the year group taking GCSE exams, Hatton asked him for volumes of data on his students' attainment, progress, behaviour and attendance, all of which needed to demonstrate constant improvement over the previous three years.

As constant improvement hadn't always taken place, his job was to manipulate the data to show it had, creating additional workload and anxiety.

Two days later, Hatton asked to see him urgently. Sitting behind his desk, he looked exhausted and nervy.

"I've gone through the new Ofsted schedule in detail, Robert. Arrangements for ensuring pupils' health and safety have been given much higher significance, and if we fail in that category, we fail overall. I need you to prepare a report, as soon as possible, on that 1994 school summer camp. I know it was nearly two years ago, but it's within their rights to go back that far; if we get a punitive lead inspector, they might do that. When could you let me have it?"

Luckily, this wasn't a complete surprise to him. He'd read through the new framework yesterday evening—probably one of the few teachers to have done so, outside of the senior team—and noticed the increased emphasis on health and safety. He'd wondered whether the inspectors might ask about the summer camp incident.

"I could get you a draft by next Wednesday, Tom."

"Could you make it Tuesday afternoon, please Robert, so that the senior team can study it at our meeting that evening?"

Robert worked ten- to twelve-hour days for the next three weeks. By the weekend before the inspection, he was exhausted.

"I haven't seen you this stressed since the council hearing nearly two years ago. Is there anything I can help with, stuff you want to run past me?"

Emily had brought two glasses of Burgundy into the front room. She'd done most of the cooking over the last three weeks so that Robert had something decent to eat when he got home; most days, he was living on sandwiches, coffee and crisps.

"Probably lots of things that I haven't thought of, but my brain is too addled to remember. I know I haven't been easy to live with over the last three weeks; you've been brilliant, as always. God knows whether they'll bring up the summer camp incident. If they do decide to go for it, I'm pretty sure Hatton will leave me to take the blame."

"That would be so wrong. If you sense that might be happening, tell me. We'll fight it."

"I will. You're the best girlfriend in the world and I love you very much. Just talking to you about this calms me down. Have you heard any more about the partner vacancy?"

"No, I don't think it will happen until the summer at the earliest."

On Friday afternoon, at the end of the inspection, staff waited in an atmosphere of suppressed anxiety and forced jollity for the head teacher to give them the verdict. The Ofsted team had been in their meeting with Hatton and his Chair of Governors for over an hour, which was longer than expected. Robert had picked up rumours in the last couple of days that the inspectors had been raising serious concerns.

His own experience of the inspection had been positive; his teaching had been graded 'Good' and 'Outstanding'. He'd acquitted himself well in his interviews with inspectors. The incident on the summer camp hadn't been raised.

He was particularly pleased with the way he'd handled the meeting about his year group. The lead inspector came armed with a huge file of pupil data and follow-up questions.

"While the progress data on Year 11 shows positive overall, Mr Mason, the performance of Irish and Somali pupils isn't so good. What's going on there?"

Robert handed the inspector four sheets of A4 paper, on which he'd broken down the performance of every pupil from those ethnic groups since they've been at the school. Those who'd been at the school since Year 7 were better than average; only those who'd joined in the last two years brought the figures down.

"Where pupils have been here from the start, they do very well. It's not statistically valid to expect the same rate of progress for those who've just joined us."

Robert had continued to rebut the inspector's points with detailed evidence until he left, clearly impressed.

The room hushed as the head teacher and Chair of Governors walked in. Robert saw immediately from the look on their faces that the judgement wasn't good. Hatton took a deep breath, then began.

"I want to thank everyone for the hard work you've all put in over the last month, particularly during the last week. Unfortunately, in spite of that, the inspectors have judged the school to have serious weaknesses, a judgement the Chair and I feel is very unfair. We argued our case strongly with the inspectors, but I'm afraid there was no budging them. The main areas of concern were leadership, pupil progress in years seven and eight and maths." He paused a moment, his voice starting to break.

"I'm confident that working together as a staff, we can fix these issues quickly and get the school back on track. For now, you all deserve to enjoy the first relaxing weekend you've had for over a month."

Robert noted the Chair's body language. It showed little confidence in Hatton's optimism that things would be sorted quickly. But judging by what he'd just heard, the outcome could be useful for him. His areas of responsibility had been judged good, and the findings on leadership could open up opportunities as people were 'moved on'. Sacked, in other words.

Many teachers were angry when the report was published three weeks later. The verdict on the school was harsher than they'd been led to believe and a sense of injustice took hold. Headlines in the local press fed into this.

"Popular local school fails younger pupils with weak leadership. Head teacher and governors insufficiently aware of the problems."

The Council and the governors were ruthless. Hatton resigned after a deal was negotiated with his union. It wasn't an offer he could refuse, and he cleared his desk immediately. A school inspector and the first deputy head were drafted in to run the school jointly until a new head teacher could be appointed. One of the deputy heads suffered the same fate as Hatton, leaving a gap in the senior team.

The report's conclusions were the opportunity Robert had been waiting for. He discreetly set up a meeting with the first deputy head, who was now the acting head teacher, effectively running the school. He'd previously been Robert's line manager, and they'd always got on well.

"Have you thought about what you're going to do about the vacancy in the senior team, Sam? I assume you won't be leaving it empty, given the challenges the school's facing? I wanted you to know I'm interested in applying if it's advertised. We've always worked well together, so if I was appointed, you'd have someone watching your back on the senior team. I think the way some staff are blaming you for helping to get rid of Hatton stinks."

"Interesting idea, Robert. It would be good to have you with me. I've finally convinced the Chair and the council that we need to enlarge the team, and I'm sure they'll agree to another assistant head post. If they do, the advert will go in next week; show me your application before you send it in."

"I'm not taking anything for granted; I understand there has to be a competitive process."

Sam looked at him with a wry expression.

"Just make sure you show up."

Robert was one of three teachers who went for the job. The days when he screwed up interviews were now in the past, and he was appointed a week later, for six months initially. The permanent job would have to wait for the new head teacher to be appointed.

When he got home that evening, Emily told him it had been confirmed that she would be made a partner on the first of August. *Thank God I persuaded Sam to create that promotion.* He knew her success would have left him frustrated and begrudging otherwise.

After two weeks, he began to wonder whether the new job was such a good idea. The pressure on the senior staff to push through Ofsted's recommendations was intense and involved frequent monitoring of those teachers identified as under-performing. Unfortunately, Sue was one of them. Their first meeting in his new role didn't go well, leaving him exasperated.

"So, you've well and truly joined the other side now, Robert. How can you live with yourself, putting your old friends through this farce? You know my targets are set up to fail me and give you lot the excuse to sack me. God, you've changed."

"This isn't easy for me either, Sue. I'm going to do everything I can to help you get through this, but it's going to be difficult if you take that approach."

"There you go again, trying to make out this is the same for both of us. It isn't, and the fact you're so dishonest with yourself shows how far you've sold out."

Their meetings carried on like that until, on the penultimate day of term, Sue told the acting head she was resigning. She bitterly resented Robert's role, accusing him of helping to end her career.

His capability meetings with other colleagues became increasingly confrontational. It was an open secret that their targets were set unachievably high, to ensure that they failed. While Robert felt some sympathy for those teachers that didn't deserve to be dismissed, he knew his job depended on failing most of them, however good they were. He didn't question the unfairness; his future career was all that mattered, and he couldn't afford to care about theirs. As a result, he was increasingly resented by other staff.

Emily noticed a change in his mood.

"You seem less positive about the job these days. Is there anything happening at the school you'd like to talk about?"

"Nothing I can't deal with. I think you know there's huge pressure on the senior team to demonstrate that the school is making progress on Ofsted's performance targets, which is leading to bad feeling between us and some of the staff. Petty stuff, really, like moving away when I go into the staff room. Once people feel that the school is improving, most of it will be forgotten."

"I had no idea it was that punitive. Maybe I can help you find a way through. Decide who deserves to succeed, agree an achievable timescale with each of them and help the rest with an exit plan."

Robert knew it wouldn't be that easy and sensed the sour atmosphere could get to him eventually. He would often feel depressed after a particularly confrontational meeting. But during the last weeks of the summer term, with Emily's help, he was able to chart a path through his doubts and anxieties. Once again, he realised how important her support was to achieving his ambition.

Two weeks later, sitting in their tiny, parched back garden on a sweltering Sunday afternoon in the '96 heatwave, Emily put down the Observer travel section and proposed that they splash out on a three-week trip to Kenya, splitting the time between the Masai Mara game reserve and a resort on the Indian Ocean.

"I've wanted to go for years but couldn't afford it and had to find the right man to go with. Now we've got two good salaries coming in, money isn't a problem. I guess one out of two isn't bad."

"Have I ever told you it's your sense of humour that I love most about you."

"Seriously, what do you think? I know it's late in the day to book, there might not be any flights left, but I could spend time tomorrow finding out. Do I have your permission to go ahead and book if there's availability? I know it will be madly expensive, but we're doing fine financially now."

"It sounds fantastic, sweetheart. We haven't had a real holiday since we started living together, and I've always wanted to visit a game park, so let's do it. I'll ring you at work tomorrow to see if you've got anywhere. Sounds really exciting."

Five weeks later, four days into their stay at the idyllic resort Emily had found, Robert lay on their bed, looking out at the Indian Ocean through the open veranda doors. Emily was asleep next to him, looking serenely untroubled. He'd woken from his afternoon siesta twenty minutes ago and was mulling over thoughts he'd been having since they'd arrived. Is it time to have that conversation yet?

They'd first talked about having children when he moved into her house and both agreed that they wanted to have children at some point. That was eighteen months ago, and every conversation they'd subsequently had about their future carried the assumption that they would stay together. Emily would be thirty in little over a year and he knew that a woman's cycle took time to stabilise after coming off the pill. The holiday had been everything they'd wished for; the stress of the summer term just a memory for both of them. They couldn't leave each other alone.

At dinner that evening, Emily looked at Robert across the lilies arranged in the middle of the table and said, "I've been wondering for a few days whether this is the right time to ask you something and decided that there won't ever be a better moment. We've hardly talked about it since we started living together, but I wanted to ask—"

"My answer is yes."

"You don't know what I was going to say!"

"I think you were going to ask if I wanted us to start trying for a baby."

"How did you know that? That's weird. And amazing. And your answer is amazing. Do you really? Are you sure? Are we really having this conversation?"

"The really weird thing is that I've been thinking the same for the last two weeks and couldn't decide whether to ask you or not. Lying in bed this afternoon, looking at you asleep, I decided to ask you this evening. I couldn't believe it when I saw where you were heading. Luckily, I was right. God, Emily, I'm so happy. Come here."

She went around the table, sat on his lap and kissed him.

Shortly after the new head teacher was appointed in October, Robert applied for the permanent assistant head post. He got the job, in spite of the rumours that some governors were concerned that his approach with teachers on capability procedures had been too punitive. Knowing the issue could be raised, he'd crafted a response.

"I saw it as my job as a manager to support those that demonstrated they were capable of improving, while being straight with those that didn't. Our pupils deserve to have excellent teaching, every lesson."

The new Head had been impressed.

The constant pressure could leave Robert exhausted, though, which was unfortunate on those occasions when it coincided with Emily's fertile days. She wouldn't take 'No' for an answer.

"Emily, sweetheart, I'm really tired. I need to go to sleep."

"Not before you've fulfilled your only useful, male function, my love. This woman has chosen you, out of a cast of hundreds, to be the father of her children. This is the moment when the chances of impregnation are at their highest, so we have to mate, mate."

"You've put it so romantically, how can I refuse? But you'll have to do all of the preparatory work."

"That's a deal, providing you keep going until the end."

Slowly, Ofsted's judgements on the school's progress began to improve, reducing one pressure on Robert, at least.

13

A New Beginning

Emily discovered she was pregnant in January 1997, shortly after Ofsted judged the school to have improved enough to be rated 'Satisfactory'. The reduction in Robert's workload no doubt helped the conception. Ten weeks into the pregnancy, she suffered a miscarriage. They hadn't told anybody she was pregnant, and colleagues at work became concerned by her sudden, unexplained, moments of distress. Even when she became pregnant the second time, a few months later, she continued to grieve for the developing life she'd lost, something that Robert struggled to understand.

"My love, I'm so sorry we lost our first one. But we know that a high percentage of first pregnancies end in miscarriage, and you mustn't blame yourself. Now you're pregnant again so soon, we know there's nothing wrong."

"I know you find it hard to understand, but it's not about blaming either of us or worrying there's something wrong. The fact that I've been lucky enough to conceive again so quickly doesn't take away my grieving for our first one. It will fade with time, I'm sure, but I doubt it will ever go away completely. I hope you understand that."

"Of course, I do. I love you." But he wished she could put it behind her, just as he had.

Emily was due to give birth in February the following year. She continued to work normally for thirty weeks into the pregnancy, when she handed over her three remaining cases. On her last day at work, at the end of November, the partners gave her a moving 'farewell and good luck' send-off at a local Italian restaurant.

Jonathan, the senior partner, gave the speech.

"I know I speak for all of us when I say that you're going to be sorely missed. We hope you're not gone too long, not only because you're such a great lawyer but because you're such a supportive colleague to everyone at Pearson, Shallice and Grant. Lawyers are often accused of forgetting that their clients are human beings when we get submerged in the legal intricacies of a case, but you're an example to us all. Your clients all seem to adore you.

"Can we please raise our glasses, to Emily, Robert and the baby. Good luck and good health to the three of you."

For the first time in eight years, she found herself with time on her hands and suggested to Robert that they should invite as many close friends as possible around before the birth as they probably wouldn't feel like entertaining in the first months afterwards. There were also parental pressures. Robert's mum had been asking to visit them since he'd told her, and that was now fixed for next week. Emily's mum was waiting until after the birth before arranging her flight from Australia and her dad had already made the trip down from Dundee and stayed for a couple of days.

Although Emily had continued to meet Maria regularly for lunch, the dinner party this Saturday was the first time the four of them would have met in months. She warned Robert that her pregnancy had brought a long-festering issue to the surface for the other couple. Maria was keen to start a family, but Angus wasn't ready to commit; during the meal, their previous exuberant humour was noticeable by its absence. Angus came up to him as he was washing saucepans in the kitchen.

"I'm very pleased for you, mate, really I am, but you two deciding to have a baby has really brought things to a head for Maria and me. Hardly a day goes by without her starting a row about the fact that I don't want children yet, and it's now affecting our sex life. She's come off the pill as she says it can affect her fertility in the future, so I insist on using a condom and she throws a wobbly."

"Do you think you'll ever want children, Angus? If you don't, as much as we would hate to see you two split up, maybe you need to have that out. It's not fair on her, if you know you'll always feel like this."

"That's the problem. I know I don't want them now, but how can I be sure what I'll feel in three, four or five years' time?"

"You can't. But if you're pushing it that far ahead, you need to tell her."

As they said their goodbyes, Maria pulled him towards her and hugged him. "Emily's a lucky woman," she whispered.

Two weeks later, just before her weekly check-up, Emily began to experience stomach pains and nausea. She could see the nurse was concerned as soon as she'd taken her blood pressure.

"I'm going to send off your urine for further tests, as I suspect you may have pre-eclampsia. We'll get the result back in 24 hours; please rest until then. Depending on the result, we may want you to come into hospital until the birth."

She told Robert that evening.

"So, I'll hear within 24 hours whether I have to go into hospital and be monitored up until the birth. I hope not, as I can't stand hospitals, but it's for the best if the results are concerning."

"What do you mean, concerning? Is the baby at risk? Are you at risk?"

"Calm down, Robert. Apparently, the condition is caused when the placenta doesn't function as well as it should, which can then affect my kidneys' ability to get rid of waste from the blood. It's only serious if it becomes eclampsia, which can happen quickly sometimes, and that's why I might need to be in hospital."

The nurse rang early the next morning, before Robert had left for work.

"I'm afraid the test showed there's a high level of protein in your urine, so we need to admit you from today, up to the birth. I've alerted the maternity ward, they're expecting you this afternoon. Is there someone who can bring you in?"

"My boyfriend can bring me, thanks. Is there any risk to the baby at the moment?"

"Almost certainly not. You're into your thirty-sixth week, but you need to be in hospital in case the condition suddenly deteriorates."

Robert rang the school to tell them he wasn't coming in. As they drove to the hospital, he asked so many questions that she lost patience.

"For God's sake, Robert, you can ask the doctor when we get there. You know as much as I do at the moment, which is that nearly ten percent of women can get this condition in their first pregnancy and in almost every case it disappears after the baby is born. There are no implications for the baby's health."

A few days later, on the 25th January 1998, her kidneys began to fail. Emily was rushed to the operating theatre, where her daughter was delivered by emergency caesarean. Lily was three weeks premature and perfectly healthy, but Emily was already showing signs of eclampsia. Her joy at touching her daughter, as the midwife held her close, was short lived. As poison spread quickly around her body, she was sedated and admitted to intensive care. For the next twelve hours, her body continued to swell from the retained fluids.

The hospital had contacted Robert at work as soon as Emily went to theatre, but by the time he got there, she was already in intensive care. When he was finally allowed to go in, he was warned not to disturb her as she was sedated. As he entered the intensive care unit, he was surprised by the subdued lighting and quiet atmosphere within, interrupted only by beeps and pings from the monitoring equipment around every bed. He immediately noticed Lily in a small plastic crib alongside one of the beds, but he hardly recognised Emily, still unconscious, her hands, arms and face grossly swollen.

Confronted by his tiny, new born daughter sleeping next to her critically ill mother, the woman he'd fallen in love with, Robert felt unanchored in a way he'd never experienced. Trying to take in the brand-new life and potential mortality in the same moment, he felt completely lost, unprepared and strangely disengaged by the existential moment. He realised that his life had changed irrevocably, in the most fundamental way, and it overwhelmed him. From this moment, the freedom to shape his life selfishly, without considering the consequences of his actions for others, would never be the same. He now had responsibility—possibly his alone if Emily died—for this beautiful little girl. He would have to be there for her for the rest of his life. Fucking hell.

He stood there, willing Emily to recover, crying silently from a combination of fear and joy.

One of the ICU nurses approached him.

"This is your first one, I think? It's overwhelming, I know, especially as your wife has developed eclampsia. Please don't worry about her; the doctors expect the swelling to go down in the next twenty-four hours, as the poison starts to drain. We'll bring her out of sedation as soon as that happens."

He turned to look at her. She was in her mid-twenties, with the easy, re-assuring manner of someone confident in their role, confident of their expertise.

"How can you be so sure?"

"Because we're used to seeing women with this condition and they've all made a full recovery."

"Every one of them?"

The nurse considered her reply, weighing him up.

"All but one. But that patient had complications."

"Thank you for being honest. What about our daughter? She's looks tiny."

"She's five pounds ten ounces, which is about what we'd expect for three weeks premature. Three weeks means nothing, they're fully cooked by then."

He smiled at the nurse's phrase.

"I assume Lily doesn't stay here all the time? Who cares for her while Emily's in intensive care? Sorry if that's a stupid question."

"Not at all. We brought her in here an hour ago, in case Emily had begun to improve, but we'll take her back to the special care baby unit now. The midwives will look after her until your wife has recovered."

"Would it be possible for me to stay in here tonight, sleeping next to the bed? On a chair?"

"I think so. We're not full now, but you may not get much sleep if we have an emergency admission. I'll find you something comfortable."

A nurse took Lily out ten minutes later. Robert sat down, looking at Emily more closely. She looked awful, really unwell. There was a tube going into her arm from a drip, another device on the end of one finger and three electrode pads on her chest, wired up to two monitors. A thicker tube, coming out from the bottom of her gown, fed into a clear bag at the end of the bed, slowly filling with yellowy-brown liquid. *That must be the drain from the catheter going into her bladder*, he thought. *My God, what has she just been through, giving birth to our daughter?*

He went to the toilet around one in the morning but couldn't get back to sleep for hours, terrified by the recurring thought that Emily could die. How would he possibly cope? He woke to the sound of doctors conferring around her bed. He forced his eyes open and tried to sit up.

"Good morning, Mr Mason. I don't need to ask how you slept, but I can give you the good news that the swelling is down, and your wife's body has begun to rid itself of poison. We're going to slowly bring her out of sedation, so why don't you freshen up and get a cup of coffee? She should be awake by the time you come back."

A huge sense of relief burst through him; she was going to be fine.

"Thank you, that's wonderful news. I'll take your advice about freshening up."

He'd always been impressed by the way senior doctors could make a suggestion sound like a command. He wanted to learn how to do that. Half an hour later, feeling slightly more human, he went back to the ICU.

When she saw him, Emily smiled as broadly as her re-sculptured face allowed. He kissed her gently on the cheek and held her hand.

"We've done it, Robert. We've got a baby daughter," she said in a half whisper.

"You've done it, Emily. You've been amazing. She's absolutely beautiful. Like her mum."

They both had tears in their eyes.

"She is, isn't she? Beautiful, I mean. I saw her briefly after the delivery, before I came in here. Christ, I felt fucking dreadful. Still do, just not quite as bad. It's so lovely to see you here, what a surprise. Where did you sleep?"

"In that chair. I asked to stay with you and the nurse said it was OK. I'm so relieved, you worried me last night. I'll always to be with you. My amazing wife."

Emily looked surprised, then Robert realised what he'd said and laughed.

"The nurse kept calling you my wife and it seemed too much hassle to correct her. It must have stuck in my subconscious, sorry. It wasn't a proposal."

"That's a shame," she said and closed her eyes.

They were married three months later in a low-key ceremony at Islington town hall, Lily gurgling through everything in a sling around Robert's neck. They persuaded a middle-aged couple sitting in a nearby coffee bar to be their witnesses and told their parents two days later. Emily remained Emily Fowler.

While they coped with baby Lily no better, and no worse, than the average couple, Emily did almost all of the coping. Robert's mother came to stay for a couple of weeks soon after Lily came home, although Robert argued against it, much to Emily's annoyance.

"I understand you've got a right to express your view, but when it comes to support for Lily's care, if I'm saying that this is going to make a difference to me, you need to back off. I never thought I'd say this, but I don't think you realise the extent to which my life changed the day Lily was born, whereas yours has pretty much stayed the same."

Robert said nothing, even though he'd felt his life had been turned upside down since his daughter arrived. And he had to admit that his mum had made a real difference to Emily's level of exhaustion, although he didn't, shamefully, translate that observation into giving Emily more support. From his perspective, it had been a mutual decision that she would take at least six months maternity leave to be full time with Lily, as they could just about survive on his salary. Of course, her life has changed. He began to feel resentful that his time together with Emily had to be shared with Lily, who inevitably came first.

Her dad came down for a weekend with his girlfriend but stayed in a hotel.

"Lovely to see you two and the baby, but I thought we'd see some of the sights too." Her dad's girlfriend made it clear, in a nice way, that she wasn't really a baby person.

One evening in March, working in his office after an unpleasant, backbiting, senior team meeting, his mobile rang. They'd bought mobile phones after Emily's miscarriage the previous year.

"Hi, Robert, it's Maria. How's everything with Emily and the baby?"

Robert's mood dipped further. Emily had told him that Maria was finding it difficult to deal with her feelings now that Lily had arrived and had left the house in tears on the last two occasions she'd come around.

"Hi, Maria. Everything is fine, just the usual: no sleep, no money and no sex." Robert regretted the last words.

"But it's all worth it, yes? I'm ringing you to ask a big favour, please say no if you're not happy about it. As you probably know, Angus and I are almost at the end, arguing constantly about starting a family. I want to have a last attempt to talk him round before we call it a day, but whenever I've tried, it's ended in a terrible row. I wanted to get your advice, as a bloke, about what I'm planning to say."

"Does Angus know about this? I wouldn't want to go behind his back."

"Of course he knows. I'm not going to hide anything. Could we meet for a coffee next week sometime?"

After their meeting, he was left wondering why she'd contacted him. Emily had thought it an odd request but encouraged him to go. He left the coffee shop after little more than an hour, feeling sad for Maria and Angus. He liked them both enormously, but the longer she'd talked, the more it seemed obvious that she should end the relationship if having children was overwhelmingly important to her. He told her as much, as gently as he could. Angus had made it clear he couldn't commit. As they left, she gave him a hug and said, "Thank you. You may not realise it, but you've helped me make my decision. Whatever happens, I hope we'll stay in touch."

14

Life Moves On and On

Four months before Lily's first birthday, Emily went back to work for three days a week. She'd managed to set-up a nanny share with another family to cover her days in the office, and though the nanny's wages took up half of Emily's salary, that was a better deal than many other families. Like many couples their age with young children who'd moved into their rapidly 'improving' neighbourhood, Robert and Emily's life increasingly revolved around maintaining and developing local networks of mutual support. Robert's expectations of their roles were clear; you've got the part-time job so it's fair that you're responsible for managing Lily's care.

Emily became increasingly irritated with his attitude. While he was completely engaged with his daughter at weekends and holidays—the joy, the moments of terror, the cajoling, the changing and bathing—they argued constantly about his assumption that all this was ultimately Emily's responsibility during the working week.

"Men just don't seem to get how knackering it is to look after a one year old all day. Believe me, my days at work are far less stressful. And I still do most of the childcare in the evenings on the days when we both work."

They were in the kitchen, arguing. It was Emily's half day at work and she'd come home, looking forward to a rest, before their nanny returned at tea time. Dawn had taken Lily to the park, and Robert had come back around three o'clock, straight from a meeting at the education offices that had finished early. Emily was in her underwear, having got out of bed to make a cup of tea.

"Hi there, sexy, guess who's home early? How do you feel about going back up to bed?"

"For fuck's sake, Robert. Sex is the last thing on my mind at this moment. I got back at 2 o'clock, knackered and went for a nap. I've just come down to make a cup of tea and I'm going back up—alone. Dawn will be back in an hour, so perhaps you could look after your daughter in the afternoon for once."

"Christ, Emily, anyone would think I'd just suggested you provide a freshly ironed shirt every day and a cooked meal on the table. Apologies for showing that I still fancy you and want to have sex. Of course, I'll look after Lily. That was a snide remark."

"I still fancy you, but now we've got Lily. I'm more exhausted most of the time than I ever used to be. You just need to be more understanding."

Their feelings for each other remained strong, but Emily grew weary of the arguments about childcare and sex, and she began to feel frustrated with aspects of their relationship. She accepted, sadly, that Robert was fundamentally selfish; he would always put himself first, although she acknowledged he loved his daughter unconditionally. Their social circle changed as single friends drifted away and new friends, mostly couples with children that Emily met in cafes and later at nursery, came on the scene. Emily and Maria tried to keep their friendship alive, but gradually saw less of each other. Angus and Maria split up two months after Robert had met her in the café.

His affair with Maria was entirely predictable.

He'd seen Angus twice since the break-up of his relationship with Maria. The last time they met in a pub around the corner from Angus's new rented flat, it became increasingly clear that he partly blamed Robert and Emily for the break-up. Robert was furious, given the time he'd spent with Angus talking about his options, and he decided to stop seeing him.

Two weeks later, he got a call from Maria.

"Hi, Robert, how are you? Long time, no see. I hear things are good for you and Emily. I'm still in touch with Angus and he told me that you two aren't meeting up anymore. I wanted to ask you if you'd re-consider; he's pretty low, and I know he looked forward to your pub sessions."

"It's true. I don't think I'll be meeting Angus anytime soon. He seems to be blaming me for your separation, which is so ridiculous that I decided to call it a day. If he gets himself through those feelings, then perhaps I'll see him again. How are you doing?"

"Not so bad, I'm keeping busy. I've had some fun nights out with my single friends, all of us bitching about the lack of fit blokes around. Been on three dates so far, all of them a disaster. Not how I was hoping things would work out, of course. It would be lovely to see you, just for a coffee, if you fancy a chat."

"Sure, that would be great. We could meet in that café 'round the corner from your place after work, if you like."

Robert had few illusions about where this could be heading.

A week later, he finished work early and drove over to Walworth. He hadn't mentioned their meeting to Emily. Maria rang as he was on his way,

"Hi, it's me. I've been to the café and it's closed. Why don't you come 'round to the house instead?"

Maria greeted him warmly and took him through to the garden. He watched her as she walked ahead, the outline of her figure thrillingly clear under a light cotton dress. It was a warm, late summer afternoon. A jug of Pimm's and two glasses were placed on the patio table.

"Why not, I thought?" she smiled, pointing at the Pimm's. "It was such a lovely afternoon, this seemed a much better idea."

"So, the café closure was…?

"A little fib. Cheers, Robert, it's lovely to see you. You're looking good."

"You too. Cheers."

So, this is how these things happen. He looked at Maria; her dress had ridden up and was exposing her tanned thighs. *Why not? I've been so fucking patient for months, putting up with Emily's moods and reluctance to have sex. Maria's clearly up for it. What's wrong with a no-strings fuck? I deserve it.*

Later, Robert wouldn't be able to recall a single word of their conversation in the garden, such was the intensity of the sexual tension between them. When he'd followed her into the kitchen, a few seconds after she went to refresh the Pimm's, she was standing at the island unit in the middle of the room, cutting fruit, her back towards him.

He walked over and wrapped his arms around her, hands covering her breasts, kissing the back of her neck.

"I've fantasised about this for months," he said as she turned around and kissed him ferociously, pushing herself against him, feeling his arousal. She broke away, undid his belt and began tugging his trousers down. Robert pulled her dress over her head, then wrenched his shoes, boxers and trousers off.

Maria slipped her knickers down and bent forward across the island unit, sweeping pieces of fruit aside. She popped a couple of strawberries into her mouth, savouring their intense sweetness just as she felt him pushing inside, overwhelming her senses.

Looking down at the cleft between her buttocks, Robert knew he couldn't hold on for long. Less than a minute later, he pulled her against him, his head exploding. As he fell forward against her sweat-covered back, Maria began to laugh.

"Blimey! You needed that, didn't you? If you were trying for the kitchen-fuck speed record, I think you've broken it."

"I'm sorry, that must have been disastrous for you. Pretty amazing for me, though."

"Disastrous isn't quite the word I'd use. How long before you're ready, again?"

"Twenty minutes."

"Then we'll take the Pimm's upstairs to the bedroom, and this time, I'll show you what I need."

They met only twice after that. He felt no guilt about cheating on Emily. He adored her, still wanted her, needed her, but didn't believe his feelings were compromised by his affair. Maria meant nothing to him, and he strongly suspected he meant little to her. It wasn't as if he'd planned it to happen, and anyway, Maria had made the first move.

He ended their affair after their third meeting, even though he missed the thrill of illicit sex. He was terrified that Emily might find out, knew how much he needed her and was sure she'd leave him, taking Lily with her.

Robert was lucky. He was obsessive about cleaning away the smell of sex, and after his third and last time with Maria, he'd gone straight to the bathroom to shower. Watching Channel 4 News in the lounge downstairs, Emily noticed. He'd never done anything like that before, and she casually thought that this was classic behaviour for a bloke after screwing someone else. She didn't believe Robert would cheat again but was aware that their sex life had become an issue for him.

After a chance meeting with Maria in Putney High Street three weeks later, her anxieties returned. Emily was genuinely pleased to see her after such a long break and suggested a coffee. For ten minutes or so, their conversation flowed like old times. Then Emily said, "We were both sad that you and Angus split, though I understand you couldn't carry on without a commitment from him about children in the future. You had no choice. Mind you, combining just one child with a part time job is life changing, Maria."

"But you've got Lily, and the joy she brings."

"I know, and I didn't mean to be insensitive, sorry. But I'm so tired most of the time. Robert complains about our sex life, or lack of it. I know this sounds corny, but a couple of weeks ago I even found myself wondering if he was having an affair, when he came home and went straight upstairs for a shower. It's crazy, I know. I do trust him."

Emily saw the blush spreading around her friend's neck.

"Are you OK?"

"Sorry, Emily, I'm not feeling so good. I think I'd better go, but let's meet up again soon. Remember me to Robert, it would be good to see you both in the future, when I'm feeling less upset."

What was that about, Emily thought, as she watched her leave.

That evening, as she thought more about Maria's odd reaction at the end of their conversation, she became more convinced that Robert had slept with her old friend. And he'd cheated before, of course, right at the start of their relationship. She thought seriously about confronting him, but what real evidence did she have? She couldn't face the rows and turmoil that would result if she accused him, so she said nothing. Their sex life became more joyless and infrequent; Emily simply participated, and as making love became a faint memory, she felt a distance begin to open between them for the first time since the incident with Molly.

Two months later, before Lily turned two, a deputy head job came up in the school that had provided support to Robert's after its inspection. He'd got to know the head teacher there well and knew that he rated him highly. It was a perfect opportunity; Robert had only ever worked in one school, which could count against him when he went for his first headship job in the future. After making the usual enquiries, he put in his application.

He'd worked hard to strengthen his position on the senior team, lobbying the head teacher to give him more challenging responsibilities, building an impressive CV, so he wasn't surprised to be shortlisted.

He took up the opportunity to look round the school before the interview. As he was taken around by an articulate Year Ten pupil, he saw a familiar face, teaching in one of the classrooms.

"How did the tour go; what do you think of the place?" Emily asked when he got back that evening.

"It had a good feel. I'll definitely go for the interview. The kids seemed happy and alert. I was impressed by the Head. You'll never guess who I saw on my tour."

"Go on, tell me."

"Your friend at the party where we met. I might end up managing him if I get the job."

Emily laughed.

"You're joking! That would be so funny—well, maybe not. But it would be Karma."

Two weeks before Christmas, Robert got the job. He was jubilant, and while Emily was pleased for him, his mood threw the problems in their relationship into stark contrast. She was becoming concerned that Lily might pick up on the tension between them caused by her unresolved suspicion that he'd cheated with Maria. She knew she had to get over it and put it behind her, or confront him and risk splitting up. It wasn't really a choice – Lily's happiness came first,

She realised that by not having things out with Robert at the time, her sense of betrayal had festered and grown out of proportion. There was no evidence, after all. Wasn't that what lawyers believed in, evidence? She eventually reached an accommodation with herself over the doubts that she'd been harbouring since her meeting with Maria months ago. It was time to move on. .

In the early morning of the new millennium,, she made love with Robert for the first time in weeks. Before they went to sleep, he turned and looked at her.

"I don't need to know where you've been for the last few weeks, but I'm glad you've come back. I love you."

You'll never know, she thought. "I love you, too."

But their relationship never fully recovered its former intensity. How could it? Emily did what all grounded, rational people with secure, fulfilling and generally happy lives would do. She focussed on her good fortune, accepted the man she loved with all his faults and made sure Lily felt loved and safe. As the bond between her and Lily grew stronger, they developed the ability to read each other's moods and feelings to a telepathic degree. To his surprise,

Robert overcame his feelings of being the marginalised parent. He came to realise, and accept, that while the paternal connection might not be as deep as the maternal one, providing a strong, funny and caring role model brings all the rewards the father of a daughter could wish for.

He adored Lily and felt enormously protective towards her. She was sharp and funny and could talk fluently by two and a half. He was enthralled as the character that would become his grown-up daughter developed, marvelling as their early exchanges evolved into proper conversations.

Emily and Robert continued to benefit from being in the right place at the right time, as big changes in education and the law were introduced by the New Labour government. They became known among their friends as the lucky couple. A new National Curriculum increased pupil testing and a focus on improving results brought increased accountability and stress for schools. Academy schools provided greater competition, and senior teams became increasingly focussed on marketing their schools. Some hated it, but Robert thrived in the new culture.

Emily had been preparing for the Human Rights Act for nearly a year before it became law in 2000. She realised it would have a big impact on her work, introducing the concept of human rights into British Law for the first time.

She even tried to convince a sceptical Robert it could affect his job.

"One section gives people accused of something the right to a fair hearing, including the right to question witnesses. Say a parent feels that her child has been excluded unfairly. They can now argue that they have the right to directly question the teacher that's accused the pupil of wrongdoing, in front of the exclusion panel. I don't think schools allow that to happen at present?"

"Too right they don't. I see what you mean about a big impact."

By the summer of 2002, they'd been together for eight years. Lily was about to go into Year 1 at the local primary school, and their social life now revolved mostly around couples with children, about their age, whom they'd met as neighbours or through Lily's school. Robert was approaching thirty-four, Emily had just turned thirty-six.

When Emily reflected on her life, and their life as a family, she would say that they were fortunate and privileged; they had fulfilling, well-paid jobs, enjoyed living where they were, in fine health and blessed with a beautiful daughter. Robert was less satisfied; life was generally good, but they should be earning more, given how hard they work. He'd only worked in London schools and fancied a change and had started to worry about his daughter's safety. Most importantly, if he was going to get a headship at a decent school in the next couple of years, he had to look at opportunities across the country.

Emily reacted with amazement when he first mentioned the idea of moving away.

"You mean, for good? How long have you been harbouring this idea?"

"I suppose a part of me has always wanted to live somewhere less frenetic, more beautiful, less corrosive on the lungs and safer for Lily. I could ask you if you thought we'd never live anywhere else?"

He kept silent about the real reason—his determination to get his own school within the next two years.

"Pretty much, yes, at least until Lily goes to university. We've got a great life here, haven't we? What about our jobs? I'm not sure which part of the country you've got in mind, but assuming it isn't suburbia then the commute on its own would rule it out. And where does this concern about Lily's safety come from?"

Robert showed his irritation.

"Well, I certainly hadn't thought we'd be here for another fourteen years. Surely, in our jobs, we can find work almost anywhere?"

"But I love working for Pearson, Shallice and Grant, and they don't have an office anywhere else. And what about all our friends, and Lily's friends? She'd be devastated."

But Robert wouldn't let the idea go, so when Emily's practice opened a branch in Manchester, an increasingly exasperated Emily made him an offer.

"I'll consider moving up there if you do all the research on schools and transport, the partners agree to me transferring to Manchester and Lily is completely happy with the idea."

A year later, in spring 2003, Robert got the job of head teacher at Preston Park comprehensive school, near Macclesfield. They sold the Brixton house for twice what they'd paid for it, paid off the mortgage and moved to a large house near Bollington, on the edge of the Peak District.

Emily was surprised by how quickly she began to enjoy the variety of working in the city and living in the countryside, commuting to Manchester four days a week by train. They made good friends quickly, Lily settled easily into her new school and started to become a country girl. Emily's colleagues in Manchester seemed less frenetic in the way they went about things; the office culture there suited her.

Act 3

15

Four Years Later

Robert hung the keys to the Ford S Max on the hook above the hall table and rushed upstairs to change into his running vest, shorts and shoes. It had taken longer than usual to drive Lily to the Macclesfield performing arts centre and he was running late, but he could just fit in a run if he was quick. Three weeks ago, Emily had reminded him that they owed several friends an invitation to dinner. When she'd said that she would do the emailing to arrange a date that worked for everyone, his excuses ran out. They would need all afternoon to get everything ready for ten people, especially with four vegetarians and a vegan. *Meat eaters will soon be a persecuted minority*, he thought.

As long as he was back before Emily returned with the shopping, he'd avoid an argument. They argued more since Lily had moved up to Year 1 in primary school. Emily had made it clear she wanted to go back to work full time and expected childcare to become a shared responsibility, which meant more juggling for him.

He cut short his warm up—at thirty-eight, he needed it more than ever—turned right onto the Rainow Road, then left onto the gritstone trail, heading for the country park. He pushed himself up the steady climb, his legs feeling unresponsive after a sedentary week of meetings with the secondary head teachers' conference committee. In spite of the fuss he'd made about the dinner party, he was looking forward to it; he enjoyed these occasions where he could observe people's behaviour, watching their inhibitions melt away.

They'd invited four couples. There was Jo, a young lawyer from Emily's practice in Manchester, with her boyfriend. Emily was unofficially mentoring Jo, in whom she saw a younger version of herself. He'd met Jo at a barbeque in the summer, but he'd never met her boyfriend. Emily had run across him once after work and thought he was OK.

They'd met Sheila and Andrew soon after they'd moved here, when they'd got involved in the couple's successful campaign to stop a farmer closing a well-used public footpath. They were left wing, politically committed and good fun. He would probably flirt innocently with Sheila throughout the evening. Then there was his deputy head Rachel and her partner Jane, who would, no doubt, behave inappropriately after a few drinks, though he was sure the others would take it in their stride.

Finally, there were their neighbours, Graham and Christine. He and Emily hadn't ever been close to their immediate neighbours before, but when they'd moved up to the Peak District nearly four years ago, they'd come around with flowers and a bottle of bubbly to welcome them to the village and remained close friends. Graham ran his own small ICT consultancy and Christine was a social worker.

Glancing at his watch, he picked up his pace and headed back home, making sure he'd be there before Emily returned. He'd just got out of the shower when he heard her Mini Cooper driving up; throwing on a T-shirt, jeans and trainers, he ran downstairs just in time to hold the door as Emily brought in the first bags. She gave him her 'you may drive me mad at times, but I still love you' smile.

"Hi, did Lily get there OK in the end? I got a text message from her to say you were stuck in traffic. You shouldn't cut things so fine; you know what it means to her, to be there with the others before the start."

"No problem, sweetheart, we had five minutes to spare in the end. Susan's dad is picking her up as she's having a sleep over there, as you know. Did you get everything we need?" Her little lectures annoyed him, but he let it pass.

"I sure did. I'm looking forward to this evening—it's going to be fun."

"Me too. How much do you know about Jo's boyfriend? If he's the serious type, he might get a shock."

"My only concern is the war—Blair, Bush, the whole Iraq catastrophe. Sheila, Andrew, Rachel and Jane are all against, whilst Graham and Christine are for. We've all been round the table before with this, you know how strongly I feel about it, but I'll tone it down so as not to make Chris and Graham uncomfortable. Jo is also against. I think her boyfriend is a member of the Socialist Workers Party, so things could get heated."

"Great, well I hope Jo keeps him the right side of the class war, otherwise one of us will have to."

"She's my friend so I'm responsible for that. You can sometimes come across like a rather right-wing head teacher in those situations, darling husband."

"You love it when I'm commanding and forceful."

"Oh, you mean when you and the idiot who cut us up in his GTI nearly had a fist fight in the middle of Whaley Bridge? That would have looked good in the local paper: 'Head teacher assaults young driver in High Street'."

"You're never going to let me forget that, are you?"

"Let's say I've not seen you like that for a long time; it was a shock seeing you so angry."

Robert prepared the fish part of the meal from a favourite Delia Smith recipe, Emily the vegetarian dish. By the time the doorbell rang, they'd got everything ready and were drinking their first glass of wine in the lounge.

Rachel and Jane stood at the door—Rachel holding a bag with wine and chocolates, Jane flowers. They'd both dressed up.

"Hi, Emily. Thanks for inviting us; we've been looking forward to this evening the whole week. We're such stop at homes usually. I promise I won't say anything outrageous, though you've never seemed to mind my indiscretions in the past, Robert." Rachel was getting her apologies in early.

Robert had formed a particularly close relationship with his deputy over the last three years, which some staff might have questioned, but for the fact that she was a lesbian.

The other three couples arrived within the next ten minutes and were efficiently seated around the dining table by Emily.

They'd been eating for about a quarter of an hour when Andrew used the occasion to lobby Robert on behalf of his son.

"This is delicious, compliments to the chefs. We hear very good things on the parent grapevine about your school, Robert. Jamie is fixed on going there in a year's time, so I hope you've got no plans to leave."

Rachel was touchy about remarks that gave too much credit to Robert for the school's success and jumped in.

"Can I respectfully quibble with 'your school', Andrew? Dynamic head teacher he may be, but the rest of us who slave away every day play a role too. Not that we see as much of him these days, now that he's on the government's anti-bullying task force."

"Thank you for those kind remarks, Rachel. Like every head teacher, I simply sit around all day and take the plaudits for the tremendous work done by my staff. It's great to hear that Jamie wants to go there in a year's time. Andrew; he should get in, from where you live."

Christine joined the conversation. "We just wish that you'd been the Head when Natalie was choosing secondary school, Robert. She looked around the school twice before secondary transfer and was adamant that she didn't want to go. It had such a dodgy reputation, so we agreed to send her to Hazlehurst instead."

Emily could see Rachel frowning. She'd had been there at the time Christine was referring to, so Emily jumped in,

"Is she happy there, Christine? How does she like being at a girls' school?"

"That's a private school, isn't it?" Jo's boyfriend, who'd introduced himself as Max, interrupted abruptly before Christine could answer.

Graham and Robert looked up from their conversation, alerted by his jarring tone.

"It is, Max. We wanted Natalie to go to the local state school at first. Most of her friends were thinking of going and so was she, but one by one they decided not to. And to answer your question, Emily, yes, she is happy there, though financially it's been tough."

"You're not expecting us to feel sorry for you?" said Max, sounding incredulous.

Emily caught Robert's eye. His expression was unmistakeable: 'If you don't shut him up, then I will'.

But it was Graham who spoke first.

"Sorry if you don't approve of our decision, Max, but I feel that's exactly what it was—our decision—and we don't have to account for it to anyone. We're not the only ones here whose children don't go to state schools."

Max turned to Jo, making sure everyone heard what he said.

"I came along because you said they're all interesting people, but apparently their kids go to private schools. Who are you calling your friends these days, Jo?"

Emily had heard enough and broke in before Jo could reply.

"The kind of people who don't only want to speak to others who think exactly like them, Max. And who don't rush to judgement about decisions other people take before knowing more about the reasons."

"Oh, liberals you mean?"

"That's right, Max, you're among middle class, comfortably off liberals. But then you should feel right at home as I guess you're from a pretty comfortable background yourself?" said Robert.

As the others fell silent, Max rose from his seat. Turning to Jo, he said,

"Can we go? This is my idea of hell, sitting here listening to these privileged wankers moaning about their lot when there's so much real hardship in the world. I don't know why you asked me along."

As Max left the table and walked out, Jo turned to Emily, apologised and followed him.

Robert went to the front door and watched as they got their jackets and left, then went back to the others.

"Safely off the premises?" joked Rachel.

"Just wanted to make sure he didn't liberate anything of ours on the way out. You can't say our dinner parties aren't entertaining."

"Sorry about that, everybody, I'm surprised Jo's with someone like that. It's not so much his politics, more the faux anger that annoys me. Anyway, where were we?" said Emily.

"I think Andrew was making the most of this opportunity to schmooze Robert about our school in order to increase Jamie's chances of getting in," said Rachel.

"What a cynic, the thought never crossed my mind. Tell us more about this committee you're on, Robert, sounds as if you're getting known in high places."

"It's early days yet. My hope is it won't turn out to be another talking shop but will actually produce practical guidance. I'm not sure it says much about my profile, though. I think the Department for Education asked around for names and my Head Teachers' Association probably put me forward as I'm on their curriculum committee."

"Wow, next thing we'll be seeing you on the telly. 'And now we go to Robert Mason, head at Preston Park Comprehensive, for his analysis of the Government's White paper'."

"Thank you, Rachel. I thought you'd been a bit quiet for the last few minutes," Robert replied.

Emily took the opportunity to change the subject, which she thought might be starting to embarrass him.

"I didn't dare ask this before, but what do you think about the news this week about Blair's announcement that he's standing down?"

"Talk about changing the subject, Emily!" said Christine.

Everyone had an opinion and the last guests didn't leave until 1 a.m. Robert and Emily got to bed just before two in the morning, deciding to do the worst of the clearing up first. As they moved around the kitchen, they would occasionally brush against each other, touching an arm or a shoulder. While their sex life was less frequent these days, physical intimacy had remained important for both of them in their relationship.

"I think we should thank Max; that was one of our best ever dinner parties," joked Emily before she fell asleep.

Robert wasn't sleepy. He hadn't been embarrassed by the conversation about his career, though he knew that's why Emily had changed the subject. He thought about the last twelve years—their prosperous careers, his growing national profile, successful marriage, lovely daughter, good friends—and felt pleased with himself. *Luck has played a part, I suppose, but I've made my own most of the time. Coming up to the Peak District was a great move, though it took all my guile to break Emily's resistance. I even got away with that stupid affair with Maria.*

The next morning, he made Emily breakfast and took the garden rubbish and empty bottles from the party to the council's recycling centre. He'd just finished unloading it all when his mobile rang. He didn't recognise the number.

"Hello, Robert Mason."

"Hello, Robert. It's Sue. Sue from the Brecon camp."

16

Surprise, Surprise

'Sue from the Brecon camp.' For a second, his brain stopped working—on hold until a response crystallised. *This can only be bad news, so be cool. Don't get angry, don't be off hand, don't provide more information than necessary and stay in control. Let her do the talking, remember how unstable she could be.*

"Hi, Sue, this is a big surprise." He heard the slight tremor in his voice. *Take deep breaths, Robert, you have to stay on top here.*

"Hello, Robert. I'm afraid I took the liberty of contacting your school to get your number. I hope no one gets into trouble for releasing it. You're quite famous, it seems. I only had to put your name into Google and you came up all over the place. Head teacher of Preston Park School, member of the Government's Advisory Committee on Combating Bullying, member of the Head Teachers' Association executive. How are you?"

"I'm very well, thanks, Sue. It's true, I've been fortunate in my career. I find my job fulfilling; I love it in fact. So, what prompted you to look me up after all this time?"

"It's a long story. I haven't had much good fortune since we last saw each other ten years ago. I was diagnosed with clinical depression in 2005, and I've been living on benefits since then. If you can call it living."

Christ, nothing's changed, he thought. *The same self-pity, blaming others for decisions she's taken. If she wants money, she can fuck off.*

"Anyway, enough of the sob story, which I suspect you're already tired of. I'm ringing to suggest that we meet

190

soon, as you have the right to know that I've decided to tell the truth about what really happened the night Tom died. I know the implications aren't good for you and your family, so I need to explain face to face why it's so important for me to do this. You deserve that, at least."

Robert suddenly felt unsteady and grabbed the car door for support, as a cold sweat broke out across his forehead. *She cannot, she must not be allowed to do this. I'll lose everything.* He knew he had to control the anger that was close to overwhelming him, sound calm and buy time to think this through. Feeling his hands trembling, he took a deep breath and said, "You're right, Sue, this is devastating news. I'm struggling to take it in, to understand why you'd do this after all this time. Obviously, we need to talk, the sooner the better. Where do you live?"

"Not very far from you, assuming you live somewhere near your school. Why don't we meet in Lyme Park, by the lake? I'm free any time next week; as the head teacher, you must be able to slope off during the day, surely?"

Robert ignored her bitter sarcasm. *I'd better get used to it.*

"I'll see you there on Tuesday around 4.00 pm. I can't say when exactly so please don't leave, even if I'm a bit late."

"I won't. I'll see you then."

Robert drove out of the recycling centre, carried on for half a mile, pulled into the country park and parked the car. He needed to walk and think; he was facing a situation that could destroy him and everything he'd achieved. If she went ahead, the scandal would cost him his job, at the very least. But it wouldn't stop there. The negligence charge would be re-opened, and Tom's family would pursue it to the bitter end. The father might even be prepared to risk exposing his past crime and accuse Robert of blackmail. That would mean prison. Emily would leave him and take Lily with her. Actually, she would insist he left the house. The fact that he'd hidden the real story of that night from her for thirteen years, then blackmailed Garner would be unredeemable for her.

He hadn't been taking in the view but suddenly found himself at the vantage point. You could see for miles in every direction, over to Snowden on a clear day. An awful sadness came over him as he remembered the many occasions he'd come here with Emily and Lily and pointed out the landmarks. Lily had been fascinated at first but quickly lost interest, failing to see any point in seeing it again and again.

This didn't feel like blackmail; she didn't seem to want money, just to get the truth out. But surely, she can't have really thought through what the implications would be for him and his family, otherwise she couldn't be doing this. She may be mentally ill, but she's not a cruel person. That was the line he'd take when they met—convince her of the harm her revelations would cause to Emily and Lily. He'd persuaded her before and he was sure he'd be able to again. *I just need to buy more time.*

He drove home slowly, sitting patiently behind a huge Massey Ferguson tractor towing a muck spreader. *How appropriate. I've got to try to keep up my post-dinner party mood in front of Emily; she's very perceptive about noticing small changes.*

Lyme Park was just under thirty minutes' drive from Tuesday's head teacher's meeting. No one asked questions when he left the meeting fifteen minutes early; he'd told his deputies he wouldn't be returning to school. He rehearsed his lines as he entered the park and drove down the long drive to the gatehouse. *Be patient and let her talk for as long she wants*, he told himself. *Don't get angry, whatever happens.*

He paid the entrance fee at the gatehouse to the grounds, drove on to the lake and parked. It was a warm, dry day, but the car park was nearly empty as it was Tuesday. As he walked towards the lake, half-covered with a bloom of algae, he realised that her appearance had probably changed in ten years; he might have trouble recognising her. But then he saw her. *She has changed; the last ten years haven't been kind, but it's definitely her.* As he got to within twenty metres, she half turned in his direction, appeared to recognise him and raised her hand. She was in her early forties now but looked older. Her hair, cut above the shoulder, was prematurely grey and hanging lankly from a centre parting. Even with a half-smile, her face gave away the sadness that had been with her over the years, with dark rings under hollow eyes. She was wearing a shapeless kaftan over faded jeans.

Robert guessed the impression his physical appearance must be making on her.

"Hello, Sue." He walked straight up to her, holding out his arms to embrace her. Awkwardly, she returned the hug.

"Hello, Robert. Don't you look the successful executive on the way up?"

"Don't let this uniform fool you. Not quite how I see myself when I'm chasing truants round the local flats. How have you been?"

"Let's get a coffee and sit down over there. I know this has come as a shock and I appreciate you responding so quickly."

They took their coffee and cake to a table out of earshot of other customers. He looked at her, trying to hide the disgust he felt at her self-indulgence, her self-pity, the neglect of her appearance.

"It's certainly been a shock; I've hardly slept for the last few nights. It would help me if I understand why, after all these years, you want to tell the real story about the night that Tom went missing."

Sue paused, taking a sip of coffee. "I agreed to go along with your version of what happened that night, even though I was conflicted about it, because I felt it wasn't fair that you'd be held responsible as well as me. As you know, I had some wobbles before the hearing but did my best. The trouble was, while I convinced the panel, I never convinced myself that I was doing the right thing by lying about that night. Remember, as the special needs teacher on the camp, I had a personal responsibility for Tom's welfare.

"Then it all went pear-shaped at the school. I was put under close monitoring—I don't blame you for that—and I left at the end of 1996 without a job to go to. For the next six years or so, I held down a number of supply posts in special needs departments, unhappy and unfulfilled. I had a few relationships, mostly with men, a couple with women, but I was lousy company and a lousy lover too, I expect. My self-respect went off the scale negative; it was only a friend suggesting therapy that stopped me from killing myself. The therapy has helped, though I was diagnosed as clinically depressed by a psychiatrist two years ago and have been on anti-depressants ever since. My therapist doesn't approve, obviously.

"In the last few months, I've finally been able to talk to my therapist about the decision I made eleven years ago to cover up my involvement in Tom's death. I haven't gone into details and I certainly haven't mentioned any names, but she's said that I don't stand a chance of conquering my depression until I confront my actions that night honestly and tell the truth. I know that if I don't, I'll continue living in this twilight, which isn't living at all."

Sue stopped, aware that she needed to let Robert respond.

"So, who are you planning to tell, and when?" said Robert.

"The only thing that's been holding me back is the need to tell you. I knew I couldn't go public with this until we'd made contact. Now I've told you, I'm going to write to the Council in the next few days and tell them I want to make a new statement about what happened the night Tom died."

He couldn't believe what he was hearing, uttered in such a matter of fact way, as if she was discussing the weather. Robert felt like smashing his fist into her face and only stopped himself by gripping the edge of the metal table until it dug into the base of his thumb.

As calmly as he could, he replied, "I'm so sorry that your life has been that way for the last few years, Sue. I can't take away what you've gone through. Part of me can see why you want to do this, even though the consequences for you and me will be severe. And maybe we deserve to face justice. But please think about the consequences of your decision for two completely innocent parties—my wife and daughter. Obviously, I'm thinking about myself too—career ending in disgrace, prosecuted for lying at the inquest and tribunal—but that's nothing compared to the potential impact on my nine-year-old daughter. We live in a relatively small community; all her friends know her dad's the local head teacher and if her father goes to prison, her life will be hell. To say nothing about—"

Sue interrupted him, furiously,

"I knew you'd try to guilt trip me, Robert. It's shameful of you to blame me for any consequences that your wife and daughter might suffer. They may be innocent, but you're certainly not. Any fallout for them will be down to you. You know, deep down, that you persuaded me to make up that story. I would have told the truth back then, if you hadn't pressurised me."

"And God knows what careers we'd have had if we'd done that at the time. I'm just asking you to think through the possible consequences of doing this, for everyone."

"Oh yes, our careers. Well, mine certainly couldn't have turned out much worse, could it? Your precious career was always uppermost in your mind, starting the morning after we found Tom's body."

Sooner than that, he recalled.

"Perhaps I was thinking about the consequences for my job. Is that so terrible? I agree that I was the one pushing for us to make up a story, but remember that it was you that left your duty that night and came into my tent, uninvited, trying to persuade me to have sex. I didn't deserve to end up in such a serious situation."

"Come on, Robert. I didn't have to try hard to persuade you. You were totally up for it."

Robert stared at her, stunned, horrified by what she'd said. He knew, immediately, it changed everything. If a second tribunal heard they were having sex at the time Tom left, it would make their punishment much harsher; not only that, God knows what other stories she might make up. With a sickening feeling, he realised that he'd run out of options. When he drove into the park half an hour ago, he was optimistic that he'd talk her round. But she'd left him no choice; he'd have to silence her, permanently. His priority now was to buy time and find out where she lived.

"I think we both know that didn't happen, Sue. I can understand why you won't listen to me about the implications of your intentions, but surely you can talk to friends, get their advice."

"Now you're saying that we didn't have sex? Unbelievable. You haven't really been listening to what I've been saying, have you? I don't have any friends, I live alone. The only people I talk to are my therapist and a couple of shopkeepers in Tideswell. I don't want company or conversation; I can't face people—I'm too depressed."

"What about your therapist; does she know you're seeing me?" Robert was thinking clearly now—he had to know if anyone else knew about his role.

"No, there's no need for her to know. She knows that there were other staff involved in the camp, of course, and that the two of us faced the most questioning, but that's all."

Robert was relieved. He'd heard what he needed to know.

"I can see you're not going to change your mind, but can I at least ask you to reflect on what I've said about the wider consequences until the weekend? That will give me time to prepare the ground if you do go ahead."

"I'm definitely going ahead, Robert, you mustn't be in any doubt, but I agree to wait until after the weekend, if it will help. I'm very sorry for the pain this will cause Emily and your daughter, but I'm going to put my needs first, for once."

"I'd rather you didn't ring me again, in case Emily is around, so can I have a number to contact you on Monday, so that I'll know when the police are likely to call?"

"I'd rather not give you my number. Just assume I'm going to contact the local authority on Monday. If I change my mind, I'll call you. If anyone else answers, I'll say it's a wrong number."

Robert sat looking at her across the table, feeling a hatred he'd not experienced ever before. He wanted to kill her, and if they weren't in such a public place, he knew he could.

"Good bye, Robert. I suppose we'll next see each other in court."

He watched her as she walked up the path towards the car park, a pathetic figure. It was a beautiful afternoon, the gardens looked stunning. He'd guessed she was unlikely to give him her number. Now that she'd refused, he had no more cards left to play. When he'd realised, over the last couple of days, that she might insist on going ahead, he'd started to put a plan together. He felt sick with anxiety and completely focussed at the same time. He knew what he had to do, starting now: follow her to find out where she lived.

He left the bench and walked slowly towards the car park, occasionally glancing in her direction. He saw her get into an aging red Fiat Panda then heard the engine fire after several attempts. Careful to keep to an ambling pace as she drove out of the car park, he ran to his car as soon as she was out of sight. He knew he had to have her in view by the time she got to the junction with the main road.

He raced up the road, narrowly missing an older couple coming the other way in an old Rover, went through the gatehouse at twice speed the limit and was within sight of the Panda as it neared the exit. But a combination of a rise and a bend in the road meant that she disappeared out of sight, just before she got to the A6. As he pulled up to the junction, there was no sign of the Panda in either direction. For a moment he sat there, frozen with indecision. A lorry was approaching from the left with a queue behind it, so he let the clutch in rapidly, lurched forward and turned right towards Buxton.

For nearly half a mile, he feared he'd made the wrong call. On the point of turning around, he came up behind cars queuing at traffic lights. The red Panda was three cars ahead in the queue. The lights changed; the Panda went through, followed by the car behind her just as the lights went to amber. He could tell the driver in front of him was going to stop, so he swerved round and went through on the red.

He managed a smile. *Breaking the law, Robert, you'll get into trouble for that.* There was now only one car between them: a large Ford Galaxy people carrier, which suited his need to remain unobserved. The Galaxy stayed behind Sue's car up to the roundabout after Chapel-en-le-Frith, when it turned off to Buxton. She went left on the A623 to Baslow, leaving no vehicles between them, as he followed her onto the Baslow Road.

All he could do was stay 50 metres back and hope she wasn't paying much attention to her mirrors, though he needed to get close enough to read her registration number in case he lost her. As they came to the hairpin at Sparrowpit, she slowed enough for him to read it. *V659 HJA.* The Panda was misfiring, barely accelerating up the hill away from the hairpin so he was gentle with the Saab's throttle. Three miles before Baslow, Sue turned right onto a B-road. He waited a few seconds before turning so that it wouldn't be obvious that he was following her. It had been steadily clouding over since he left Lyme Park, and spots of rain began to appear on the windscreen. *Good*, he thought. *Anything that helps to obscure her view.*

After five minutes, as they approached a hamlet of five cottages, one of the brake lights on the Panda came on. She began to slow and pulled over, so he drove past, parking on the verge one hundred metres along the road. He set off back to the hamlet at a half run, although there was no cover for him to hide if she suddenly appeared. As he walked round the bend just before the hamlet, he saw the Panda in front of one of the cottages, parked half onto the pavement. There was no sign of Sue, but suddenly she emerged from the middle cottage, turned to say goodbye and got into her car.

He looked around for cover as he ran back to his car, the sound of the Panda's engine turning over in the distance. The engine finally came to life, followed by the sound of her car accelerating up the road behind him. A few more seconds and Sue would see him. He sprinted to a farm track ten metres ahead on the other side of the road, vaulting the five-bar gate and crouching down just as the Panda went by. He stood up and listened, cursing when he realised he'd torn his suit, which was already damp from the rain. He heard the engine note drop, then a gear change, then the sound of the car picking up speed again. She must have made a turn up ahead, but which way?

Robert ran back to his car. After two hundred metres, he came to a crossroads. Left or right? It was nearly six o'clock. As long as he was home around seven, he would be there in time to pick Lily up from Brownies, giving him twenty minutes to find her house. He checked his phone for missed calls, switched on the heated seat to dry his suit and turned left. He drove slowly on for ten minutes, and when he hadn't seen any sign of the Panda, turned around and drove back in the opposite direction, crossing over at the junction. He was starting to panic. It was too late to ring Emily and ask her to pick Lily up. *Unless I start for Macclesfield now, I'll be late for Lily.*

Then he saw it; an isolated cottage on higher ground to his left, about half a mile away. Parked outside, the distinctive, boxy shape of the red Panda. He calculated where the lane to the cottage joined his road, then turned around and set off for home. He didn't have time to drive up there to confirm it, and it was too risky in daylight anyway. If he was lucky with the traffic, he might just make it to the Guide's porta cabin.

Robert thought of himself as a fast, but safe, driver, like most men. In his case, it was a reasonably accurate assessment. The Saab felt planted on the road at just over 100mph on the dual carriageway, as he clinically went through the plan he'd been developing from the time of Sue's phone call.

He'd recently heard of a colleague whose career was ended overnight when a case of negligence, previously covered up, came to light. The man had lost everything; reputation, job, marriage, pension and any chance of working again. He wasn't going to let Sue's sudden discovery of a conscience bring him down like that. He'd told her, honestly, what the catastrophic consequences for him and his family would be if she went ahead, but she'd made it clear she didn't give a shit. She was willing to bring them all down. OK, then she shouldn't be surprised he'd do whatever it took to stop her. Once he'd realised, with a certainty that surprised him, that he was emotionally capable of, and morally justified in, killing her, the rest was logistics. She'd forfeited her right to live!

His research had pointed to strangulation as the most effective way for a strong person to kill a much weaker one. With a suitable garrotte in the hands of a strong man, the victim should lose consciousness within ten seconds, and be dead within three minutes. Disposing of her body posed the biggest risk, but Robert thought he'd found a solution. Not risk-free—he knew that murder had by far the highest conviction rate of any crime—but as good as he can come up with in the time he'd got.

He was only three minutes late for Lily as he turned into the driveway to the Guide's porta cabin. If he harboured any scruples about what he was intending to do, they were dispelled by the thought of how Lily would suffer if that fucking bitch went ahead with her plan.

As soon as he got home, he gave Emily his cover story for the night he'd need to be away.

"Not another conference? I'm amazed the school governors put up with it—they'll be suggesting you go part-time soon. God knows what the staff must think."

He'd told her that a two-day conference had been arranged at the last minute for all secondary school head teachers in his Authority to discuss proposals for a new national school building initiative. He'd have to stay overnight in a hotel in Stockport, so was it OK for her to collect Lily from school Thursday afternoon?

"Sure, you know I'm working from home for the next few days. Just make sure that you leave me the number of the hotel. Anyone else going I should worry about?"

They had a long running joke between them about the other one sleeping with someone else at a conference. Emily never had, although as an attractive woman in her mid-thirties, she'd had offers. The closest she'd come had been with a young barrister from a radical London chambers. They were kissing outside her hotel room at one in the morning after flirting in the bar at the conference hotel. He was annoyed and surprisingly insistent when she didn't ask him in, until she'd said, "I think you're about to fail the 'No means No' test, so thank you for a lovely evening and goodnight."

When he'd cut her dead at breakfast the next morning, she'd just smiled pityingly at him and walked away.

Surprisingly, Robert had remained faithful since his brief affair with Maria.

17

The Unexpected

Emily had congratulated herself on not allowing her suspicion that he'd had a fling with Maria turn her into one of those partners who tormented themselves about imagined affairs. But he'd seemed distracted and on edge the last few days; since their dinner party in fact. Had anything happened that evening which she hadn't noticed? She didn't think so. They'd gone to bed tired but happy, spooning together as they sometimes did before falling asleep. He'd half-suggested making love, but she'd declined graciously. "Sorry, but I think I'd be asleep before the end."

She'd first noticed the change when he came back from the recycling centre. Thirteen years together; Emily had learnt to read small changes in his mood. She still felt close to him despite the different ways they interpreted the world. Still loved him despite his flare ups with Lily and his obsessive, competitive drive with his career, although that could get too much for her sometimes. But if he was having another affair, betraying her trust again, she'd leave him. And take Lily with her.

Robert realised he needed to carry out an initial check on Sue's cottage and its immediate surroundings before committing himself on Thursday night, to ensure everything went as smoothly as possible. He had tried to calculate the level of every risk, as best he could. Someone could see his car outside Sue's house; she might not be in until late on Thursday night; he might botch the strangulation; he might be seen carrying her body to his car; he might not use enough weight to sink it; Emily could ring the hotel.

Some he could minimise. He'd check-into the hotel before driving to Sue's house on Thursday evening, then leave after dark by a back entrance. He also needed to check access to the reservoir.

But a risk analysis was missing the point. Whatever the risks, he knew he wouldn't be able to live with himself if he simply did nothing and let Sue ruin everything he'd achieved.

The following day—Wednesday—he took a long lunch hour and bought the stuff he needed: an air bed, plastic sheeting, twenty meters of rope and cleaning liquid. He already had the cord and handles for the garrotte, two breeze blocks and duct tape for securing the plastic sheet. At five o'clock he left the school and drove to her cottage in order to get a clear idea of the exact location and access from the surrounding land. If her car was outside, he would park a safe distance away and scout out possible problems on foot. As he turned up the lane that he'd worked out led to her cottage, he saw the flash of a red car, driving slowly in his direction. If they passed on this narrow lane, she was bound to see him. He could carry on and chance finding a place to pull off or reverse back to the turn off. He braked hard, snapped the gear lever into reverse, turned around in his seat and reversed as fast as he could, just managing to control the car as it weaved from side to side. As he reached the junction, he saw another car about to turn in, but he kept going to the obvious anger of the other driver. He drove up the road, parked in a lay-by, waited for five minutes and drove back up the lane to her house.

There were no other dwellings near her cottage. He drove slowly past, then further on for about three hundred metres; there were no houses on this side either, but there was a bridleway, wide enough for a car, thirty metres away. He reversed up the track and parked, far enough for his car not to be obvious to anyone driving past, then walked to her house.

Lady luck is with me, being able to check out her empty cottage and find the easiest way to break in tomorrow night. As he got to the rear of the building, he could see it wasn't overlooked. There were two possibilities for breaking in. The open bathroom window on the first floor and the sash

203

window on the ground floor, which had a simple latch securing the top and bottom sashes.

He checked his watch; ten minutes had passed since her car had driven down the lane. Using a knife he'd taken from the school canteen, he slipped the catch and tried to pull the top sash down. It was stuck tight. He had more success with the bottom sash; he could push it up far enough for him to squeeze through tomorrow night, although it squeaked. He pulled the sash down and flicked the catch back to appear as if it was still in place. Not quite where it had been, but it would have to do. Finally, he checked the outhouse, which revealed the usual gardening paraphernalia and various lengths of rope hanging up.

He'd seen everything he needed and walked round to the front to leave. As he got to the gate, he heard the distinctive note of the Panda's engine less than fifty metres away. She'd be bound to see him if he left now. He ran back to the rear of the house, re-thinking his plan. It could be too good an opportunity to miss.

He took the knife out of his pocket, slipped the sash window catch and pushed the bottom sash up to free it. The car door slammed once; she was alone. He went to the outhouse, took a metre-long piece of cord and a pair of gardening gloves from a shelf and hid behind a rhododendron bush where he could watch the back of the house, unobserved.

He saw Sue through the window in the back door, which he assumed led to the kitchen. Moments later, she unlocked it and emerged, putting some tired looking fuchsias in the recycling bin, then went back into the house, leaving the door unlocked behind her. She appeared even more careworn and dishevelled than the day before.

Robert put on the gardening gloves and waited. Adrenalin had slowed his sense of passing time and increased his heart rate dramatically. When he heard the toilet flush through the open window upstairs, he opened the back door and went into the kitchen. Scruffy and basic, cupboard doors hanging open, the floor needing a wash. He stood behind the open door that led from the small hall way, guessing that she'd come back to the kitchen when she came downstairs.

As he heard the stairs creaking, he wrapped the ends of the rope twice round each hand, leaving enough cord to circle her neck. She walked into the kitchen from the hall and stopped with her back to him, less than two feet away. It was as if she sensed something in the room had changed since she was last there. A faint, unwashed odour came off her; it repulsed him that he'd ever had sex with her. In a movement that took less than a second, he stepped forward, swept the cord over her head, crossed one hand over the other and pulled the cord as tight as he could. The cartilage surrounding her trachea ruptured instantly.

Her initial cry was cut off as her windpipe was crushed, replaced by a guttural gurgling as her tongue went back down her throat. Her fingers tried frantically, hopelessly, to prise the cord from her neck as she kicked back against him, twisting her body from side to side. She tried to turn her head to look at him; for the briefest instant, before losing consciousness, their eyes met. He saw no fear, only hatred.

He let her unconscious body drop to the floor, keeping the cord tight around her larynx for a further three minutes before checking her pulse. Nothing. He straightened up and immediately felt faint. Hands shaking, he gulped one glass of water, then another and sat down on the plastic kitchen chair.

Robert looked at Sue's body. *It's done*, he thought, astonished it had been so easy. He felt no guilt, no sorrow for ending the life of this fellow human being, a person with whom he'd once been physically intimate. Why should he? From the moment she'd threatened to ruin his life, the rest was inevitable, surely? Anyone who does that must know there's a very good chance that the potential victim will do everything possible to eliminate the threat.

He realised that he'd have to leave the body there and return tomorrow night, as planned. The risk involved in carrying it to his car in broad daylight was too great, and he couldn't wait until dark to dispose of the body. If he wasn't back tonight until the early hours, Emily would become suspicious. He had his story for tomorrow, and he'd stick to it.

But now she was dead, his task tomorrow night was much simpler: to collect her body and dispose of it. Before he left this afternoon, he only needed to move her body to the outhouse, out of sight, and clean the house up.

Suddenly, he began to panic, scared that he'd miss something vital in the next thirty-six hours and leave a clue, however small, that pointed to his guilt. He looked around for a pen and paper, then began to write down the things he must do before leaving the house:

Wear gloves all the time from now on; wipe every surface I've already touched; re-lock the sash window; find an old coat and hat to wear, to walk unrecognised to the car; collect the plastic sheet and tape, wrap the body; find anything and everything in the house that might provide a link to me; wipe the answerphone in case there are incriminating recorded conversations.

Robert found a long waterproof coat and an awful woollen bobble hat in the hall, pulled the collar up and the hat down, then quickly walked to his car and collected the things he needed. He lay the plastic sheet out next to Sue's body and stood there, repulsed by the idea of touching it. A car was coming down the road, towards the house. It seemed to be slowing down. He held his breath, but the sound of the engine rose as the car drove on. The shock gave him the nerve he needed to roll the body onto the middle of the sheet, fold the plastic around it at both ends and tape it up. He was careful not to touch her skin—that was too much.

Robert cleared a space in the outhouse, then dragged Sue's body from the kitchen across the yard and propped it up in a corner. Sweating heavily, he shut the door, returned to the house and locked the window.

He wanted the cottage to look as if she'd gone away for a long time, so he went around every room, collecting personal effects such as keys, phone, diary and clothes. He worked as fast as he could, putting everything into a large bin liner, grateful for the gloves as he emptied her laundry basket. It was a small, two-bedroomed cottage but took longer than he'd planned as he went through every drawer in the house, checking for notebooks and memo pads—anything that could lead the police to him if her body was discovered. Finally, he erased the answerphone and wiped every surface he'd touched.

It was nearly seven o'clock. Putting the sack of clothes in the outhouse, he locked the door and took a small bag of her personal possessions to his car. On the drive home, he reflected on the kind of person he'd become; able to kill without remorse or feeling, drive home to his wife and daughter and act normally. He'd read about cases like this; murderers who walked away without feelings for their victim or guilt about what they'd done. He'd always wondered how anyone could do that, and now he had. If he felt anything, it was a combination of relief and satisfaction with the outcome. Perhaps he'd always been like this.

18

Subterfuge

The following morning, Robert went through the motions of packing an overnight case for the conference. Emily had noticed he'd seemed tense when he'd returned the previous evening.

"Is everything OK at work? You seem on edge at the moment."

"Nothing, really. You know what it's like near the end of term, staff are tired, exams are over, kids have had enough; it all gets a bit ragged."

"I understand. What date are we going to France? I can't wait to get away."

"We get the ferry on the 4th August, then drive through the night to Annecy. It can't come soon enough for me either."

"I hope your little conference this evening is worth it. Make sure you leave the name and number of the hotel, just in case there's an emergency. Love you."

"Love you too. Thanks for picking Lily up this evening."

Robert left his school around seven o'clock that evening and drove to the hotel. As he checked in at the desk, he made a fuss about needing a quiet room so that he would be remembered. Everything had worked out fortuitously in the end. His original plan had been to break into her cottage and kill her tonight, having checked the area around the cottage yesterday. But now, he only had to collect and dispose of her body in the reservoir. At least he hoped it would be 'only'. He laughed to himself, *Just my usual evening, really, disposing of the woman that I strangled last night.*

He left the hotel by the side entrance around nine-thirty, drove slowly to Sue's cottage and parked in the bridleway. He'd felt calm during the drive, but as he walked through the gate, he realised he was being stupidly over confident. Maybe her body had been discovered; at this moment, police could be surrounding the house, waiting to catch the murderer returning. Taking the outhouse key from his pocket, he unlocked the door and shone his torch into the corner.

It wasn't there. Panic gripped him, until the torchlight picked out her body on the floor. It had slid down from its position against the wall. Robert took the bag of clothes to the front gate, then dragged her increasingly stiff body to the front of the house, behind the garden wall. Before going back to the car, he carefully inspected the path by torchlight, making sure there were no marks on the ground.

Satisfied, he lowered the back seats in the Saab and parked it tightly against the garden wall. The next thirty seconds would be the riskiest. Opening the boot, he stood and listened for the noise of a vehicle or people coming along the lane. The only sound he could hear was the blood pumping in his ears. He picked up her body around the shoulders, dragged it to the car and heaved the torso into the boot, pushing the legs in afterwards. Just as he was putting the bag of clothes in the car, he saw car headlights turning into the lane. *I can't be seen parked outside the cottage.*

As he got into the driver's seat, he remembered he'd left the outhouse door open. He ran back and locked it, returning to his car just as he heard the vehicle changing gear before the bend. *Once he rounds the bend, he'll see me.* Robert accelerated away and was still near the centre of the road when a small van came around too fast, swerving to avoid him.

There's no way he could have seen me, the make of my car or the registration number. So far, so good. That was a near thing, though. Drive cautiously, an accident would finish everything.

His plan was to dump Sue's body in the centre of a local reservoir. The advantage of the location was access—he could get the car to a place near the water that wasn't overlooked, reducing the risk of being seen. Once there, he'd float the weighted body to the middle of the lake on an air bed with the valve attached to a long cord. When he pulled the cord, the valve would open, the airbed will deflate, and the body will sink to the bottom of the reservoir. The airbed could then be pulled back to shore.

He parked the car safely in the place he'd checked out the day before. It was thirty-metres to the reservoir, a fair distance to drag a body, and he had to rest twice before returning for the air bed, pump, rope and breeze blocks. It took another half an hour to get Sue's body roped to the two blocks, then onto the inflated airbed next to the water line. He took his shoes and socks off, rolled his trousers up and waded several metres away from shore into the reservoir, carefully manoeuvring the air bed. With the combined weight of the body and the blocks, the air bed was three quarters submerged, but stable.

He gave the bed a strong push out to the middle of the reservoir, holding onto the cord attached to the valve, but it was blown back by an on-shore breeze. He hadn't allowed for the effect of the wind. He would have to swim with the airbed, pushing it further out to the deeper water. Quickly. The longer he stayed there, the greater the chance someone would notice his car. He stripped down to his underpants, tied the cord around his waist and waded in to the numbingly cold water. After ten minutes, only half way to the middle, he realised the airbed had a slow puncture, as the body was noticeably lower in the water. He felt exposed, cold and exhausted.

This whole plan was insane. What are the chances that I won't be caught? That there's no clue in Sue's cottage revealing her intention to disclose the truth? That my car hasn't been noticed, parked here or near her house? That her body won't float to the surface as it fills with gas?

Get a grip, Robert, you're almost there. You know what to do; one step at a time. First, swim for another ten minutes and release the body; next, front crawl back to shore to warm up, and so on.

Five minutes later, shivering violently, he pulled on the cord and opened the valve. As the remaining air rushed out, the airbed rapidly lost buoyancy. The speed of the body's descent took him by surprise and, for a moment, it looked as if it would take the airbed down with it. He jerked on the cord, releasing the airbed, then swam back to shore, towing it as fast as his exhausted body could manage. The breeze chilled him further as he got out, but he'd forgotten to bring a towel, so he put his clothes on wet. Back at the car, he threw the air bed and rope into the boot, slumped into the driver's seat and turned the heated seat on.

More than anything, he just wanted to sleep, but he knew he had to get away from this spot, back to the hotel. He turned the car heater full on, opened the window to keep himself awake and slowly drove back, shivering violently the whole way.

It was nearly 3.00 a.m. when he walked up to his room. There was a note under his door saying that his wife had rung, with the message, '*Hope you're enjoying yourself.*' He checked his mobile for the first time in three hours and saw two missed calls from Emily. No point ringing now. He took his wet clothes off, hung them up, then got into bed. He was asleep in less than a minute.

Twelve miles away, Emily lay in bed, unable to sleep. She'd been crying, but her hurt was now replaced by anger. When she'd rung the hotel, they'd confirmed that Robert Mason had checked in earlier that day. No, they didn't have a head teachers' conference booked into the hotel, though there were a number of different groups staying at the moment. Yes, please, she would like to be put through to his room. Yes, I would like to leave a message if there's no answer. She'd tried his mobile a couple of times, but by now she was sure he wouldn't pick up.

Obviously, he's having another affair, she thought. It would also explain his edgy mood and those recent occasions when he'd come back later than usual with some vague excuse. She couldn't decide whether to be angrier with him or with herself for not confronting him about the first affair. *No, that was stupid; of course, I'm angrier with him. I won't be one of those pathetic women who take some of the blame for their husband's affairs. When he comes back, I'll listen politely to whatever story he comes out with, then confront him. Right now, I don't know what I want to happen; it'll depend on his reaction. He might even come back and announce that he's infatuated with some beautiful young thing and he's leaving me.*

Emily was surprised that she didn't find the last thought as painful as she'd expected.

She finally got to sleep at 3.30 a.m. to be woken up by Lily shaking her.

"Mum, for goodness sake, wake up, it's gone eight o'clock, you've got to take me into school in fifteen minutes. Wake up, Mum!"

As she surfaced, the issue that had kept her awake half the night came clearly into focus and her anger returned, only more so. Putting on a brave face for her daughter, she pulled on sweat pants and sweatshirt, checked Lily had everything she needed and walked to the car.

She's such a lovely kid, she thought, as she watched her get in, smiling at Emily. *Always optimistic, generous, happy—I can't bear to think what Robert and my splitting up would do to her. We've got to try and fix this if it's possible. It will depend on whether he tries to brazen it out and lie about last night.* In spite of throwing the Mini around on the winding lanes, they were still a couple of minutes late. She pulled in on the yellow zig-zags, incurring a baleful look from Ms White, the deputy head. She kissed her daughter goodbye, reminding her, "Dad will pick you up this afternoon," before driving off.

Her mobile went on the drive back. She saw it was Robert, pulled over and took several deep breaths. *Keep things conversational, avoid a row over the phone.*

"Hi, Robert, how was the conference?"

"Hi, Emily. A bit of a let-down, really. When I got there, I could see that it was more like a focus group with only about ten heads, the facilitator and someone important from the Department. I couldn't really leave as she was there, otherwise I'd have come home. I missed you."

Emily felt like throwing up.

"Did you get my message? I rang the hotel around midnight and your mobile a couple of times."

"Yes, thanks, a few of us went into Manchester and it turned into a late night. I didn't think you'd appreciate a call after 2 a.m. I'm about to go down to the morning session, feeling a bit hungover."

"Where did you go in Manchester—anywhere interesting?"

"It was a bit of a pub crawl in the Northern Quarter, not our kind of place, really."

"Anywhere decent? My office is near there. I'd be interested to know if there'd be anywhere good for an office lunch."

"OK if we talk about it when I get home? The morning session is due to begin, and I don't want to get a detention. I'm not going back to school. I've told them I'm going straight home after the conference, so I'll be home by one."

"Sure, see you then. Bye."

"Bye, love you."

The fucking bastard, she thought. He couldn't even be bothered to think up a convincing story. *I'll ring the hotel and do some research, when I get home.*

Robert hadn't seen Emily's response coming. He was expecting her to be really pissed off that he'd (apparently) been out drinking until two in the morning and hadn't returned her call. But she'd seemed cool about that. Except, there was something else, like that question about the pubs in the Northern Quarter; seemingly innocent, but somehow not. *I'll get the names of a couple of pubs from the hotel staff, before I leave.*

He organised for the hotel to press his suit, had a shower and went down to breakfast.

He felt pleased with what he'd achieved. Sue was out of his life. He hadn't been seen, he'd left no clues, no phone messages…

Sitting at the table, breakfast half-finished, Robert felt the content of his bowels turning to water. Sue had rung him from her phone. If her phone provider kept records of all calls made, his number would be on that list. With the date of the call providing clear evidence of when they'd been in contact. He rushed out to his car, found her phone in the bag of her effects and switched it on. Orange. He rang the provider on his phone.

"I'm sorry, sir, you're just a couple of months too early. We don't start to keep call data permanently until September. Currently, it's wiped after three days."

Instead of working on her current case involving two gay men in danger of being deported on the grounds that they were in a relationship of convenience, Emily had been on the phone to the hotel and Ofsted. The hotel confirmed that no group such as the one Robert described had used any of their meeting rooms yesterday. Furthermore, there were no meetings at all taking place this morning. She then rang a contact at Ofsted, who she'd given pro bono advice to in the past. Would it be possible to check the diaries of all female senior officers working in the local secondary schools' division to see if any had an engagement in Stockport yesterday afternoon? An hour later, the friend came back to her; unless someone was doing some dodgy unauthorised freelancing, no one had been in Stockport.

She wrote down the names of all the pubs in the Northern Quarter and waited.

"So, it was a bit of a waste of time, then?" asked Emily.

They were sitting in the lounge, across the coffee table from each other, weak afternoon sunlight coming in through the big sash window.

"Yes. We were all really fed up, having been brought there under false pretences. We let the woman from the inspectorate know it, too."

Emily took a deep breath.

"What was she called? I've worked with a few of their senior people. I might know her."

"No, I'm sure you won't, not from her division."

"But just humour me, what was her name?"

Robert looked at his wife, her mouth set in a rictus smile. But her eyes—the striking green eyes that had reeled him in the first time he saw her—weren't smiling. What was it he saw? Disappointment? Pity? Sadness? He couldn't read her; but at that moment, he realised she knew something.

"What is this, Emily, twenty questions? I think it was Macmillan or something. Do you want a list of everyone else who was there, too?"

"That would be a very short list, wouldn't it, Robert? A deceased list, in fact. I rang the hotel this morning. No group bearing any similarity to the one you described stayed at the hotel last night or booked rooms for a meeting. There were no meetings at all taking place this morning. And according to Ofsted, none of their senior officers were in Stockport yesterday. Plus, I don't think I can remember another time since Lily was born when either of us hasn't returned a missed call from the other."

"What's come over you; you're being ridiculous. Of course, I was meeting with a group of educationists. What else would I be doing?"

Emily looked at him. He was calculating his best strategy. Coldly, unemotionally. She hadn't seen that look for years, and it scared her.

"My best guess, in fact my unhappy conclusion, unless you tell me what you were really doing last night, is that you're having an affair." She felt her eyes watering and quickly wiped them.

"I swear to you, on Lily's life, that I'm not having an affair, Emily! You must believe me! For God's sake, I love you!"

"Oh, Robert, please. If that's so, just give me the names of everyone who was there, including the Ofsted phantom, and I'll ring the hotel and the Department to check. If I'm wrong, then no one will be happier or more contrite."

There was silence between them for several seconds. Finally, Robert spoke,

"I can't tell you who I was meeting last night. I'm sworn to secrecy. It was work, I promise. You will just have to trust me; I'm not having an affair."

So, this is what it feels like to play a trump card, she thought.

"I'd probably find it easier to trust you if you hadn't screwed Maria back in 1999. You thought I didn't know, but Maria gave it away once when we met."

On the point of uttering another denial, he pulled back. If he owned up, it might help to restore some trust.

"If she told you, you must know it meant nothing to either of us. I'm sorry, Emily, but it was years ago. I swear I've not been unfaithful since."

"I didn't say she told me, I said she gave it away. You've just confirmed it. Don't say anything else. I can't bear to listen. I don't know what to believe anymore, Robert. Understand this changes everything for me. 'Sworn to secrecy', is that the best you can do? I'm not saying it's over yet, but nothing can ever be the same between us again."

She looked at her watch.

"You need to pick up Lily. She's our priority now. I'm going to make up a bed for you in the spare room while you're gone. I can't sleep with you, not until you tell me the truth."

"You're completely overreacting! You already knew about Maria—so the only new piece of information is that I was out last night for work-related business that I can't tell you about. You can't unilaterally decide to kick me out of the bedroom."

"'The only new piece of information'? Is that what you're calling it? It sounds like you're giving a power point talk. Put yourself in my place, listening to your bullshit, and think very hard if I'm overreacting before you say anything else. You've never been good at understanding where other people are coming from, but this is beyond belief."

They sat looking at each other for a few seconds. Emily felt utterly wretched, despairing, lower than she could ever remember. Fighting to control her tears, she saw only anger and calculation in Robert's face before he pushed himself forcefully out of his chair, collected the car keys and left the house.

He was furious with himself. *I should have handled that better. Emily is far too smart not to have done some basic checking after I failed to return her calls. Although I didn't know she knew about the Maria affair, which made it more likely she'd be suspicious. I won't fight her about the sleeping arrangements. My priority is to get our relationship back to normal, whatever the new normal is going to be. Think long term; concentrate on six, even nine, months' time, when hopefully this will have been forgotten.*

He remembered, just in time, to take a short diversion to the recycling centre, to get rid of Sue's clothes and the airbed. He checked each item for anything that might identify her, then put them in the container chute. He'd have to hide her phone, diaries, address book and keys in the loft, until he had the opportunity to either burn them or throw them into a reservoir. A different one, obviously.

As he turned into the road outside the school, Lily was waiting at the gates, talking to her friends, Rachel and Miriam. She'll be ten on her next birthday, looking more and more like a younger version of Emily. She broke into a big smile as she saw the Saab, said goodbye to her friends and ran to the car, waving at him. *We've got to protect her from the fallout from this, whatever happens*, he thought.

19

One Last Chance

Emily impatiently pulled bed sheets and a duvet out of the linen cupboard and took them to the spare room.

"Fuck you, you deceiving bastard," she raged, her mind in an uproar that refused to still. *Who is this person I've been with for the last thirteen years? The longer he went on, the more I thought 'where's your heart, where's your conscience?'*

He was so cold. Has our whole relationship, for the last thirteen years, been based on a lie? He can be thoughtful, considerate and funny. Caring, even. But it's like that's all calculated, thought through. He does the right things, but he doesn't feel them inside. When I think about it, the only real passions I've ever seen him show are anger and sexual desire. But you fell in love with him, Emily. What was that about? Was I subconsciously looking for someone to balance me, to smooth my emotional highs and lows?

She left the sheets on the bed—he could make it himself—went downstairs and made herself a gin and tonic. She never usually drank this early, but today's events warranted an exception. Was she unfair, refusing to believe his version of events? *Don't you dare go down that path. 'Work related business I can't tell you about'? What the fuck does that mean? When have we ever not been able to tell each other about our work?* She thought about some of the confidential cases she'd shared with him—his story was pathetic.

For Lily's sake, she would try to make the relationship work in the short term, but it was going to be difficult keeping everything from her. She was bright and picked up moods quickly. If Robert owned up to an affair, they could at least talk about what lay behind his cheating; in that case, it might be possible for them to move on. If he stuck to this ridiculous story, there was no way back; she'd leave him.

For the next three weeks, up to their long-planned holiday, Robert and Emily lived separate lives, keeping arguments to a minimum. Lily noticed almost immediately and began asking them what was going on. They knew this could happen and had agreed a story. Mum and Dad were working through a misunderstanding about something that happened a long time ago and had decided that the quickest way to be happy again was to spend more time on their own, for a while. This happened before Lily was born; she wasn't to blame and they both loved her as much as ever.

It worked to an extent. Lily didn't seem to be dwelling on it.

A few days before they set off on their holiday, Emily briefly noticed a story in the local paper, hidden away at the bottom of page seven, about a Tideswell resident, Sue Goodall, who hadn't been seen for three weeks. There were no signs of a break-in at her house, nothing to suggest she'd been abducted. The police had listed her as a missing person but weren't pursuing enquiries into her disappearance. The story ended by quoting the number of people who go missing and disappear in England every year.

Robert, who'd been scanning the local press daily, was relieved to read that the police didn't regard her disappearance as suspicious.

Their route to Annecy took them to Folkestone, through the Channel tunnel, then for several hundred miles through northern France, via Reims and Dijon. It was impractical for Robert and Emily to maintain their non-communication during the two-day drive. Lily sat in the back, listening to music on her iPod and playing with her Nintendo. She was relieved to see her parents talking to each other at last. What she didn't notice was the effort they were making to keep their conversation on neutral topics, such as the landscape, where they should stop for lunch and the activities on offer at Annecy.

Except just once, when they were sure Lily was asleep. Robert said, "We haven't discussed it, but I'm assuming that we will be sharing a bedroom in the chalet. I don't think it will work if I sleep on a sofa in the living area."

Emily's grip on the steering wheel tightened involuntarily. She'd been wondering the same thing but wasn't going to be the first to raise it.

"Of course I don't expect that. Apart from anything else, it would confuse Lily even more. I've brought a sleeping bag and an airbed, and I'll sleep on the bedroom floor."

"Oh, for fuck's sake, Emily, that's ridiculous. I get it you don't want to have sex with me at the moment. What do you think I'm going to do, force myself on you? Have we really come to this?"

"I don't think, I know, you don't get it Robert. It's not about whether I want to fuck you or not. It's about re-building the trust and intimacy between us, that's currently non-existent. There's no chance of that until you either tell me who you slept with or what you were doing. Just don't say, again, it was a secret work meeting with people whose names you daren't share with me."

Robert decided to bite his tongue. He understood her position; he'd feel the same if the roles were reversed, but what could he say now? "OK, you deserve to know, the truth is I strangled a woman to death and dumped her body in a lake."

Their self-catering chalet at Arc-en-Ciel on the lake shore at Annecy was everything the brochure promised: great facilities, good food and endless activities to choose from. Some, like cycling, the three of them did together, but when Lily was signed up for a supervised activity, Robert and Emily did their own thing. Emily spent hours running by the side of the lake; she'd taken it up again in the last few months.

A deep sadness at the impending loss of the future she'd thought the three of them would share was always with her.

Although her relationship with Robert had lost its spark in the last couple of years, up to now they'd had a rewarding life, a beautiful daughter and remained attracted to each other. But until he could be honest about that night, she knew her feelings wouldn't change. His lack of empathy astonished her. He'd really thought her refusal to sleep with him was about sex. She could deal with the fact that he'd screwed someone else, just; the issue was the shredding of trust between them.

Robert remained untroubled about killing Sue. But with time to reflect, away from the pressures of work, he realised that his marriage would fall apart unless he made up a believable story. She'd made it clear it was his refusal to tell the truth about that night that was coming between them. He could see that was never going to change until he cleared it up. He could live with the monstrous act of murdering Sue; she'd been determined to ruin his life, what choice did he have? But if his marriage fell apart and he lost contact with Lily, he'd be devastated.

But he had to think of a convincing scenario.

On the fifth day, they signed up for an archery class together.

"I'm not sure this is wise, being in the same place as you with a bow and arrow in your hands."

Emily laughed, "I'm a terrible shot; you've got nothing to worry about."

"That's the first time I've seen you laugh in a month. Can we get a babysitter this evening and go out for dinner? I want to tell you what happened that night. God knows what you'll think of me when you know. It's not an affair, but you'll be shocked."

Emily felt a huge sense of release. Whatever it was, it couldn't be worse that not knowing.

He'd booked a lakeside table in the Arc-en-Ciel Brasserie. Emily raised her glass of Sauvignon and chinked it against his.

"Cheers, here's to us," she said ironically.

It was a warm, humid night. Robert took a large swallow and began.

After twenty minutes, the bottle three quarters empty, he stopped.

"So now you know. I wouldn't blame you if you didn't want to have anything to do with me."

Emily sat looking at him, aghast.

He'd explained that six months ago, the Chair of Governors had accused him in one of their meetings of falsifying school performance data for the governing body to make the results look better. 'Falsifying' was an exaggeration, but the Chair could make a case that he'd deliberately withheld important data and threatened to raise it at the next governors' meeting. If he did, it would threaten to end his career. He hadn't told Emily because he'd wanted to sort this out on his own, for once. There'd been gossip in his senior team that the Chair had covered up a serious accident at his factory. With the help of a private investigator, Robert had gathered concrete evidence that the rumour was true. He'd set up a meeting with the Chair in a hotel in Stockport, presented him with the evidence and gave him a choice; drop your plan to tell governors about the doctored performance data, or I will make sure this comes out. Following a furious row, lasting into the small hours, the Chair, building a career within the Tory party, had agreed.

"I felt disgusted with myself, but I was desperate. He was determined to get the governors to censure me, which would have been the end of my career. From the look on your face, I can see I was right when I judged you'd be appalled, so I made up a story. I swear to you I didn't have an affair."

She believed him; it seemed to ring true. She'd guessed, years ago, that he'd probably behaved ruthlessly to get promotion as quickly as he had; his moral boundaries had always been flexible. But this was extreme, not to mention criminal behaviour.

"You're right, Robert, I'm appalled by what you've told me. Do you understand how irresponsible you've been? Blackmail is a serious criminal offence; if he'd gone to the police and you'd been found guilty, you would have gone to jail for several years. The implications for me, as a lawyer, and Lily, facing taunts at school about her father, would have been terrible. How dare you take such a risk with our lives? How do you know he's dropped it?"

"At the final governing body meeting of the term, he made a speech saying how lucky the school was to have me and endorsed my proposals for the future direction of the school. There was no mention of the dodgy data."

There was silence between them for over a minute. Emily spoke, finally.

"I'm so fucking angry at the moment; it's best I don't say anything. But thank you for telling me. I can see why you didn't. I need time to think about where this leaves me, and I want your word that you will never take risks with our future like this again. If you do and I find out, we're finished, and you will lose contact with Lily. I'm not joking; I don't joke about stuff like this."

"I promise. Thank you for hearing me out, I was afraid you might not."

"And leave you with the wine? Let's be English and finish our meal. If I've managed to make sense of my feelings by tomorrow evening, we'll talk again then."

She lay awake until two in the morning, thinking about what he'd done and what it said about him. It was unfathomably reckless, utterly stupid. But there was no point dwelling on that. The question was, could she stay with him after this? If she did, she needed to be sure she'd be able to put it behind her and re-build her trust. If she couldn't, she had to leave him. Muddling along in the middle would be the worst option.

When Emily woke up, Robert had already left for his morning run. She made herself a coffee and sat on the deck and thought about the decision that she had to make. But she was really just going through the motions, and she knew it. She'd already decided to make the marriage work. Lily's happiness played a big part in her decision; she adored her dad, and it would devastate her if they split up. He'd taken a huge, reckless gamble. But she still loved him even if she didn't like him as much she used to.

When she told him her decision that evening in the brasserie, she said that she'd leave him if he ever lied to her again or took such a reckless risk with their futures. Robert appeared contrite but felt exultant. *I've done it. Sue's out of the way, I've talked Emily round and my marriage is secure. I can get on with my career.*

Back at the chalet, they paid the babysitter, checked on Lily and took two glasses of wine onto the deck outside. They chatted about their plans for tomorrow before Robert went to bed, chancing a kiss goodnight.

When Emily went to the bedroom twenty minutes later, Robert was in bed, lying with his back to her. She undressed quietly and lay on the airbed. She missed making love; they hadn't had sex for weeks. *This is ridiculous*, she thought. She got onto the bed and put her arm around him. He turned towards her, kissing her hard on her mouth and pulling her tightly against him. It was another humid night, and they were soon soaked in sweat, their bodies sliding against each other. Robert moved gently at first, then with increasing force, pushing into her with a disconnected urgency. When she looked at his face, she saw conquest, not love. At the end, she felt his hand move to the bottom of her neck, fingers tightening as he came.

They lay side by side on their backs, drenched in sweat.

"I lost you towards the end, where did you go?" she said.

He couldn't give her an answer; he wasn't sure he could even give himself one. Or wanted to.

At the end of the holiday, they took their time driving back through France, using the minor roads, stopping at a small hotel outside Troyes. Emily lay awake in their narrow bed, sunlight streaming into their room in the early morning, unable to forget the image of Robert's face that night.

20

Surfacing

The week after they got back to Cheshire was frenetic for both of them. Robert was preparing for the new school year with his two deputies, putting the final touches to the staff training day and a press release on 'another stellar set of exam results for the school'. In reality, they were pretty average, but ever since another local school began to cherry pick its results and splash full page adverts in the local press, every school did it. Emily went into the Manchester office every day, taking Lily with her on one occasion when none of her friends were around for her to play with. There was a backlog of correspondence about the deportation case to catch up on and meetings with other partners about expanding the human rights law side of the practice. She also had to spend time with Jo who was struggling with her workload.

She still felt an emotional distance from Robert and knew a return to normality would take time. It bothered her more that he seemed to have moved on completely, rarely showing any acknowledgement that his behaviour had come close to ending their marriage. Once he'd even said to her, "You seem a bit low at the moment, is anything the matter?"

She'd just looked at him and given a shake of her head.

"I'm not sure how to begin answering that question, Robert."

Robert wished Emily could return to being the woman he knew before he'd told her the 'real' reason for his absence on the night he'd sunk Sue's body in the reservoir. Occasionally, in rare moments of self-awareness, he would see himself through her eyes; an unfaithful liar so obsessed with advancing his career that he'd put her and Lily's security at risk. In those moments, he understood, but they didn't trouble him for long.

Four weeks later, walking back along Piccadilly to get the train home, she'd stopped to pick up the Manchester Evening News. The headline splashed across the front page read: 'Woman's Body Found in Local Reservoir'.

The body had apparently floated to the surface when the rope holding the weights rotted. It was too early for an identification, but a police spokesman was quoted as saying that, judging by the state of the body, it had been there for two or three months. A number was given at the end of the piece for members of the public to call, should they have relevant information. Another woman murdered by some bastard jealous partner, she'd thought. The statistics about such cases were horrendous.

Emily tossed the paper onto the coffee table in the lounge and began to prepare a lasagne. She'd just put the dish in the oven and sat down with a glass of Pinot when she heard Robert come in. There was a time, not that long ago, when that would have given her a buzz of anticipation, but not anymore.

Robert came in, smiled at her and said, "How was your day, mine was non-stop?"

Before she could answer, Robert's eye was caught by the newspaper headline. She watched as he froze and turned pale, colour leaving his face. He remained, staring at the paper, for several seconds.

"Robert, are you OK? You look as if you've seen a ghost. Some poor woman's body has been found in the reservoir. She was murdered."

As he took in the headline, he had to struggle to recover and stop himself passing out. It had to be her.

"Sorry, I felt a bit queasy on the drive home, must be something I ate at lunch. I'd better get to the bathroom."

Emily was puzzled rather than concerned. He did look very pale, but he seemed fine when he came in, smiling and upbeat. The story in the paper seemed to bring it on. Odd.

Robert sat on the toilet, head between his knees, getting blood to his brain. *You knew this could happen, that's why you took so much trouble making sure there was nothing to link you to Sue. There's no reason they'll have her DNA on the database and she must be unrecognisable after nearly three months in the water. Emily gave me a really doubtful look; she mustn't connect my reaction to the headline. I need to keep this pretence up for the rest of the evening.*

"How are you feeling, you went very pale?" she said as Robert came back.

"Still lousy. I'm afraid I won't be wanting any of the delicious lasagne that I smelt as I came in, sorry. I think I'll go up and lay down for a while."

"Sure. Is there anything I can get you?"

"It's OK, thanks, my love. I'll just take a glass of iced water up with me."

Margaret Gibson had worked as a forensic pathologist for nearly five years. In that time, she'd examined a number of bodies that had been in water for an extended period. This one was unusual, though. Cases like these made the job interesting. The temperature at the bottom of the reservoir during spring and summer varied between ten and fifteen degrees centigrade, well above the temperature needed for gut bacteria to multiply rapidly The polythene wrapping would trap the heat generated by the bacteria and further speed up decay. Given the extent of decomposition, she calculated the body couldn't have been in the water more than eight weeks. Any longer than that, and she'd just have a pile of bones to examine.

The skin and muscle had begun to delaminate from the skeleton; once the plastic sheeting had loosened, fish had done the rest, particularly around the face. It was going to be very difficult to identify who this poor soul was, as there appeared to be no recent dental work. *Let's hope that it's possible to get a DNA match from the database.*

Some facts she had managed to establish. The victim was female, about five feet seven inches tall with a slim build. Establishing the age of the corpse was harder, but she was ninety five percent sure the victim was between forty and forty-five years old. There were no distinguishing birth marks left. Given the warming effect of the plastic wrapping around the body, she narrowed her judgement about the time it had been in the reservoir down to between six and eight weeks.

The cause of death had been straightforward. Although much of the outer skin on the face had been eaten away, the windpipe and major blood vessels in the neck bore the unmistakable signs of rupture caused by strangulation. A particularly forceful strangulation, in this case. There was one final clue to the identity of the corpse. As Margaret and her assistant had peeled away the remaining pieces of polythene sheeting, they found a silver ring, lying between the remains of the right hand and the sheet. There was no inscription and little to distinguish it, save for a knot motif formed within the ring itself.

The police released a press statement two days after Margaret's autopsy, which covered all of her findings, with an attached picture of the ring. It included the usual plea for anyone who knew of a missing woman fitting the description, or who recognises the ring, to inform the police immediately. Unfortunately, there was no DNA match in the national database and no dental records.

The police carried out door to door enquiries of all the households around the lake, but after four weeks, there were no leads to the body's identity. The team on the investigation was reduced by half and the public slowly lost interest.

Except for Robert and Emily.

Robert looked every day for news of the 'body in the lake', making sure Emily wasn't around. He couldn't afford a repeat of the previous occasion, which had clearly thrown her. It was particularly fortunate that he wasn't with her when he saw the press release with the picture of the ring; he'd involuntarily called out 'you fucking idiot'. *How can you have missed that?* For the next few days, he scoured the papers every day, expecting to read that the body had been identified as Sue Goodall, from Tideswell, Derbyshire. After two weeks, he stopped worrying; no one had recognised the ring.

Robert's reaction to the story had aroused Emily's interest in the case. When she saw the picture of the ring her first thought was: *Someone must recognise that, surely?* But the story eventually died along with her interest in it. More important issues needed her time and attention, like Lily's move to secondary school. Although this was nearly two years away, Lily was getting anxious about the move; she didn't feel comfortable about going to her father's school and wanted to check out the alternatives. She and Emily were duly guided around on a number of school open days, pupils in virtual lock-down, listening to the head teacher's embellished sales pitch.

After a particularly frustrating drive from the airport along the M56, Aileen Ashby's taxi finally pulled up outside her flat in West Didsbury. She'd been travelling for thirty hours and was exhausted by the flight from Perth, Australia, where she'd been staying with her sister on an extended visit. It was the beginning of November, five o'clock in the afternoon, and already dark. And raining, obviously. Luckily, she'd thought to get milk, bread and a ready meal at the airport so she made a cup of tea and sat down to the sickly lasagne. Going through her post, she threw out the obvious junk mail and put the rest aside to read in the morning. She'd told all her clients she would be away for three months but knew there would still be an overflowing inbox in her business email address; she decided to leave that for the morning, too.

She woke at 5 a.m. after an interrupted sleep, feeling a medley of jet-lag effects; head ache, nausea and an inability to concentrate. *I can manage the post, but emails are out of the question at the moment. Maybe this evening.*

After something approaching a night's sleep, 'this evening' became the next morning. There weren't as many emails as she feared, bringing on an anxiety that some clients might be leaving her. She was surprised not to see anything from Sue Goodall. After a year of therapy, Sue had finally accepted that confessing to her role in a cover-up thirteen years ago was crucial to conquering her depression. At their final session, before she left for Australia, Sue had promised she'd be in touch, to tell her the outcome and re-assure Aileen she was OK. Aileen had thought it strange that she hadn't heard from her before she left for Australia, but a last-minute packing crisis meant she hadn't had time to follow up.

When she'd finally finished dealing with the last email at 2:30 p.m., she tried Sue's number. 'This phone is switched off.' When she got the same result again two days later, she resigned herself to losing another client.

A week later, researching information on the increase in numbers of young women seeking therapeutic help for eating disorders, she was directed to an article in the Manchester Evening News, dated the 4th of October. The data in the article itself was nothing new, but as she was leaving the site, an image on the front page appeared on the screen. The headline was: Silver Ring Clue to Body in the Reservoir.

Fifteen minutes later, a voice finally answered the number given at the end of the story. Calmly, she said, "I've just seen the picture of the ring worn by the victim found in the reservoir. I think I know who it belongs to."

The Detective Inspector on the end of the phone sighed audibly. He was hoping the weirdos who'd been phoning constantly had at last moved on to other things.

"Can I have your name please, Madam? Then can you tell me as briefly as possible why you think you recognise this ring and who it belongs to?"

Half an hour later, Aileen was collected from her house by Detective Inspector Singh in his unmarked car, then taken to City Centre police station to give a statement. *At last*, he thought, *a witness who speaks in full sentences and appears to have relevant information.*

Aileen told him how she knew Sue, the way in which she'd constantly played with the ring during her sessions, the fact that the description seemed to fit and that she was intending to reveal her role in a cover-up just as Aileen left for Australia for three months. When the policeman showed her the ring, she'd answered, "That's either the ring that Sue wore or an identical copy." She was that certain.

The mood amongst Manchester CID was mixed. Elation at the thought they'd got a name and a possible motive. Anxiety, because if this was the victim, why on earth hadn't a connection been made with the report of Sue Goodall's disappearance over three months ago? They all knew that would be the first question the Chief Inspector would ask; the second, whose responsibility was it to have made that link?

Everything pointed to Sue Goodall as the victim, so the police immediately put out a press statement. The statement included a request that anyone who knew the victim should get in touch. In the circumstances, Aileen was prepared to wave her ex-client's confidentiality and tell Inspector Singh as much as she knew about the incident in Sue's past.

"She said she'd been largely responsible for the accidental death of a child on a school trip many years ago. She'd been persuaded to lie about certain things leading-up to the accident but had never been able to come to terms with what she'd done."

The police narrowed their enquiries to the three schools where Sue had worked from 1990 to 2003; after a couple of phone calls they'd established that the incident in question took place on the Wood Vale School summer camp in the Brecon Beacons in 1994. Hackney Council responded immediately to their request for all the documentation related to the incident and to the enquiry.

As soon as he saw the latest press release, Robert knew it was likely that the police would want to speak to him about Sue's disappearance. They'd probably already contacted her previous schools. It was only a matter of time before they discovered her involvement in the school camp incident, which could lead them to him. But why go to the police before they contact him? He decided to tell Emily that he knew the dead woman from the incident on the school camp.

"You know they've identified the woman that was found in the reservoir? I think it might be someone I worked with at my first school in London. The police have asked anyone who knew her to come forward, but I don't think I need to as it's so long ago."

"That's incredible. I'm so sorry, that must have been a shock. Was she a close friend?"

"Not really, but we were both involved in that incident on the school camp, so I got to know her well."

"Oh, I remember her. Didn't she contact you constantly before the enquiry?"

"That's her."

Emily was putting herself in the mind-set of an average police detective, wondering how to advise him.

"I think it would be a mistake not to contact the police. You never know where their enquiries will lead. They might find out about the incident, your name will crop up and given it's unlikely that you wouldn't have heard about her murder, they may wonder why you didn't come forward."

Robert found himself getting irritated by the way she seemed to assume that he would take her advice, that she was bound to know better than him. But he could see the logic of what she'd said.

"OK, I'll contact them, though I'll emphasise that I haven't seen her for twelve years, so I doubt I'll be any use."

21

An Inspector Calls, Again

Calmly confident, Robert walked through the doors of the police station into the throng of people in the lobby. If they asked, he'd be frank about his involvement in the tribunal and come across as a model citizen doing everything to help the police. Deepak Singh intercepted him before he got to the duty officer on reception and took him to an interview room on the first floor.

"Thank you for getting in touch, Mr Mason, we appreciate it. Do you want a tea or coffee? No? OK, so can you tell me when you last saw Sue Goodall and where, so we can assess whether this is the same person or not."

"I last saw Sue in 1996, when she left Wood Vale Comprehensive School in Hackney, where we were both teaching. We weren't especially close—she was in special needs and I was a science teacher—but we'd been on a school camp in the Brecon Beacons together. There was a tragic incident on the camp; a boy died, there was an enquiry, none of the staff were blamed, but I know Sue found the enquiry process stressful. I think it was a factor behind her leaving; she wanted to get away from the bad memories."

"And that was the last time you saw her?"

"Yes. She rang me a few times to talk about the incident when she left, but we lost touch after a few months. Do you think this could be the same person?"

"From our enquiries into her past and what you've just told me, I think I can now say it is."

"God, poor Sue, what an appalling thing to happen. You never think that someone you know will end up being murdered."

"You live near Macclesfield, I believe. Was it a coincidence that you both ended up in this part of the North West, after you left London?"

"Yes, of course. My wife, daughter and I moved up here four years ago when I became the head teacher at Preston Park. As I said, we'd lost touch years ago."

"Can you remember anyone in the past that had a grudge against her, or had a significant falling out with her?"

"No, I'm afraid I can't. When I first thought this could be the same Sue Goodall that I used to know, I tried to remember if she'd had any enemies. I couldn't think of anyone. She wasn't the type to fall out with colleagues."

"Another witness who came forward has told us that Sue was tormented by having lied about an incident in the past, which she now wanted to own up to. Did she ever mention anything like that to you?"

"No. But then, as I say, I haven't been in contact with her for over eleven years."

"Thank you again, Mr Mason. One more question before you leave. I believe that you were the staff leader on that camp. That must have been a very stressful time."

Robert thought the police could bring this up and had prepared for it.

"Yes, it was. As the leader, I had responsibility for the safety of everyone on the camp. Tom's parents had trusted me with their son's welfare, but they never saw him again. In those circumstances, the council had to satisfy themselves that all of us had fulfilled our duty of care and that his death was accidental. So, I accepted the need for the enquiry. We were all cleared of any blame."

"Yes, I know. Thank you again for coming in, Mr Mason, I doubt we'll need to be in touch again."

After Robert left, Deepak Singh reflected on the performance he'd just witnessed. That's what he'd felt it was; a performance. Why would a man like Robert Mason feel the need to rehearse his lines for a meeting like this? There could be a number of innocent reasons. But Singh had learned to trust his feelings about the people he'd interviewed over the years; his feeling this time was that Mason was holding something back.

What did he know so far about Sue Goodall? She was a forty-two-year-old, special needs teacher who'd moved from London to Tideswell five years ago. Since then she'd worked on and off as a supply teacher, lived simply and made few friends. According to her therapist, she was troubled by a lie she'd told in her past and was planning to own up to her dishonesty. Not the kind of personal history that would normally lead to making serious enemies.

His team's interviews with her few neighbours in Tideswell and their door to door enquiries in the homes around the reservoir had produced no leads. So far, his best line of enquiry appeared to be this event in her past. Apparently, she was murdered just as she was about to reveal the truth. Coincidence? The only incident the police knew about was the death of the pupil on the school camp, which was run by Robert Mason. Who just happens to live a forty-minute drive from Sue Goodall. If only the pathologist could be more specific about the time of death.

Deepak left a message for the pathologist, made a call to Wood Vale School and booked a seat on the 7.30 a.m. train from Manchester Piccadilly to Euston the following day.

Margaret Gibson rang him back later that afternoon.

"You must understand, Deepak, given the state of the body when it was brought in, it's not possible to give a specific date. I can be sure that it had been in the water for more than six weeks and no longer than eight, at the outside. That's your window."

The school secretary was shocked when Deepak told her why he wanted to speak to all the current staff who'd been there in 1994. She'd worked at Wood Vale for fifteen years and remembered Sue well. When she'd regained her composure, she agreed to draw up the list of names and pass them to the head teacher, who would ring him back on his mobile. He got the call at eight that evening, just as he was sitting down to dinner. He stifled his irritation, then answered.

"Thank you for getting back to me, Mr Ashton. Has your secretary explained what this is about?"

"Yes, it was dreadful news. I wasn't here then, but we've identified twelve staff who were, including one who was on the camp. Some of them knew Sue well and they've been really upset. I've managed to timetable you to meet with each one of them separately for twenty minutes tomorrow. Will that be enough?"

"That should give me plenty of time. I really appreciate it, thank you. How many staff are there at the school?"

"Around one hundred and fifty."

"And only twelve still there, after thirteen years?"

"Welcome to my world. Over fifteen percent staff turnover in London, each year."

The staff were all keen to talk. Sue came across as a caring, supportive colleague who liked a laugh. She could be overly touchy sometimes, neurotic even, but someone you could rely on if things kicked off.

Robert Mason didn't come over so well. Not a team player, focussed on getting promotion and not averse to shafting his colleagues to achieve it. But the most revealing thing Deepak learned was that Mason had been very economical with the truth about the fall-out from the incident. He'd been suspended for over two months up to the date of the enquiry; the only member of staff to suffer that. Sue had been on duty when the boy went missing that night and was a key witness at the enquiry. Several teachers told him that she'd been a nervous wreck during the months leading up to it, and a friend of hers said Sue had told her that Mason was pressuring her.

On the train back to Manchester, Deepak decided to give Robert Mason another call.

"I'm sorry to bother you again, Mr Mason. We're following up the idea that Sue Goodall never got over the boy's death on the camp thirteen years ago and would like to clear up a few points with you. I went to your old school yesterday and spoke to staff who were there at the time. A number of them said that she was deeply affected by the incident and I think you might be able to add to the picture."

Once Sue's body had been identified, Robert had known that the enquiries might lead to him and he'd tried to prepare himself. There was clearly no evidence to link him directly to the crime, or they would have found it by now. And it would be impossible for them to know precisely when she was killed and put in the water. But the news that the inspector had returned to Wood Vale and spoken to his ex-colleagues had a traumatising impact. As he listened to Singh, he felt his throat drying up. Not for the first time, he had to force himself to come across calmly.

"I'd be happy to help in any way I can, Inspector. Tell me, what's the protocol here? Should I bring someone with me?"

"Only if you want a lawyer with you, Mr Mason, but I don't think that's necessary. This isn't a formal interview; I'm not bringing you in for questioning."

"That's a relief, Inspector. When shall I come in?"

"Can you make 2 o'clock tomorrow?"

"I'll see you then."

Robert decided not to tell Emily about the inspector's 'request'. How could she help him? She didn't know he was a murderer or that he'd lied at the inquest so there was a limit to how useful her advice could be. If he could satisfy Singh tomorrow and put this to rest, then she needn't know that he'd been called back.

If the line of questioning stuck to events on and after the incident itself, including Sue's state of mind, then he was sure he could deal with it conclusively. What he didn't know was whether the police had uncovered anything circumstantial, such as traffic camera footage of him driving on the night in question. He'd been watching for cameras but couldn't be sure. If that was the case, he would have said he was just going for a drive, and he did sometimes when he had an issue at work to think through.

"Thank you for coming in again, Mr Mason. I appreciate how busy you must be running a school. However, my interviews with staff at your old school revealed information about the incident and its aftermath that you hadn't mentioned in our last conversation, which may have a bearing on Sue Goodall's state of mind. Firstly, did you put any pressure on Sue to stick to a particular version of events in the weeks before the enquiry?"

"Did someone on the staff say that?"

"One of them said that Sue had implied that to her before the enquiry, yes."

"Well, that's completely untrue. In fact, the reverse is the case. As Sue was the person on duty at the time that Tom left his tent and walked onto the Beacons, she felt particularly guilty. She was very nervous about giving evidence at the enquiry and I met her several times to give her support, which included mock interviews, thinking about possible questions that might come up, that sort of thing. We wanted to make sure we said the same thing; as I'm sure you're aware, it's easy to get someone like her flustered with aggressive questioning. And the panel did just that. They were awful."

"When you last saw Sue, did she still feel guilty about the incident?"

"Yes. I suspect she felt guilty for a long time; she was that kind of person."

"You didn't tell me that you'd been suspended before the enquiry. Why not?"

"I didn't think it was relevant. It's standard practice for the Council to do that in such situations, and there's no implication of guilt, as I'm sure you know. And anyway, it's all in the records, which I'd assumed you'd read."

Deepak noted the edge that had crept into Robert's tone.

"Finally, Mr Mason, can you tell me where you were between the beginning and end of August? You're not a suspect, but it could help to stop us wasting any more of your time in the future."

"Christ, that's a long period to account for. For the first three weeks, I was on holiday in France with my wife and daughter. For the last week, I was in school every day for eight or nine hours; in the evenings we were all at home."

Deepak felt disappointed. If verified, this would put Mason out of contention for the murder. His instincts were wrong.

"Would your wife be able to verify that?"

"I'm sure she would, yes. Do you want to question her, too?"

There's the tone again.

"I think a phone conversation will cover it, Mr Mason. I don't think we'll need to see you anymore, so if you could ask her to ring me on this number tomorrow afternoon, at a time that suits her, I would be most grateful. Thank you again for coming in."

Robert had mixed feelings on the train back to Macclesfield. He hadn't put a foot wrong in the interview. What's more, they clearly don't think the body could have been put in the lake before August, which ruled him out. *I don't know how they made that mistake, and I don't care. But Emily will be furious that I hadn't told her about the second meeting, especially as she's now going to be involved.*

"What were you thinking not telling me about this? I would have advised you to take someone with you for a start. They clearly have a suspicion that you know more about her murder than you've told them so far. At the very least."

Robert felt incensed by her attitude. She was telling him off, belittling him.

"That's not fair, Emily. I don't want to bother you every time there's some legal issue that involves me."

"But this doesn't just involve you, does it? He now wants to speak to me. Why did they ask you back for a second interview?"

He was getting really pissed off with her.

"Because the inspector in charge of the case decided to go back to Wood Vale, speak to the staff that were there in 1994 and ask about Sue's state of mind after the camp. He seems to think that she never got over it, and there may be some link to her murder. One of the staff he interviewed told him that I'd been putting pressure on Sue, to agree to a particular version of events on the night Tom went missing. Which is complete bollocks; as you may remember, she was phoning me all the time, asking for advice and support."

"Please don't get angry with me, I obviously need to know where he's coming from if I'm going to speak to him. What's he going to ask exactly?"

"He wants you to confirm that you were with me throughout our holiday in France, and during the evenings in the last week in August."

"The whole of August? Do you realise this is to eliminate you as a suspect? Which means, currently, you are one? He's going to ask me precisely what we were doing that week, so we'd better try to remember."

Emily rang Inspector Singh the following afternoon from work and went through her movements during the evenings of the last week of August. Fortunately, they'd either been at home together, out shopping, or at the cinema with Lily. Shortly after the start of the call, when he'd asked her what she did for a living, his approach had become friendlier.

"Thank you for going through that, Ms Fowler. I know a couple of your colleagues and your practice has an honourable reputation. I'm sure I won't be bothering you anymore."

"I'm puzzled by the length of the period you wanted verifying, Inspector. I presume this means you don't have a more accurate estimation for the time of death?"

Deepak Singh smiled to himself.

"You may think that, but I couldn't possibly comment, Ms Fowler. Let's say we're being as inclusive as possible at this stage, but your husband isn't a suspect."

"Any longer, you mean?"

Another smile. "It's been good speaking to you, Ms Fowler. Take care."

Emily opened the case file she was working on. Robert was picking Lily up and she was intending to work late into the evening. But something about this didn't make sense. Robert had clearly been a suspect, but on what evidence? Living reasonably close and being involved in the same tragic event thirteen years ago was incredibly flimsy. Was that really all they had? It's ridiculous, anyway. Whatever else he's done over the years, Robert's not capable of murder, even if he had a motive, which he doesn't; there's no way he could do this.

A week later, Emily was attending a 'Causes of and Myths about Youth Crime' conference in Manchester. It wasn't her area, but a colleague had a family crisis and it was important for Pearson, Shallice and Grant to be represented. During the coffee break, she found herself standing next to a tall, attractive man wearing a turban. Even upside down, she could read 'Insp. Deepak Singh' on his name badge. She held her hand out and said,

"Hello, I'm Emily Fowler, your chief suspect's partner."

He looked puzzled, then smiled at her.

"Deepak Singh. Delighted to meet you, Emily, but that was a little below the belt."

"So, have you made any more progress?"

"Is this just between us? And I mean just us."

"You have my word."

"Very little. Our main problem is that the pathologist can't narrow down the time of death with any precision, given the deterioration of the body. Personally, I would have thought it could have been in the water longer than her outside estimate, but she seemed sure about that. Something to do with decomposition speeding up significantly above seven degrees."

"And the reservoir is above that in early summer, even at the bottom?"

"Apparently. So, we've no date, no motive and no material or witness evidence. We are, as my colleagues would say, stuffed."

"I'm sure that some of your colleagues might use an even less technical phrase."

"They would, but I'm not going to use such language in front of you, unshockable as I suspect you may be."

"You could always take the temperature at the bottom of the lake yourself, just to check."

A conference organiser announced that the next session was about to begin.

"Lovely to meet you, Deepak. Good luck with the case."

"Likewise, Emily. Take care."

22

Empty

Sitting in a half empty train carriage that evening, thinking about her conversation with Deepak Singh, she remembered that was the second time he'd told her to take care. Some people use the phrase casually, instead of good bye, but he didn't seem the type. Did he still harbour doubts about Robert?

Inspector Singh had returned to his office immediately after the conference with an unusual request for his boss. He wanted two officers to row across the reservoir several times in a small boat, taking the temperature of the water at the top and bottom with a digital thermometer. His boss needed convincing, but once Deepak had explained why, he agreed. Emily's remark about the temperature at the bottom had triggered something. How could the pathologist be so sure about the water temperature in that reservoir? And why did I take her word for it? We should have checked it weeks ago.

The results came back four days later. Margaret Gibson had been essentially correct about the temperature of the reservoir; it varied between thirteen degrees at the surface to eight near the bottom. Given that it would have been two or three degrees warmer in July, this seemed to confirm her original hypothesis. However, the two constables that had been given the unpopular assignment had found that in a deeper area at the centre of the reservoir, the temperature dropped to five degrees. Furthermore, at that depth, there would be less change between July and October.

Singh had rung Margaret Gibson immediately he'd got the results.

"If those readings are accurate and the body had been in that area of the reservoir, Inspector, then the rate of decomposition would have been slower, and it could have been placed in the water several weeks earlier."

"So, the body could have been placed there at least four weeks earlier, sometime in July?"

"Exactly."

Singh knew immediately that this could put Robert Mason back in the frame. But that was all. There was no new evidence connecting him to the murder. All he had was Mason's previous relationship with the deceased, the fact they'd both faced disciplinary proceedings as a result of an accidental death and the therapist's testimony that Sue had been thinking about revealing a secret she'd hidden since the incident. If he pulled Mason in again, what grounds could he give? He'd appoint a lawyer immediately, claiming he was being victimised.

He had to find something specific that could connect Mason's movements in July to the body being dumped in the reservoir. There was someone who might be able to do that, of course, but why would Emily Fowler help to convict her husband? If he approached her, she was far more likely to go straight to Robert and alert him. Then he'd be back to square one. But he could ring and thank her for her remark about checking the temperature at the bottom of the reservoir, then casually mention that, as a result, they now know the body could have been put in the water in July. It might plant a seed of doubt in her mind.

Emily pulled the Mini over to answer her phone, cursing. She was running late for an appointment with another lawyer involved in a similar deportation case to hers, but she never ignored her mobile during the day. There was always the chance that it could be about Lily.

"Hello?"

"Sorry, is this a bad time? It's Deepak Singh. This is just a quick thank you call. When we were chatting at that conference recently, you raised a doubt in my mind about the reservoir temperature. As a result, I initiated a survey of the reservoir and it turns out that it's much colder than we thought, in one particular spot."

"Deepak, I'm sorry to interrupt, but I'm late for a meeting. Is there something important to all of this?"

"Apologies, Emily. Only that we now know that the body could have been in the water for considerably longer, which could help our enquiries. I'm sorry to hold you up. I just wanted to thank you. Bye."

"Goodbye, Deepak."

Her appointment had just arrived as she turned the Mini into the car park, having scared herself several times by driving too fast round the blind bends on the B5470. It wasn't until she got home that evening that she had time to think about Deepak's call. What was the purpose of it? She didn't buy his line about wanting to thank her—it was just an observation anyone would have made, given time. *He certainly wasn't coming onto me either.* His point seemed to be that the poor woman could have been dumped in the reservoir much earlier, in July. Previously, July had been ruled out.

Was he trying to warn me? You're getting paranoid, Emily. Don't be ridiculous.

She went upstairs to look in on Lily. She was lying on her bed, laptop resting on her legs.

"Hi, Mum. Catherine's got her new puppy called Ruby. I'm just looking at the pictures. She's so adorable, Mum. Can we get a dog, please?"

"Sweetheart, you know Dad and I have always said that when we think you're ready to take on the responsibility for feeding, walking and brushing him, then we'll discuss it. But you've got to be sure, as Dad and I are both working full time and you'll be doing most of the caring. Did Dad say when he would be back?"

"That's not fair; Catherine says she won't have to do all those things. Dad said he'd be home around nine. Bye, Mum."

Emily smiled at her daughter and closed the door behind her. *She's grown up so fast in the four years since we've been here. We're both really proud of her. She's caring, fun, popular at school and sharp as nails, and she loves her dad. She'd be devastated if anything happened to Robert. How can I doubt him—he'd never do anything that would risk damaging his relationship with Lily?*

As she went downstairs, she thought about Robert's fictitious conference in Stockport. That was in July. In spite of herself, she got her diary and looked up the dates; the seventh and eighth of July, within the period that the body could have been in the lake. He'd said he been at a meeting with the Chair of Governors, effectively blackmailing him into dropping the issue of falsified exam results. At the back of her mind, she'd always found this to be far-fetched but had chosen to believe it. There was a way to check. Robert had said that the Chair had made a statement at the last governors' meeting, putting on record his view that Robert was doing an excellent job.

The minutes of every school's governing body meetings were publicly available.

The following morning, she rang the local authority to ask for a copy and was told where she could find them on their website. As she read them, Emily was desperately hoping that she'd see a clear statement praising Robert, but there was nothing like that from the Chair, or anyone else. As she scanned back to the first page, she read something under 'Apologies' that caused her to cry out involuntarily.

The Chair had given his apologies. He wasn't at the meeting—the Vice Chair was standing in. Robert's story about that night was a lie. Another one!

Emily felt the blood pounding in her temples as cold sweat broke out on forehead. Her hands were shaking, even though they were still resting on the keyboard. She forced herself to breath slowly and deeply.

Will I ever get to the bottom of his lies? The question answers itself—I have to. She poured herself a glass of the red they'd opened a couple of days ago and sat in the lounge.

You have to finally confront this, Emily. He's got a fundamental problem with the truth. At the least, he's now lied to you three times about what he was doing that night.

On that basis alone, you can't ever trust him again, and you can't share your life intimately with someone you can't trust. Much worse, there's circumstantial evidence that he might have been involved in the murder of that poor woman. What the hell am I going to do with all this? Where do I begin? Think everything through before you speak to him; what are you going to say, what aren't you going to say, what are you trying to achieve? You've got to do everything possible to protect Lily.

At all costs, make it about his lying and your inability to trust him anymore. However much he goads you, don't reveal your suspicions that he could be involved in a murder. You don't know what he might do.

She felt scared and desperately sad. There would be no confrontational scenes this evening; she'd go to work tomorrow and start to make enquiries about separating. Until then, she'd say nothing.

When Robert came home around nine-thirty, she told him about Lily's request and they discussed again the practicalities of having a dog. She said nothing about the phone call from Deepak Singh or the governors' meeting before they both went to bed around eleven. Unable to sleep, Emily went over the unexplained days in July again. If he wasn't meeting his Chair of governors, having an affair or dumping Sue Goodall's body in the reservoir, what had he been doing? Why make up such an implausible story which wasn't true anyway?

Thinking about Sue Goodall, her thoughts went back to that awful time, soon after they'd met, when he was facing a tribunal that could have led to his dismissal. She remembered how frequently Sue contacted him during that period and how he'd always agreed to meet her. Her heart missed a beat as she remembered a conversation she'd overheard at a lawyers' conference nine months after the tribunal. The lawyer was from a teachers' union and was telling her colleagues about two people she'd represented some months previously who'd been involved in an accident on a school camp. She'd felt strongly that there was collusion between them, led by the man, but didn't have enough evidence to confront them.

Although she'd guessed then that the chances were high that it was Robert, she was too busy falling in love with him to believe it.

If they had colluded in a cover up, and if Sue had contacted Robert and told him she was about to own up to the authorities, would he try to silence her? As she lay in bed next to him, feeling sick at the thought of what he might have done, she couldn't honestly answer 'impossible'.

At work the following morning, she was too distracted to do any research on divorce. Questions about the man she'd lived with for twelve years went around and round in her mind. What did she know as a fact and what was merely conjecture? Once she was clear about that, she could begin to plan her next steps. She forced herself to concentrate.

Thirteen years ago, Robert and Sue were investigated for possible negligence during a school camp, on which a thirteen-year-old boy lost his life. Robert was tense and anxious during the period leading up to the tribunal, but no more than you'd expect in that situation. Emily remembered Sue demanding a lot of support from Robert and they met frequently at her request. Other than the unguarded conversation with the NUT lawyer, there was no concrete evidence that they'd colluded in a cover up. After they were cleared, there was a difficult period for Robert at the school as the boy's father waged a campaign against him, but that died down.

To her knowledge, he'd met Sue again a couple of times, at her request, but hadn't heard from her since then.

Sue's body was found in a local reservoir. She'd been living in Tideswell, about half an hour away. From what Emily had read in the press and something Inspector Singh let slip, Sue was depressed, lonely and obsessed with guilt about an incident from her past. The chances that it was the school camp incident are high. If she had decided to confess, it would be in her character to contact Robert and tell him what she planned to do. He was easy to trace, and they could have met, given the short distances involved. If they did, and if she'd told him she was going to own up to colluding with Robert in a cover up, he would have a strong motive to silence her.

Then there are those two days at the beginning of July, when Robert's whereabouts are unknown. He'd seemed unaccountably edgy in the days before. Without any notice, he'd told her that he had a two-day conference in Stockport. When she'd rung the hotel he was staying at, there was no one in his room and he didn't respond to her message until nine in the morning. He could have been out most of the night, just about long enough to go to her place, kill her and dump her in the reservoir. His account of what he was doing that night, forced out of him, is a lie. When, by chance, he saw the headline in the paper about a body being found in the reservoir, he was shocked.

So, he had a possible motive, and the time to carry out the crime on the 7th July, a period he still hasn't accounted for. She wasn't achieving anything by staying in her office and decided to go home and work out how to tell him she'd found out his story about that night was a lie and she wanted a separation. She'd say nothing about her further suspicions.

Her phone rang as her train pulled into Macclesfield station.

"Hello, Emily Fowler."

"Hello, Emily, it's Inspector Singh. I wanted to tell you there's been a development with our enquiries into Sue Goodall's murder. You don't have to respond, it's just something I thought you should know."

"If you just hang on a minute, Inspector, I'm leaving the station and walking to my car."

"Sure."

As she walked to the Mini, she wondered what he was up to. It was dubious practice to contact the wife of a previous suspect with an update on the case, to put it mildly.

"OK, I'm in the car, please go ahead."

"We've been carrying out follow-up enquiries with homes around the reservoir and along the lane where Sue Goodall lived. A guy who lives in a cottage about half a mile down the road from Goodall's house, who wasn't in when we first called, has told us that around midnight on the night of July 7th, he nearly hit an oncoming, dark-coloured car being driven along the lane, away from her house towards the main road. He couldn't see the driver and didn't recognise the make, though he did say 'I'm sure it was foreign, you don't see many of them about'. The thing is, his is the last cottage along the lane; the driver had almost certainly come from Sue Goodall's house."

The second she'd heard the date, adrenalin had begun to pour into her bloodstream, and she had to make a huge effort to control her voice.

"Can I ask why you're telling me this, Inspector? Given that I imagine you've just broken any number of operational protocols with this call."

There was a long pause.

"I desperately want to arrest the person who murdered Sue Goodall in cold blood. He is clearly a danger to the public; but I believe he could pose an even greater threat to those close to him. I thought you should be aware of the new development, in case the date means anything to you."

"Thank you, Inspector, I mean it when I say your concern is appreciated. I will think further and let you know."

"Please do, Emily. Take care."

She pulled up outside the house, the journey home a complete blank. She remembered leaving the car park, but then nothing. Unlocking the front door, she put her bag on the hall table, walked through to the kitchen and poured a gin and tonic.

Why didn't I tell Deepak about that date?

You know why, of course. After all his lies, I must be the one to confront him with this, face to face, to see his reaction and watch him concoct another ridiculous story. What can he do? He won't hurt me. Even if he felt like it, he'd know Lily would never forgive him or see him again.

She went upstairs to change out of her suit, feeling faint when she reached the top. *Steady, you're in shock.* She took several deep breaths, splashed cold water on her face then took her jacket and skirt off. She knew she should ring Deepak and tell him that Robert had lied to her about that night. But once she'd done that, she'd lose control, and events would be out of her hands. Deepak would come around immediately to arrest him, and she'd lose the only chance she had to persuade him to tell the truth, face to face. At this point in their relationship, after everything he'd put her through, it was more important to her than anything else.

She sat on the bed, tears running down her cheeks, furious, scared. She had so many questions.

What kind of human being have I been living with for all these years, for god's sake? Who is he? How can I have got him so wrong? I've born his child, shared so many intimate moments with him. What does this say about me, that I didn't pick up the signs? Maybe he wasn't like this before he met me?

I wanted him so much, I didn't want to face the obvious truth about him; I've been living a lie for the last thirteen years.

Hearing the key turn in the lock, she blew her nose and wiped her face.

"Hi, there. I wasn't expecting to find you home. Where are you?"

"I'm up here. I had a headache, so I came home early. I'll be down in a minute." When she looked in the mirror, it was clear she'd been crying. She washed her face again, pulled on a sweater and jeans and went downstairs, still shaky, but resolved. The next few hours would be awful, but she knew she had to confront him; she wouldn't be able to face herself if she didn't.

He was making a cup of tea in the kitchen as she walked in.

"How come you're home so early?"

"I decided to skive off and work from home this afternoon. Is everything OK? You look tired; would you like a cup of tea?"

"Yes, please. Let's take them into the lounge; we need to talk before Lily comes back."

"OK, that sounds ominous."

They sat across from each other, the coffee table between them. Emily looked at him, feeling sad, fearful, yet resolute.

"So, what would you like to talk about?"

He sounded calm, but she knew that could quickly change.

"I need to know the truth about where you were on the night you supposedly had a meeting with your Chair of Governors, Robert. I checked the minutes of the meeting, and your Chair of Governors wasn't at the final meeting of the year; he'd given his apologies. Nor was there any record of the Vice Chair making a speech about you. You've lied to me. Again."

He looked directly at Emily, a calculating blankness behind his eyes she'd only noticed once or twice before. She could see he was shaken, weighing up whether to bluff things out again, or tell her the truth.

"You've been quite the amateur detective, haven't you, Emily? You want the truth, I'll tell you, but you won't like it. I've been having an affair with a married colleague for several months. It began when we went to the pub after work one day and shared our feelings about our relationships with our partners. We were both in steady, comfortable but unexciting marriages. And really missed that excitement. We drove to a secluded spot and had the most thrilling sex, there in the car, which I've ever had. It blew my head off.

"But all good things, as they say. She realised her husband was becoming suspicious, so we decided to end it in style with a night together in a hotel. Of course, I lied to you, it was over by then and I didn't want to hurt you. Or risk damaging our marriage; I've still got strong feelings for you, Emily. But let's face it, you haven't been the most responsive lover over the last few months, and I needed this. Most men need this, and I've strayed less than most blokes I know."

She sat there, taking it all in. *God, he was good at this.* If she hadn't had the phone call from Deepak about a car just like his being seen near Sue's house, she might even have believed him. Not this time, though.

But what to do? She could play the trump card that Deepak's message had dealt her. Tell him that his story doesn't remotely fit with the recent news which she'd had from the police that a car matching his was seen leaving Sue Goodall's cottage on the night he claimed he was with his lover in a Stockport hotel.

Or she could say nothing and play along with his story until tomorrow morning. If he did have something to do with Sue's murder, she couldn't predict his reaction to the new information. While Emily felt sure he wouldn't harm her—assaulting her would solve nothing and make his situation immeasurably worse— she didn't want Lily to witness a terrible row this evening. She would ring Deepak first thing tomorrow morning.

Robert tried to read Emily's reaction, but she wasn't giving anything away. He'd realised that she might do some more detective work and discover that his account about meeting the Chair of Governors didn't hold up, so he'd thought through a cover story. *I think I was pretty convincing. If she wants to know the name of this woman, I'll say that I'm not prepared to tell her, in case she decides to confront her, or tell her husband, in order to get back at me. Which even my morally unimpeachable wife could do, if things get unpleasant between us. Which they might, if she demands a divorce and we start to fight about the terms.*

Emily took a swig of tea, put her cup carefully on a coaster, leant forward and said in a calm, measured voice,

"So, you swore on Lily's life that you weren't having an affair when you were? You say that most men feel the need to screw other women, but I didn't marry most men, I married you. I can't trust anything you say anymore, and I can't share my life with you and bring up our child together with no trust left between us. I didn't think I'd ever say these words, I can't believe I'm saying them now, but I want a divorce, Robert, on the grounds of your adultery.

I'll start the process next week, but there's no rush. I'm sure we can carry on almost as usual until the hard decisions have to be made, for Lily's sake at least."

"You really are quite a bitch, aren't you, Emily, under that holier than thou exterior? Fine, but don't think I won't fight all the way for equal custody of Lily."

"I hope we can sort out our differences without a fight, Robert. Of course, I know you love your daughter, and she loves you. My assumption is that we'll go for joint custody, if she's OK with that."

"She may surprise you and ask to stay with me for most of the time."

"Great. True to character, my husband's first response is to attack. Let's try and maintain civility between us, for Lily's sake."

"Don't play the 'we must protect Lily' card, Emily; you're the one who wants to turn her world upside down by divorcing me."

"Unbelievable. Are you incapable of honest self-analysis? From your perspective, your behaviour over the past thirteen years can't have played any part in my decision? Molly, after three months? Maria, soon after I'd given birth? Now this latest affair, covered up by one lie after another? And these are the ones I know about! I'm going to pick up Lily from Miriam's, Robert. Perhaps you could make up your bed in the spare room while I'm gone?"

Robert was about to spit out a vicious retort, then swallowed it at the last moment. He realised this was one deceit too far for her, though ironically not the deceit she thought it was. While the case against him for Sue's murder seemed to have run into the sand, it's not over yet. He couldn't risk a bitter divorce becoming the back story over the next few months to a continuing police investigation.

As she turned the Mini out of the drive and headed for Miriam's house, Emily knew she'd made the right decision. Better to do these things in stages, although she knew it had only put off confronting the consequences that will follow once she contacts Deepak.

It was a fifteen-minute drive to Miriam's house, and by the time Emily turned into the neat close of five detached, modern houses and pulled up outside number four, the implications of what she was about to set in motion had sunk in. Robert has no idea that the police have new information that puts a car like his at Sue's house at the time of the murder, and as soon as she tells Deepak that he'd spent an unaccounted-for night away from home on the night of 7th July, he will be brought in for questioning. God knows what story he will make up.

Would he be stupid enough to give me as his alibi?

"I was with my wife at home all night, Inspector, I'm sure she will confirm that."

Deepak would have him cornered; he couldn't keep my name out of it, and Robert would know I was responsible for shopping him—as he would see it. He could be charged with Sue's murder and wouldn't get bail. She would then have to tell Lily that her dad, who she idolizes, had been arrested for murder.

Maybe it won't come to that. Maybe there's a genuine reason for his absence that night, unconnected with Sue Goodall's murder, but so despicable that he couldn't tell me about it. *But I have to stop denying the truth in front of me; his adultery story is a fantasy.*

Hands gripping the steering wheel, her mind playing with the awful possible scenarios ahead, Emily was brought out of her trance by an increasingly persistent tapping on the window.

"Mum, what are you doing? Open the door, Miriam needs to go out soon. I've got to go."

She looked at her daughter's pretty face, etched with anxiety, and felt an intense loathing towards her husband. She hugged Lily as she got into the front seat, then drove slowly home. Her daughter was too smart not to pick up the tension between her and Robert, and she decided she had to say something.

"Dad and I have been having some arguments recently, Lily, and we've decided to sleep in separate rooms for a while. It doesn't affect how we feel about you and we will both always be there for you—we both love you more than anything else in the world, you know that, don't you?"

When Lily didn't respond, Emily turned to look at her. Tears were rolling down her daughter's face.

That night, lying alone in bed, Emily reflected on the events of the last few hours. Robert had swept Lily up in his arms as soon as she came through the door and spent the next hour playing scrabble with her. After Lily went to bed, when Robert asked Emily what she intended to do next, they managed to have a reasonably calm conversation about the options for ending their marriage. Robert seemed to accept the inevitability of her decision, given that he'd strayed once too often; it suited them both.

Thinking about the events that she was about to set in motion, she felt oddly calm about her decision to contact Deepak and tell him that Robert had spent an unaccounted-for night away from home on the night of 7th July. She slept well.

23

The Truth Hurts

"Hello, Deepak, this is Emily Fowler. I've been going through my diary since our conversation yesterday, and I wanted to tell you that Robert was away from home on the night of the date you mentioned. He'd previously told me he was at a Head teacher's meeting in Stockport, but I recently found out that was a lie. I had assumed he was having an affair, but the information you gave me yesterday has shone a different light on things. I can't believe my husband is capable of murdering anyone in cold blood, but it would be wrong not to tell you."

Deepak finally released the breath he'd been holding, exhaling as she finished speaking.

"Have you told Robert about our conversation yesterday, Emily? This is really important."

"I thought about it, but no, I haven't. What will happen now?"

"I think you know the answer to that, Emily. I will have to bring Robert in and question him under caution about his whereabouts on the 7th and 8th of July. What happens next will depend on his answers. I know I don't have to say this, but please don't contact Robert and tell him what's about to happen."

"I won't. But if you go to the school, please try to be as discreet as possible. I'm thinking about my daughter and what other kids will say if her dad is led away in handcuffs."

"That won't happen unless he refuses to come in. If he did, I'd have to arrest him."

Surely, he wouldn't be that stupid, she thought.

Looking out of his large office window overlooking the road in front of the school, Robert clocked the grey Ford Mondeo with its two male occupants as an unmarked police car, even before he saw Deepak Singh emerge from the passenger seat. He realised immediately that this had to be more serious than a request to clear up a few details; Singh would have phoned him, as he had on previous occasions. Unnerved, he felt his skin prickling as a shiver ran down his back. What new evidence could they possibly have? It had to be something that either placed him at Sue's house, or connected him with the corpse. If it was the former, he had to speak to Emily fast and persuade her not to tell Singh that he'd been away that night.

Pausing just long enough to 'remind' Patricia, his PA, that he was running late for his meeting at the town hall, he walked, then ran, to the car park at the rear of the school and was on his way as Deepak walked up to reception. *Hopefully Patricia will convince him that I've gone to the town hall.*

There was no answer from Emily's mobile, though he knew she was working from home today. He'd be there in ten minutes, tractors and muck spreaders permitting.

The relatively calm mood Emily had managed to maintain up to and during the phone call to Deepak had become one of rapidly heightening anxiety. *Have I done the right thing?* Intellectually, she'd been fully aware of the gravity of the potential consequences of that phone call; emotionally, the implications for the three of them, if Robert was found guilty of killing Sue Goodall and sent down for life, were terrifying. Particularly for Lily.

She was in her study, attempting to read her latest brief, when she heard Robert's car come to an abrupt stop in their drive, wheels skidding on the gravel. She realised that Robert must have somehow found out that Deepak was coming to question him about the night of Sue's murder and needed her to back him up. *Well, it's a little late for that, I'm afraid, Robert. That must have been him ringing just now.* She heard his key in the lock followed by the door slamming.

"Emily, where are you, I need to talk to you now," he shouted.

"I'm working in the study. I'll come down."

She braced herself for what was about to pass between them. There could be no going back from this moment, whatever the truth about that night. She would have to tell him she'd already told the police he didn't come home that night.

He was pacing around the lounge, clearly agitated. His appearance shocked her; he seemed to have aged ten years since yesterday.

"I tried to ring you, why didn't you pick up?"

"Sorry, I must have left the phone on silent. Why are you home?"

"The police arrived at the school this morning. Luckily, I saw them in time and managed to leave before they saw me. I told Patricia I was going to the town hall. God knows what they want to ask me now, but if they ask you about that night when I was in the hotel with another woman, I want you to back me up and say I was here, with you."

Looking at the man standing in front of her, Emily couldn't help feeling some compassion. Frightened and haunted, events were slipping out of his control. She sat down, motioning for him to do the same.

"If the police ask about that particular date, I don't see the problem of telling them where you were and what you were doing. I don't believe cheating on your partner is a criminal offence, and clearly, you've got a witness to your 'movements'" —Emily smirked at this point— "on that night."

"She's married, and I can't bring her into it."

"Well, I think you're going to have to. I'm afraid the police rang me yesterday to ask me if I could confirm that you were with me on the night of the 7th July. Another witness has come forward who's told them he saw a dark-coloured foreign car driving away from Sue Goodall's house late that night. They wanted to eliminate you as a possible suspect. Obviously, given that I knew you had an alibi, and given my position as a lawyer, I had to tell them that you'd been out the whole night. I didn't say you'd told me you were screwing someone else."

As she was speaking, watching the colour drain from his face, she knew beyond doubt he'd killed Sue.

Emily heard her phone ringing from the bedroom upstairs.

"You fucking bitch! How could you do this to me? You're smart, Emily, you must have realised why they were asking you about that date, and could have lied for me. For your husband!"

Any remaining compassion for the man she'd been living with for thirteen years was gone. He'd killed another human being, yet he was furious with her for not colluding by lying for him.

She saw the look of shock on his face, the hatred in his eyes. And the fear. He was sweating. He knew she knew, and he was afraid of that.

If not now, when? she thought.

"Why would you be so worried about this woman giving you an alibi? Any problems that might cause her are nothing compared to you being unjustly accused of murder. Or me being struck off, prosecuted and jailed for covering up for you. I think it's time for the truth, Robert."

"Which is what, exactly?"

"That there was no night of passion with a mystery woman or a meeting in a hotel blackmailing your Chair of governors. I think Sue Goodall recently got back in touch and told you she was going to own up to colluding with you to lie about events that night on the camp. You knew that would destroy everything you'd worked for; unbelievably, you decided the only solution was to eliminate her. On the seventh of July, having checked into your hotel, you drove to her place, killed her, drove with her body to the reservoir and dumped it. I'm not sure how you got it to the middle, but you're nothing if not resourceful. For a while, luck was on your side. The pathologist got the water temperature in the middle wrong. She thought the body couldn't have been in there longer than eight weeks, which meant you weren't a suspect. But the police took more temperature measurements and realised it could have been in the water for longer. You're going to need a cast iron alibi for that night, Robert, particularly now a car matching the Saab was seen speeding away from her house."

It's done, she thought. She felt utterly drained from the release of nervous energy.

"How the fuck do you know all this? Have you been helping the police?"

"I haven't had to, Robert, they've been piecing it together for a while. I've just filled in a few of the details for them. How could you kill her in cold blood? What's happened to you? Or have you always been prepared to eliminate anyone standing in your way, whatever it takes?"

They stared at one another for several seconds, then she got up and went into the kitchen. Her tea was cold, and she needed another cup. As she re-filled the kettle, she noticed the parts from the food processor that she'd left to dry on the draining board. *I should put those away.*

Robert looked at her, suddenly consumed with hatred for the woman he'd fallen in love with. Not just for her treachery, but for all the sanctimonious, liberal - lefty nonsense she'd preached at him all these years. And he'd just gone along with. *You're pathetic, Mason.. I've given my life to her, yet she's been working with the police, behind my back, to convict me. I'm going to lose everything while she'll be free to have a wonderful life with Lily. Well, she won't. I will fucking well make sure of that.*

He took off his tie and followed her quietly into the kitchen.

As she clicked the kettle on, she sensed a movement behind her. Before she could turn, something came over her head— a tie, how could that be? — followed by intense pain as her windpipe was crushed with shocking force. She tried to speak—*This is so stupid, Robert, think of Lily, alone, you in prison for life*—but no sound left her crushed windpipe. She knew she had just a few seconds of consciousness left; she'd learnt that when she'd worked on a murder trial involving a strangulation. The pressure was blurring her vision, but she knew that what she needed lay on the draining board; she grasped it with her right hand.

Holding the spindle of the processor blade, she reached over her head and slashed at the tie, but he saw it coming and moved his arm. She tried once more, knowing this was her last chance as she felt herself slipping under. This time she felt the blade meet resistance as she swept it round and down but the tie stayed tight around her neck. As her legs gave way, she smelt the sweet, metallic smell of blood and felt something warm spreading down her back. His tie had already loosened by the time she slumped to the floor, just conscious, taking huge gulps of air.

She looked up to see Robert standing, holding his arm, frantically trying to stop blood gushing from the deep cut along the length of his brachial artery. She'd heard about this, too. Unless the artery was closed, he only had a few minutes to live. He crashed to the floor in front of her, staring, uncomprehending. In the background, she heard a police siren coming closer, then the sound of the front door splintering. *Take your time, Deepak, there's no rush.*